The Devil's Masquerade:

The Poison

JENNIFER LOREN

Books by Jennifer Loren

The Devil's Eyes Series
THE DEVIL'S EYES
THE DEVIL'S REVENGE
THE DEVIL'S SON
THE DEVIL'S MASQUERADE: THE REMEDY

The Finding Ava Series
FINDING AVA
RECKLESS

THE HAND THAT HOLDS MINE

http://www.jenniferloren.com/

First published by Jennifer Loren, 2013

ISBN-13: 978-0-9888027-1-1

Representation and Management, More & More Professional Literary Services
http://www.moreandmorepls.com/

Acknowledgements

Content Editing: More & More Professional Literary Services http://www.moreandmorepls.com/

Copyediting: Erinn Giblin, Yours Truly, The Editor

Proofreading: Jacqueline Tria

Cover Model: Lionel Clerc

Cover Design: Hang Le, By Hang Le
http://byhangle.com/

Interior Design: Polgarus Studio
http://www.polgarusstudio.com/

Prologue

Dark venom, the black poison that is the name to which his servants call his toxin which *he* administers through the teeth of his ruby-eyed dragon. By the time you hear the squawking dragon take flight, it is too late; the venom has already entered through a main artery and is creeping through your veins with a slow burn until it reaches the ends of your soul. Its goal is to render you powerless, to break down all of the barriers and defenses that keep you from becoming the killer Asmodeus wants you to be. Then, it is just a matter of time before your heart begins to harden, your soul to become his, and you forget all that you had once held dear. There is no fighting it. There is no recovery from his darkness or running from his evil. The best you can do is not fight it at all, allowing yourself to succumb to death. However, the strongest and the ones with the most to live for fight; they fight and try to hold on, and that's what *he* wants. He wants you to fight, to show strength that is like no other, to show that you cannot be defeated. It is the unyielding that can be changed into the most deadly of killers. Asmodeus will be unstoppable once he has the absolute warrior to help him control and to kill.

Even if you are aware of what he wants he will find a way. He will distract you; make you believe that he is your friend that he is going to help you survive. You begin to think he is going to help those you love and once you believe in him, you turn your back to him. When your vulnerable back is left defenseless that's when you hear it and then you feel it. The slow burning poison changes into a raging fire that brings you to your knees, your eyes become black and overcome with darkness, you can hear nothing, but your own screams of torment. It is days before you awake again, and your mind is weak and dazed while he fills you with thoughts of violence and control and devotion, to him. Numb, closed off from all else, you are completely vulnerable to the poison's will. Your final transformation is complete when the poison kills any last fragment of the life you had, when you are broken, destroyed and your heart is hardened, and you are left as nothing but a merciless disciple of Asmodeus.

No there has never been a cure to his poison, there has been few to live through it. However, one found a way to not only live through it, but to escape it after a remedy. The love of one woman stopped the poison's hardening of his heart, revived his life and gave him a new mission, a new mission to kill Asmodeus, otherwise known as, Dennis Savage.

Chapter 1

Dante

This is only the fifth day of my training, and there is still so much I have yet to learn. My father, however, seems pleased, pleasing me. There have been many days of exhausting tests of my will and my strength, but today, I am expected to practice battling one on one. My first competition is not an easy one; it is against my brother, Saldean. My little shadow, and Saldean's full sister, cheers us on from the sidelines. My half-brother is older than me, and my half-sister is younger. Being right in the middle of the two puts me at odds with my stepmother on a daily basis. She dotes on my brother and sister every chance she gets, but I am her biggest disgrace. I don't see eye to eye with Belinda, and if there is one thing I know with certainty, it is that she would love for him to kill me to restore her dignity. My adoring sister is torn between her mother and the brother she follows around. I don't know how much longer I can hold off my older sibling. He is getting stronger by the day, and my father is becoming more supportive of him. Saldean is only a few years older, but it's just enough for him to work me over a couple times. My father finds weakness a detriment to the family and has no problem ridding himself of it if necessary. The only way I stand a chance is to deviate from brawn and use my head to gain power. I know my brother well. I spend time watching his moves and learning his first step, his second, and every one thereafter. Before long, I know every step he is going to take before he takes it. I use this knowledge to plan my attack on him, and I beat him to his position, dropping him before he can react. My tactical approach secures win after win. Saldean never learns; he only sees what is in front of him, believing his strength should assure a victory. As strong as he is, he is predictable, and I am able to out maneuver him before he can change his strategy. To my father's surprise, my wit outdoes my brother's strength, time and time again; however, he seems pleased. Brains beat strength every time, and every time, my father moves a little closer to the edge of his cushioned seat. He never thought it was possible, but now that it has happened, he has all the more reason to go against my stepmother's wishes and make me next in line for head of the family. The only thing that keeps my stepmother from suffocating me in my sleep is my father. She knows her death would instantly fall upon her if she laid a hand on me, but that doesn't encourage kindness on her part. In fact, the circumstances remind me of growing up.

My brother and I have always gotten along, and my sister has followed me around like a lost puppy most of our lives, maybe because I had more patience with her than anyone else. The three of us were brought up sheltered from most of the outside world. We were properly and privately educated by the best instructors money could buy. We were cared for by many servants, and never once do I recall any of them denying a request. However, father would not allow any of us to get out of line, even for a moment. Discipline was important to him, and only he was allowed to dictate our punishment. My stepmother was never more than a figurehead, a caring mother to her children and an evil witch to me. Belinda always had something nasty to say to me, and I allowed it until I finally realized that my blatant displays of obedience and unwarranted kindness were getting me nowhere. The verbal abuse from her lasted until I was fifteen, until the day I had enough. That day, we were all sitting down to dinner, and she decided to prove how smart her son was to Father. She would ask him question after question, all greatly simplified for him. Father was pleased and congratulated Saldean for his advancing education. The witch could have ended it there, but instead, she decided to try to humiliate me by posing questions that even she didn't know the answers to.

"That is not correct Dante. Why don't you do something simple like eat your food without spilling it," Belinda says, shaking her head with a laugh.

"Actually, he is correct. You are the one that is wrong." Father replies. *"Perhaps you should try eating your food without spilling it."*

"How did you know that?" she asks with her usual pointed stare. *"I know, for a fact, that your studies have not reached that level yet."*

"Just because my studies stop, that does not mean I am incapable of learning on my own. Unlike Saldean, I don't spend my free time playing with my penis," I answer, drawing a rare laugh from my father and even more rare silence from my stepmother.

She never bothered to directly speak to me ever again, and I have been perfectly fine with that.

After that dinner, father took a special interest in me and hired an elite assistant. Oliver Rabbie is one of the most intelligent men available, a highly-skilled professor from one of the top universities in the country. He is well-bred and speaks as if he stepped out of a traditional English novel. With Rabbie, I learn more than I ever could have from any other tutor. He has been a proud attendant at my battles whether it is with one of my father's assassin's or with my brother, and he is always an ally against my stepmother whose silence does not stop her from trying to distract me during battles. Throughout this battle session, one of my father's top assassins gets the best of Saldean. I am only allowed to know that my brother was outdone and defeated; I am not allowed to know how he was defeated so I am given no advantage when I step into the room to begin my own battle with the man. The moment I step out in from of him, the man salivates. My father sits back and watches with no emotion, my sister hides her face in her mother's arm, and Belinda smiles, assuring me that this is not going to be an easy fight.

Rabbie pulls me to his side. "Think, plan, be patient," he says before glancing over at my stepmother, "and be prepared for distractions. That witch brought in a whistle." I nod and move towards the lunatic who's ready to tear my head off. If I fail, I don't know if father will stop him or if the disappointment will be enough to justify my death.

The man blazes from one side of the room to the other before suddenly stopping much closer than I expect, but I don't move. He dashes around once again then darts at me, tumbling over my head when I duck. He looks a little shocked but once again begins his dizzying attack. He lunges, trying to force me to move; however, I jump and allow him to slide under my feet. I don't understand his motivation to get me to move until I realize he is trying to get me to run, to turn my back on him just once. When he begins again, my stepmother blows her whistle, catching only my opponent's attention. I use that moment to take hold of his face and jerk it towards mine, capturing his eyes. "Die!" To my feet, he falls. I turn back towards my father and nod at his now standing figure.

"Yay, Dante!" Galena yells, clapping for me. "Great battle brother!"

Father smiles and nods back towards me. "Ma Joie," he whispers.

The strength I feel, the desire I have, and the fire in my veins all feed a hunger to kill again.

Chapter 2

Dante

Now that my father understands my abilities, he has decided to put me in charge of the family business. This is my first chance to associate with people outside of our realm, beyond servants and paid employees. It is odd, at first, dealing with people who want to say no to me, who want to deny me what I want. My growing strength and knowledge helps me improve my family's territory and our stronghold over the city. I break one barrier after another in a much shorter time than expected. Our once unnoticeable territory now controls the city. Even the elected officials answer to us. My next order of business is to build a tower of respect to represent our family, or rather, my father. The tower, a high-rise of immense radiance, will sit on the highest part of the city and be named "Sovereignty." We have already begun construction, despite there being one obstacle that is giving me trouble. One small business is unwilling to sell their building, forcing us to share our triumph on the hill, not something my father is willing to do. This land has been dismissed up until now because the owners have been a mix of ex-cops and other public servants. However, we were able to get them all to sell to us by offering a price they couldn't refuse. That is, all except for the busy mechanic's shop, Simone's Auto Body. Simone's is being supported by the police department, feels no need to bow down to anyone, and is not swayed by any amount of money we offer. The nuisance has forced me to take care of this one in person rather than sending my usual assistants. My father believes I should have an easier time of it since the owner recently suffered a severe heart attack. The owner's misfortune has left his daughter in charge. I have never had a problem dealing with women. I ask, and they do. Sometimes, I don't even have to ask. My father always had women around us while we were growing up. Since we were home schooled and were never allowed to leave the compound, we couldn't meet girls of our own age, so father had women brought to us. We were encouraged to learn how to pleasure them properly. Some would pretend they didn't want to be there, but one look in their direction and a simple kiss to their cheek, and I easily lured them back to my bed where I would fuck them all night and throughout the next day. Soon, sex and women were easy for me. All I had to do was glance in their direction and they would run to me, dropping to their knees and begging to suck my dick. I never had to do much of anything other than say what I wanted, no matter how awkward or vulnerable it made them feel.

Now, I have to negotiate with the daughter of our enemy. Knowing my usual success, I plan for an early end to my day. I walk into the shop with all the confidence in the world, and why shouldn't I? No one has ever denied me. I am a Savage, the devil in disguise. The moment I feel her presence though, something inside me begins to crack.

"Hi, can I help you?" she says without much acknowledgment to my existence. I wait until she finds it necessary to meet my eyes. The moment she looks up, a lump forms within my throat that I can't swallow fast enough to speak. She breaks the awkward silence with a smile, "Cat got your tongue handsome?"

"No. I … I. I need to talk to the owner of this establishment," I say resuming a tall stance.

"Well you got her. What do you need?"

Breathing in deeply, I look into her eyes, "I need to buy your business today." She laughs, forcing me to stand back, unsure how to react. "I don't think you understand. I am not telling you a joke, I am making you an offer …"

"*I am not telling you a joke* … wow, you are so serious. I heard you sweetie. I am just not interested in selling. My grandfather started this business, and I am not about to give it up. Too much history, you know. This place means something to my family, especially to my brother and me." She smiles before turning her back to me and rushing around as if we have finished our conversation. She is talking to her employees and discussing changes to the disgusting place while I can do nothing more than follow her around like a puppy. She suddenly turns back to me, "Do you need something else because I have a lot to get done today?" I shake my head, and she… smiles. I don't remember much after that.

I somehow managed to make it back home. I couldn't give my father much of an explanation as to why my mission at the garage was unsuccessful. All I could do was say that I thought the situation was in need of some serious investigation before we can go much further. He believes our enemies are behind the trouble, and even though I know better, I am not about to tell him any different.

The next day, I try several more times to speak to the frustrating woman, but every time, she dismisses me or, even worse, ignores me. I have never in my life experienced such a frustration. Galena suggested I come up with a backup plan. *A backup plan?* I know what she means, but it is not something I have ever had to consider. I don't know what other kind of backup plan I could come up with that would help me with the horrible woman, so instead, I create a plan to go around her. I spend the next few weeks making side deals and organizing a solution that will work around the small body shop rather than attempting to face-off with *her*. The solution works well for me. I can oversee the construction of our great building and watch her at the same time. There has to be a reason why she can deny me. I have heard of people being able to do this, but I have never seen it in person.

This woman, "Sophia," I say, whispering her name whenever I see her just to enjoy that divine feeling that rushes through me. The syllables of her name graze my tongue with delicate softness and a warming breath. She is distracting, and I find myself having difficulty doing even the simplest of tasks. She looked up at me today and waved, and I waved back just before running into a wall. The only thing that hurt worse than my pounding head was the bruising of my ego, pummeled by the sound of her laughter. I think the only way to cure this insanity of mine is to concentrate on work and forget about her, something I manage to do until she surprises me. Covered in grease, hair tied in a mess, and eyes focused hard on mine, she marches straight toward me. My heart skips a beat, and for the first time, I have trouble breathing. Her dreadful wears are powerless against her beauty.

"Why are you doing this?" she snaps with no fear. I cock my head in confusion. "You are not going to force us to move by building your monstrosity around us. So you can just stop this bullshit right now! And stop watching us! If you think you can intimidate me, you better just forget it, asshole!"

"I don't want you to move. In fact, I would prefer you to stay. If you would look at the plans, you would see that I am not building completely around you, only in front of you to hide the eyesore."

"Eyesore? What is an eyesore?" the mess shouts at me. She continues yelling and swearing like a drunken sailor for quite some time before stopping abruptly. "Why are you looking at me that way?"

"You don't care about what I want at all do you?" I curiously ask.

"Why would I care what you want?" Sophia says, coming with her arms crossed.

"Everyone else does," I say simply.

"Well, lucky you, Rich Boy. I don't know why I should care about what you want when no one has ever cared about what I want."

"I do. I care very much about what you want," I say, and for the first time, she is silent. I could get used to this, the ringing in my ears finally has a chance to clear. "I think you should have dinner with me, and then, we can discuss what it is you want, Sophia. I will have some people come clean you up and make you more presentable for me."

"What the hell is that supposed to mean? Clean me up ... for you? What am I ..."

"You're disgusting, as you can clearly see. Just look at the grease on your face and clothes and even in your hair," I say with a scrunched up nose. "I would kiss you now, but I don't want to get any of that on me," I continue pointing out her issues. She rubs her face, smearing the grease across her skin and onto her hand. "See, you must not be very good at your job, to be such a mess. I assume you make a lot of mistakes. I could have someone teach you how to do it properly?" Suddenly, her face turns red, and her eyes burn, I look closely at her, wondering if she isn't a child of one of the Lords from my father's court, but she fails to inflict any pain on me.

"You are not much of a demon. I don't feel any pain at all," I say before she perks up and punches me in the gut. *Okay, I felt that.*

She growls, fisting her hands, "You are the most aggravating man I have ever met! Listen, you spoiled brat, I wouldn't have dinner with you if you paid me."

"You work as a whore, too? I don't usually pay for such things, but surely I can afford you. How much?"

I'm lucky I have quick reflexes and am able to stop the flying fists coming at my face. "I am not a whore, you fucking bastard. Let go of me." I hold tight to her and enjoy it so much that I smile at her until she kicks me in the shin and stomps away.

"So, I will see you tonight?" I yell after her, receiving a wave of her finger which I take to mean yes. *Yes, she waved again to assure her answer. I must make sure tonight is perfect.*

I arrange for a nice dinner to be delivered to her place of work, and I show up in my finest attire. "What are you doing here?" she huffs as I come through the door.

"We have dinner plans, and since it looks as if you will be working late, I made arrangements to have dinner brought to us. You don't even have to look nice if you don't want to. There is no one here for you to embarrass me in front of."

"You are so charming! It's amazing you are still single," Sophia says, crossing her arms.

"Thank you," I say with a smile. After my assistant sets up a table for us, I motion for her to sit, but she continues to stand with her arms folded. "The sooner you sit and eat with me, the sooner I will leave," I bargain.

"Promise?"

"I don't say things I don't mean," I reply, cautiously helping her into her chair so as not to transfer her greasy filth to my imported suit. I look up at her and take my napkin to wipe the smudge of grease from her cheek. "Even though the grease is an interesting accessory choice, I prefer to see all of you, including your beautiful face." A smile slowly emerges from one corner of her lips to the other, and something inside me fights its way from my chest. I encourage her to eat, and she slowly begins to do just that. She doesn't say much, allowing me to admire her beauty up close and without the interference of her mouth and opinions. As I promised, I have our dinner cleared and prepare to leave, but before I go, I leave Sophia with a simple kiss on her grease-stained, pink cheek. I even allow myself to linger against her skin for a moment while I inhale her essence.

The moment I walk through the door, my father's ire is clear. "Dante! How dare you defy me!" he yells, slamming his cane into the floor and vibrating the walls around us.

I shake my head, looking at him in confusion, "I don't know what you are talking about?"

"Where have you been?" he seethes.

"I was having dinner."

"With our enemy?! That is not something I approve of."

"But she is not the enemy, she is simply ..."

"She is not the enemy? Does that not go against what you told me in the first place?" I sink into my body, avoiding his glare. "That woman has made you confused, distracted you from your own family."

"She has done nothing of the sort. I am doing everything that you have asked of me."

"Are you? Was there not a man that came down to the site today to protest the use of non-union workers? He threatened you, threatened our family, I hear. Tell me. How did you handle the situation?"

"I found him a job through one of our government contacts. He's a good man, a good worker. He showed determination and strength, something I thought worthy of a job. So, I helped him find one, and guess what? No more protesting."

"He was worthy? He who threatened our family was worthy?"

"Yes! Why is it that you want to put down anyone who shows strength against us? Maybe we should start using these people rather than destroying them," I say, watching my father steam as he crushes the glass within his hand.

"Everything I have taught you has been to protect your family, our family, at all costs. Never ... *ever* consider any possibility other than death for anyone who threatens your family. Where was this woman when you offered the man a job?"

I look away from him, and answer, "Behind him. She had come to retrieve some of her mail that had gotten mixed up with ours." He instantly slams his fists into the wall near me.

"Dante, you tell me right now what your plans are for this woman!" I look up at him, and as soon as I open my mouth, he growls. "Damn you!" he yells, angering me.

I step to him, my eyes swirling with rage, "No! You don't tell me how to live my life anymore. She is my choice, and there is nothing you can do about it." Before he can say another word, I stand tall and look over him. "I am your son, and I will forever be your son, but you must allow me to make my own decisions or kill me right now and risk the family's business and future on Saldean."

My father's steaming figure calms, and he slowly sits in his chair, looking me over. "Very well. I will give you six months' time to enjoy this woman, but at the end of that time, you must decide, will it be her or will it be the woman of my choosing? I have found the perfect one for you, the perfect mother for the children *you* will have for me. If you will see them both, I will give you a choice Dante, but once you choose, there is no going back. That woman will be your destruction if you are not careful. Enjoy her Dante, but then I advise that you be done with her or else, I will be done with you." He leaves me speechless, with my stepmother smiling jubilantly.

"I am sorry. Mother has been following you for weeks, and she told him what you have been doing," Galena says, sliding up to my side. "But you should have known better. That woman isn't worth angering father over and losing your position, I assure you."

"And you sister? Have you been following me, too? Or have you been too busy with Marius?" I say, glancing down at her shocked expression. "Don't pretend that you are concerned for my well-being when all you want is to ride my coattails in hopes of gaining your boyfriend a higher position within the realm. I am your best chance Galena, knowing Saldean would soon rather have you killed than deal with you and your extracurricular activities outside of the family business."

"Dante! Now you listen to me, despite my mother, I have done everything I can to help you. I idolize you. I would do anything for you. Yes, I am loyal to my mother, but I am more loyal to you. Don't be angry with me because of what she did." I turn to look her in the eyes and realize my sister is all I have. I apologize to her with open arms, but still, how can I trust her when I know she is weak to father's will. Everyone is weak to my father, including me at times, but I do test his patience more than any of them, something that should have done me in a long time ago. I am not sure why my father continues to believe in me, but I have a feeling it has something to do with my mother.

Dennis Savage, my father, has been powerful and wealthy since I was born. My stepmother, Belinda, was arranged for my father by his own father. She was expected to make a strong match for him. Belinda is, and always will be, loyal to my father — her one endearing quality. She would never betray him, and she has strong connections with the High Council which gives my father the edge over all the other Lords. His need for my stepmother, however, didn't stop him from satisfying his sexual desires.

My mother, Sancia Jayzon, was so beautiful that every man that saw her wanted her, and my father was no different. Despite my stepmother's protests, he pursued my mother anyway. My mother is said to have fell hard for my father. She adored him, and he loved being with her, craved her even, but he refused to love her. He refused to show any sign of weakness to a woman, to a simple, non-powerful woman. Only, he had no idea how much power she did have over him. He was ready to have me killed after I was born, but she, yes she, the simple powerless woman, stood up to him and said, "If you take my child, I will take your heart with me, to my grave." The only sign of his heart ever beating is me.

Unfortunately, my mother died of an illness no one could seem to heal. No doctor, or hospital that my father took my mother to could help her. The day she died, the harshest storm ever formed hitting our city and destroying much of it. The leftover rubble was cleaned up, and out of the ashes, my father began to rebuild, and he rebuilt an empire that could not be fractured.

My father has never approved of any relationship my siblings or I desired to have. He only approves the ones that are arranged for us. I have to wonder if his heart was taken to the grave with my mother, like she threatened to do. All that is left of him is a heartless, vindictive soul. No one can be happy if my father is not.

While my father built his empire, I was brought in to share his home with my half-brother, half-sister, and detestable step-mother. My younger sister, Galena, has been more motherly to me than my stepmother has ever been. I guess I can understand why, not that it made things any easier for me. I grew up sheltered from the world until my father decided I was ready to be Pasha: a sultan, a prince to his kingdom as he saw it. It is an honor to be believed in by him, for him to call me, "Ma Joie," French for, "My Joy." I am his joy, and for anyone to take that joy away from him is considered a direct attack. I smile with happiness every time he honors me this way. I know what I mean to him, but I can't imagine I can push much further. I need to tread carefully and give his choice for me a chance while I pursue my own.

Chapter 3

Dante

I don't know what it is I am feeling, but I do know Sophia makes my every day better than the day before. I try to keep calm around her and not look too eager, though she catches me smiling at her more than once during our work day. At the end of my day, I approach her once again and ask her to join me for dinner. She smiles but tells me she has a lot to do before she can leave, rambling on and on about the long list of duties she must complete. There is no way she can finish all of her work in time for dinner. I understand her issue after looking around the garage, so I change into one of the many uniforms she has available and begin cleaning up, doing the odd things she mentioned. I don't plan on having dinner alone tonight.

"What are you doing, Dante?" Sophia asks as she emerges from her office.

"You said you couldn't leave until you were done, so I am helping you leave earlier in hopes you will have dinner with me," I say, trying to look my best whilst holding trash and a broom.

Her expression leaves me confused, and I prepare for another one of her harsh gut punches as she quickly approaches. Only, Sophia smiles and wraps her arms around my neck. "Oh my gosh! You are so adorable." I feel a smile coming over my face, but I don't want to look ridiculous. I try to force it back, but it keeps fighting its way through. She lets go of me and laughs for some reason. *It's the damn smile… I know it.* "You are a big spoiled brat, and you talk strange, but at least you care about something other than yourself."

"Of course. I care about you, Sophia," I say, feeling good about my answer when she leans up on her toes and kisses me on the lips. I don't let her simply taste my lips and run; I bring her back in and press my lips against hers. The wondrous sensations running through my body give me reason to hold her tight, massaging her lips open so I can slip my tongue between them, urging her to give me more. I pick her up, sit her on the hood of one of the cars, and pull her legs around my waist. She leans back and allows me to feel her breasts, but the moment I start to rip through her shirt, she hesitates to go any further. I press my erection against her and watch as her eyes flutter and her mouth quivers, a subtle invitation. Her body heats up with mine, and her clothes begin to stick to her skin. I unzip the top of my grease-stained coveralls, allowing the pants to hang halfway off my hips while I push her shirt over her head. Her nipples tease me as they press boldly against her tank top. I take hold of the fabric between her breasts and tear it from her body, releasing her breasts into the open air. She gasps but settles in as I massage one breast after the other against my lips. My cock frees itself, wanting its own desires to be satisfied. Our skin is wet and heated, and I have to peel her pants from her legs, but I make up for it by holding them up and kissing every part of them from the tips of her toes to her barely-there panties. I lick the outline of her pussy against the fabric before slowly edging them down and out of my way. I force my tongue inside and send her reeling backwards, but my tight hold on her thighs keeps her from getting away from me. Sophia reaches out and fists my hair, but she doesn't beg me to stop. I feel the rush of her pleasure against my mouth and proudly lick my lips as I rise up. Still gripping her legs, I give my cock what it has been wanting. Feeling inside of her, my dick has never felt so good. I look down at her and smile, but when she opens her eyes to me and reaches out for me, I instantly collapse into her arms and kiss her deeply, whispering my secret desires before coming inside of her with a whimper.

"Ummm ... well that was an interesting first kiss," she says.

"I liked it," I reply with a smile. "I can't wait for the second."

She smiles but straightens up with an attitude. "No second kiss until I get my dinner." I help her off the hood of the car and kindly give her another kiss.

"That one was only for inspiration."

"Inspiration for what?"

"To decide where I want to take you for dinner."

Smiling beautifully, she looks over me and laughs. "You are a mess, you are going to have to clean yourself up before we go to dinner because I simply cannot have you embarrass me." I lean over and look into some shiny rims she has displayed to see the grease on my face and my hair a mess. "Don't worry. You can clean up at my house while I make us dinner."

"But I was going to ..."

"Shush! The last thing I feel like doing is getting dressed up and going to one of your hoity-toity restaurants." I would argue but something tells me it would be best to just shut up and follow her.

Sophia's home is small, but refreshing and warm. While she prepares dinner, I take a shower and scrub the dirt and grime from beneath my fingernails. I walk out of the bathroom with a towel wrapped around my waist, searching for my clothes that seem to have disappeared. "Sophia, where are my clothes?"

She runs in and looks down at my towel and smiles, "Wow, ummm. What was your question again?"

I shake my head at her wandering eyes. "Where are my clothes?"

"Oh yes, your clothes. I hid them. I laid out some more common people clothes there for you. Try them, or wear your towel if you prefer, and then meet me in the kitchen for dinner." I look down at the odd wears and pick them up in horror. "Don't look at them that way. They are my brother's, but they should fit you fine. They are sweats, something you should try once in a while to relax a little." I refuse to wear such things, so I sit down to dinner in my towel to her instant humor. "Stubborn ass."

"I would be fine naked if you prefer, but I was trying to be respectful, and those clothes are nowhere near respectful."

"I'm not complaining, Dante, the towel is fine with me. Perfectly fine," she says with a suspicious smile. "Now that you are here, can you help me by getting that dish on the top shelf?" I do as asked and notice her staring at me. "Nice ass," she laughs, putting the dish aside and sitting down.

"You didn't need that dish?" She shakes her head and waits for me to sit. I narrow my eyes in her direction, wondering how this woman is causing me to be so under her power.

This time during dinner, we enjoy some polite, and somewhat flirtatious, conversation. At one point, I find her hand in mine and enjoy rubbing circles with my thumb more than I do eating. When we finish dinner, Sophia leads me to another room where she sits down close to me. I invite her to share my towel, but instead, she has me toss it aside.

Sophia tempts me by running her fingers over my arms, my chest, and down my neck until I can't take it anymore. I grab her hips and sit her square on my lap. She asks me to slow down before she moans my name and whimpers, "Mmm, don't stop."

She pushes me back but then pulls me forward again, straddling me with growing pleasure of her own. Sophia slips out of her shirt and breaks free of her bra while I enjoy watching her control me. "I want you, Sophia. I want to be inside you," I say between soft kisses and disrespectful touches. "Do you want me?" I ask, sliding my hands into her pants and watching her carefully.

"Dante, I have only been with one other man in my life, and it ended terribly. We are moving much faster than that relationship. You shouldn't be here now, and I certainly ..." She begins moaning again as I lift my hips up into her. I pick her up and find her bedroom. Placing her on the bed, I slide off her remaining clothes.

"I promise you, Sophia, I am not like any other man. You won't ever need another. I will take care of you forever and beyond," I say as I reach down and into her hot, wet desiring place that she happily opens up wide for me. "Let me inside of you Sophia, let me come inside you and feel you come on me," I whisper against her ear, and she continues to search for control of her emotions. I won't let her maintain control. I go down and pleasure her until she gives in, until she is completely mine. Her exhaustion is my success, and now I can have more of what I want. She rubs her hands down my erection and licks her lips. "No, no I think my cock is better served somewhere else." She releases her grip on me and lies back, closing her eyes and breathing heavily as she awaits me. I find my place in her arms, and my cock finds it way so deep inside the tight, warm center that I have to let go of my emotions and groan my appreciation for her.

"Dante, please don't let go of me," she cries out, holding onto me with everything she has.

"Never, my darling, I will never, ever, let you go." She smiles, and I follow. I feel so good. The emotions running through my body are like nothing I have ever felt before. The moment I feel her come on me, I release into her, holding her close and respecting her breathless requests by wrapping her in my arms. I can't imagine anything feeling more wonderful in my life.

As opposed to my perfect night last night, tonight I am forced to stay home and have dinner with a woman that my father finds more suitable for me. Wendy is the well-bred daughter of one of my father's friends. Wendy's father is an advisor to the High Council and, therefore, important to my father. She is an attractive woman which gives me a slight hope for the evening, but the woman takes my hand without looking my way and sits as though she has a pole extending through her body. She seems as if she is waiting for someone to let out the seams of her dress so she can breathe. When we are left alone to talk, I do my best to try to find some endearing quality about this woman for my father. "So what do you enjoy doing?"

"I enjoy nothing. My existence is simply to be and breed with my match. To respect my husband and follow him wherever he goes," Wendy says with little emotion.

"You don't do anything all day then?"

"I study and prepare myself to be the perfect mother and wife," she says. "I assure you, no man could want for much more than me."

"Really?" I ask, looking over her stiff posture. I can only imagine taking her to bed. The thought sends chills down my spine.

"Yes, whatever you need, I can do. Whatever you care to discuss, I can discuss, or I can simply listen to your wonderful ideas and feel great pleasure in hearing your intelligence be spoken."

"What if my ideas are terrible though?" I ask.

"I am sure they are not. I am sure whatever you say should be heard and executed without question."

"What if I told you stand on your head?" I ask, receiving a slightly puzzled expression. However, I have to hand it to her. Whatever I tell her to do, she does, and by the time my brother comes in to check on me, Wendy is balancing on one foot with a book on her head and an apple in her hand while reciting her favorite poetry. Saldean looks her over and nods with approval.

"Very nice. All I could get my date to do was polish my shoes. I never thought of entertainment," Saldean says. "She is going to have to leave soon though, so you might want to say your goodbyes now." Shaking his head at the awkward woman, he exits the room.

"I guess you better go."

"So, I will be seeing you again soon?" she asks.

"No, I don't think so. You're really boring and not even interesting enough to want to fuck, but thank you for coming over and wasting my time." I escort her and her astonished expression out of my house. One thing Father taught me is to always tell people exactly what you want and what you think. That way, there is no way they can misunderstand you.

Chapter 4

Dante

I spend my days working at the site and keeping an eye on Sophia. She has started bringing me homemade lunch. It is barely edible. Sophia is a horrible cook, but I eat it anyway to make her happy. She always delivers it with a smile and a delicate touch to my hand, but I don't let her leave without pulling her into an out of the way corner and taking in her lips. Our secret flirting becomes a game that we both seem to enjoy. Whether I sneak up on her or she surprises me with a kiss, it doesn't matter to us. Every time I see her look up at me and smile, I can hardly remain focused on my overseeing of the building. She clearly has my attention, and it is a good thing, too. She has a lot of unruly customers come through. Anytime I hear someone raise their voice to her, I rush to her side, but she continuously holds me back with a hand on my chest.

"Dante, this is my business. You have got to let me handle it."

"But he was being rude to you."

"He was upset about his car being in bad shape, he doesn't have enough money to fix it and, he needs his car to get to work. Of course he was angry, but not with me. He was just taking it out on me. It isn't the first time, and it won't be the last."

"I don't like it," I say. "I think I should go get him and make him apologize."

She rolls her eyes and turns me around. "Will you please go back to your job and let me do mine. I promise you, I can handle myself without your help." Hesitating to move, I look back at her. "Dante, go back to work!"

I leave, but I keep an eye on her each day, making sure things don't get out of control. She says she can handle it, but I have my doubts, and my suspicions prove true. As Sophia begins to close up one night, I notice a man sneak into the garage. The bays are empty, and the only person in the building is Sophia, finishing up some last minute business matters in her office. I can only imagine what his intentions are, and that alone is enough to ignite my veins. The man waits for Sophia to step out of her office while I wait in the dark, staying out of her business as I was told to do.

Once she exits, the man surprises her. "Hello Honey, remember me? I would like that special deal you offered me earlier with a little extra," he says taking hold of her.

"Let go of her," I say with a rugged growl.

"Dante, be careful. He has a gun!" Sophia yells as he spins around, clutching her neck within his beastly arm.

He has a plan to use her to kill me, but his mistake is made when he meets my swirling angry eyes. The sight of Sophia in fear and being handled so inappropriately pushes me into an uncontrolled rage. His stunned fear gives me ample opportunity to take hold of her before he drops to his knees. I whisper his death sentence, and he dies at our feet. His lifeless body is nothing new to me. I have killed before, and this man is certainly deserving considering his intent, but Sophia backs away, looking me over with fear in her eyes. Suddenly, I realize she doesn't know me, not who I really am. "What did you do Dante? How?" I try to approach her, but she continues in her retreat.

"I won't hurt you."

"I don't understand ..." she says, avoiding looking directly at me. I beg her to listen to me, to try and understand what I am telling her. No matter how much begging I do, she still fears me, and I can see her desire to flee in her eyes.

I drop to my knees in front of her, with tears in my eyes, "Please, please Sophia, don't be afraid of me. I would never hurt you. I only want to protect you from the rest of the world, to give you everything you have ever wanted. I want to marry you, to live a long life with you. Please don't run from me. I would die inside." Her feet catch my tears, but I fear she isn't truly hearing me. "I can't help who I am Sophia; I can only help who I love." I look up at her with pleading eyes, and she looks down on me, falling to her knees with me.

"I love you too," she says, embracing me. "I promise to allow you to hold and protect me and our child for the rest of our lives, Dante."

Our child, my child, I look down at her and feel the need to quickly bring her back to my chest, to wrap my arms protectively around her more than ever. I know what this means, and I am going to do everything possible to make sure she never knows the threat of my father and his need to be the ultimate decider of who lives and who dies in his family. The only hope of protecting my family is to deal with my father face to face, bargaining for my future.

I tried to keep it simple, keeping my distance from her in hopes that I would be able to lose interest in her at some point, but nothing worked. So instead, I am diving in head first, hoping that I can talk my father into accepting our relationship, but I abstain from telling him about the child we are expecting.

"Dante, this woman is not right for you! You did not give my choice for you a chance."

"She was boring and no challenge at all."

"She would do whatever you asked her to do, Dante!"

"Exactly! Father, I love Sophia. I am going to marry and be with her. I don't care what you say."

My father doubts my love for Sophia and threatens to disown me. His fiery anger is directed at me with more force than ever before, but I remain solid in my decision. I want to marry her and be with her forever. When my stepmother comes in the room with Saldean, my father smiles and gives me last warning. "You either leave that woman and stay here and see to your responsibilities to this family or I force you out and make Saldean in charge. You will never be allowed back and will receive no protection from me or any of the other Lords who will surely want you dead the moment you step out that door. So what will it be Dante?"

I look over my stepmother and brother before looking back at my father with my head held high. "I choose her. I choose my freedom, and I know for a fact that no Lord will come after me if they know you have disowned me. I am no threat to them then. Don't try and fool me Father. I am the smart one remember?" I grab my things and walk out of my longtime home with no regrets.

Chapter 5

Dante

Since leaving the family, I have been working with Sophia, helping her until I can find a more suitable job for myself. The few things Father let me take are moved into Sophia's house. I leave with very little money. My father cut me off from all accounts, and I am forced to depend on Sophia, something she doesn't mind, but I do. I try and do everything I can to find a better life for us. Every possible opportunity I attempt, my father blocks. He threatens anyone who helps me, and his efforts are beginning to affect Sophia's business. She will be forced to close soon if I don't do something.

If not for my sister, I would know nothing of what is happening with my family. If my stepmother has her way, I will be killed, but for some reason Father resists this idea. I have never understood why he protects me from her, or why he seems to prefer me over my siblings. He never speaks of my mother, leaving me to assume she didn't mean that much to him, but maybe she meant more than I realize. I am hoping that, whatever is keeping him from killing me, is something I can use.

I show up at my father's door, and my old tutor answers. Rabbie stares straight ahead and shows no emotion. "Hello Rabbie," I say, but he says nothing. "I would like to see my father." He nods and shows me to my father's office. "Thank you, Rabbie. Please have some refreshments prepared for me and my son." Rabbie nods and leaves us.

"What is wrong with Rabbie?"

"My assistant is now perfect. After you left, there was no reason for him to be here any longer, but I hated to let a good man go. So, I turned him into my new aide," he says, looking up at me with no concern of how I would feel about that. My punishment. He seeks to cause pain to everyone around me to punish me. My anger builds, and I have a difficult time speaking. "I assume that you have left that woman and are ready to do as I say?"

"No, I have not left her. I love her, but I have come to make a deal with you since you feel it necessary to suffocate everyone around me."

"I don't make deals."

"You don't make deals that don't benefit you. I know that, and I have come to offer you a deal that will benefit you. I will come back and work for you, offering the benefit of my intelligence and negotiation skills to use as needed for the family. In exchange, you allow me the family I want and you leave Sophia and I alone with any children we may have."

My father instantly stands. "Children? She's pregnant? Oh wonderful Dante! I swear, you will be the death of me." He sits back down, swearing at me under his breath. "The child will need to go through judgment."

"No, not my child," I say, causing him to sit back with wide eyes. "We work together, but you leave my family alone, all of them, or else ..." I feel my mother taking me over, and her spirit within me forces my father to accept my terms.

With my deal with my father behind me and my accounts available, I withdraw some money and buy a ring. Before I finish my plans for the night, I make one call to Sophia and ask her to accompany me on a special date. She meets me at the door in a red dress that nearly brings me to my knees. Our dinner is set up on a private balcony where we can feel free to do as we please. The dinner is perfect, but she is even better. There isn't much room on the balcony, but we manage to dance together to the music flowing from inside the timelessly charming restaurant. I breathe in the scent from her neck and rest my heavy head against hers, her velvety hair cushioning the pain of my heart as it begins tearing its way through my chest to get to her. "Who are you?" I whisper through the foggy night air.

"Sophia, Sophia Simone. And you, who are you?" she asks, looking up into my eyes, awakening a soul within me I didn't know existed.

"I am, yours. Forever and always, your Dante." I reach into my pocket and get down on one knee. Looking up at her with pleading, loving eyes, I profess, "I love you Sophia, marry me, and be forever *my* Sophia?"

Her tears nearly drown out her gasping, "Yes, a million times, yes." A thousand kisses from another could never equal one from my Sophia. I am sure my father must be wrong about her. There is no way someone that gives me such amazing feelings could be harmful to me. *Yes*, he must be wrong, and if he isn't, then I will die never regretting loving her.

Working for my father is not difficult, except I do find myself debating him often on how to handle things. His frustration with me is building, and he continues to persuade me to rid myself of Sophia before it is too late, before she completely takes over my thoughts and turns me into her servant.

I love waking up with Sophia in my arms, but today, we are awakened by my father. I ask her to stay in the bedroom while I deal with him, but she wants to argue with me, suggesting that, maybe if he met her, things would be different. She doesn't know him like I do though, and I insist with a kiss that she stay out of sight for her own good. When I open the door to him and his new aide, Rabbie, he looks over me with disgust. I nod in his direction while blocking him from entering our home.

"Cheap clothes my son? Is that what your life has become? Cheap clothes and cheap women... I am so proud of how far you have lowered yourself," he says, looking around the neighborhood. "And what amazing creativity the poor have. It is simply marvelous that they are able to make do in such wretched conditions."

"Is that why you're here? To criticize me? To judge people you don't even know?" I step back with a long sigh. "I have made my choice Father. I am marrying Sophia. You can accept it, cut me off again, or kill me if you prefer. We go through this every day. Why today are you bringing it to my home?" Sophia sneaks up under my arm and wraps her arms around me. She never listens to me, but nonetheless, I am happy that she is at my side. "Father, this is Sophia. Sophia this is my father, Dennis Savage." The corners of his lips tense as he looks her over and notices her growing belly. "I would invite you to our wedding, but it doesn't seem as if you are too happy to hear about my good news, so I won't bother with the stamp on the invitation."

"Dante, I am not here to cause trouble, despite what you may think, and I am not here to force you out of the family, though I see that you are determined to try to leave us. I need you, Dante, no matter your decision. I need your help dealing with situations your brother is obviously not suited for." He looks over at Sophia, but she stands strong against his glare. "She is a strong woman, I see. I couldn't be more excited for you, for you both," he says through his teeth. Not exactly the warm welcome I had hoped for, but I guess for him to say it at all is somewhat of an accomplishment.

I ask her to let me speak with my father alone, and I step outside with him. "What are you doing here Father, and no more of your snide comments about the way I am now living? Tell me why you are really here."

"Dante, I took you in as a child when I didn't have to. I made you my top son despite my wife's wishes. You are not the oldest. You are not the strongest, but you are the smartest, the most strategic, and therefore, the best of all my children. I need you, Dante, and I am not willing to give up on you because you are taken with some … woman," he says delicately.

Something inside me begins to tense, and I feel trouble creeping up from all sides. I back away from him with a watchful eye all around. My mind begins to swarm with questions. Why is he really here? Why is my brother hiding in the car? Why is Barr at the side of the house? Rabbie constantly looking through the windows? My father constantly trying to turn me into another direction by pacing away from me? I block out his words and pay attention to his actions. Dennis Savage is never above deception, even with his own son.

He must have forgotten that my training was completed. He must have believed that I am my brother and would not comprehend what was happening around me. I am trained to fight, but I was born omniscient of my surroundings. As my father walks away from me in one direction, I step into the other and throw Rabbie into the air before sliding across the front deck to catch my brother sneaking around the side of the house. "Where are you going Saldean?" He stands, looking through me as if I am nothing to him. His response to me catches me off guard, and I nearly miss his quick step to attack me. While I battle my brother, I keep an eye on Barr as he moves from the car. "Sophia!" Throwing Saldean off his legs, I rush through the front door as Barr has Sophia cornered. Barr is my father's deadliest assassin. He has no fear and no use for bargaining; he only follows orders, the orders of my father. If I have to kill him to save her, I will. I move on him as my father rushes more men in at me. I battle one, then three, then five, and more and more until I hear a high pitched squawking coming my way. I don't have a chance to turn before I feel the paralyzing pain surging through my body.

"Dante!" I hear her scream for me as I try to find my way back to protect her. Sophia's screams echo in my head as I go blind and begin to feel my body being taken over by some kind of poisonous demon. *I have to help Sophia.* "Dante!" I hear her broken voice slowly fade to the back of my mind as I feel someone take my hand and kiss my cheek. The swirling voices in my head and rushing of energy around me dissipate.

Ever since I met Sophia, her presence has had a calming effect on me. I had no desire to fight or to kill for my father anymore. I have killed for her and felt the need to beg for forgiveness right after doing so. It has always been the more I killed, the more I craved it until I was no longer killing for my family. I killed for Sophia, proving my heart beat only for her. Now as much as she screams for me, I can do nothing but fight through the darkness around me. My love, my child, and I can't find either as my energy fades, "I love you Dante."

I don't know how much time passed while I was asleep, but when I awake, the sun is shining on the opposite side of the house. The silence in the room does nothing to help my pounding head. I slowly open my swollen eyes to see her hand still reaching out to me, but her broken neck twists the rest of her body away from me. My father sits in a chair, watching me with a simple expression. He knew what he was doing all along. I try to shake the groggy feeling in my head as my father directs Barr, Saldean, and Rabbie back to the car.

"Get up, and let's go home Dante. You have no reason to stay here any longer. You have done your job, now we must get back to our other business," he says, waving his hand for me to follow him to the car. I manage to sit up, looking over her body sprawled out over my own. I touch her and feel over her, searching for any kind of life within her. My father stands, looking over me with concern. "I assure you that you killed her. We can go now."

"I killed her?"

"She attacked you, and you had to defend yourself. No need to worry. She is no one to worry about, and the child she was carrying died on its own, so you will not be held responsible. Just push her to the side and dust yourself off. I will have our people come and take care of the mess."

I look up at him in shock, "She was the love of my life, the mother of my child."

My father stands back with wide eyes, "You remember her?" I nod and pull back the hair from her face and hold her against me. "How can that be? You shouldn't remember anything. You shouldn't have any feelings at all for her. The poison, the cravings I caused you to have should have taken care of all that for you."

"You did this to me? You took everything from me so I would come back to you?"

"You belong to me. You're my son. No one else should matter to you other than me," he says with no sign of sorrow or regret. "You're my son!" He screams at me.

I rage at him and knock him back into a wall. "I hate you! I hate everything about you! Why would you do this to me? Why, because you're jealous?"

"You are my son, Dante, and no one else will take you from me. You will do as I say, and what I say only." I slam him backwards and fight him with everything I have until Saldean comes in. The brother I used to share toys with now has vengeance and hate in his eyes for me. I realize I don't have enough energy to fight them both, so I run. I run, planning to never return, to go to a place he could never find me, but the image of her eats me alive, and I want nothing more than to let my father find me and put me out of my misery.

I manage to contact my sister, and she brings me enough clothes and money to get by. She begs me to return and not make father any angrier, but I refuse. Galena finally tells me that my brother, Saldean, was influenced by the same poison that father inflicted on me. He remembers nothing of our childhood and has become an unstoppable killer. She says, if I don't return, she fears Father will demand that he hunt me down and kill me. With the pain I feel from losing my Sophia and our child, I would almost prefer it. That plan would have surely come true if not for my father being distracted by an attack by Rein Lorid, the Lord of the 8th. I still wait, and I wait, but he never comes for me. Galena is the only one I stay in contact with, though she is limited in the time she can give me and even more limited on what she can tell me about our father. He doesn't trust her to know much about his business.

The more time that goes by, the more I drink, and the more women I take to bed until I realize that fucking, for me, is a calming relief from my pain and anger. I would have self-destructed if not for Galena. She contacts me in a panic one day after not seeing or hearing from her for some time. I wanted nothing to do with her by then, but she was relentless in her pursuit and tracked me down on her own accord. I thought, for sure, she was setting me up for her brother or for Father, himself, to kill me. I was ready to kill her for betraying me until she handed me a secret to protect for her. My sister needed me, and as if that wasn't enough, her secret meant betraying my father's wishes, giving me new reason to recover my strength and help her the best way I can. Only, the daunting secret becomes too much for me to handle on my own, and I worry I won't be able to keep the secret from my father if he ever comes after me. So, I search for some place and someone I can fully trust to hold our secret while I develop a plan to take a stand against my father. The process doesn't hinder my desires though. The women I encounter become nothing more than stress relievers, but some end up becoming more important than expected.

I wasn't thinking with my first child, Connor. His mother was nothing more than a conquest to prove a point to a rich brat that swore I could never have what he had, so I took his fiancé to bed. The child was beautiful, and his mother desperately wanted me to take ownership of him, but my father would have never allowed him to live. He would be a drain on his power or so he would say. You have children to increase your power, so they must be strong or else you must have them killed. I would have many more siblings if not for this rule of his. I never saw him do it, but I heard. I finally asked him one day.

"Why would you kill your own child?"

"Because Dante, if they are not strong enough, they will die anyway from the poison that will eventually spread through their veins. I kill them now to prevent inevitable suffering. You understand, don't you?

I believed him, until I realized the poison was not one we were born with but one inflicted by our own father. My father killed his children for his own gain. Only the strongest survive because only the strongest can help him gain more power. All the others drain him, leaving no opportunity for him to gain anything. I decided to leave my children alone and let them live, but without me being involved in their lives in hope that my father will never know about them. That idea changed when Nicholas was born.

His mother caught my attention, and I felt bad for her life. No one wanted her because of her condition, but she was too beautiful to be left alone forever. She was never capable of much emotion until me. I found it odd, but giving her pleasure and happiness made me feel good about myself, so I stayed with her and watched over her. I loved her like a friend, and she gave birth to the son that opened my eyes to love again. Nicholas had a power over me, something I hadn't felt since Sophia. I love my children, but Nicholas is special. I knew from the moment he looked me dead in the eyes and I saw his swirling displeasure with me for not paying enough attention to him that there was something different about him. Ignoring him was not going to be possible. No, I had to stay with him and protect him from my father. I stayed within the city and raised him, while keeping an eye on my other children.

Ryan's mother was the only woman since Sophia that has gotten to me. Although I never quivered in her presence, I was always excited to see her. I still care for her, and even love her as much as I allowed myself to love anyone after *my* Sophia. She was a great mother, and because of her, Ryan was the first of my children I rocked to sleep. Ryan had the sweetest hold on me, and it was hard to let go of him. The last time I held him, I said, "I love you," and handed him over to his mother. I cried all night from the pain of having to let him go. I was not overly supportive of Nicholas taking care of him for me. I was afraid of the attention it might bring to Ryan, but at the same time, it made it easier for me to keep an eye on them. I spent a lot of time following those two around. The things they got into still make me cringe, but somehow, they survived. I wanted to make sure their lives would be great ones, and the only way I could do that was to find a way to kill my father, to kill Dennis Savage. Once and for all. My failure to do so will eliminate my chance of ever having a life of my own, and my children will be haunted by his looming shadow, especially Nicholas.

Chapter 6

Dante

My death was unexpected. I should have prepared my son better. I shouldn't have protected him for so long. I wanted him to live as normal of a life as possible. It is unfortunate though, that he had to endure the pain of who he is without his father. I would have done anything to change that, and now, I have only one opportunity to help him. I go before the High Council and beg them to let me live again; to let me have another chance to save my children from the evil that haunts them. My father still holds the highest of positions amongst the Lords of the Realms, encouraging the council to make the difficult decision. Not only do they decide to let me live again, but they allow me to spy for them. If my father is doing acts that are not acceptable, that are against the rules of the High Council, then they must know so they can remove him and replace him with another. The High Council were once highly regarded leaders of the world before their deaths, and now, they sit in the in-between, in between right and wrong, heaven and hell, or however you to choose to see it. They are not privileged to the all-knowing, only to the ways that any human could possibly learn information, through talk and what they see first-hand. They deal with a lot in their position, and my father takes advantage of them every chance he gets. The Council is continuously made to look like fools by him, and they know it. However, they have neither the proof nor power to do anything about it.

I am, in the end, granted an opportunity, and if I succeed, I could win favor with the Council. I am grateful for the opportunity and for the offer of a favor from them, but more importantly, I am concerned about my children and protecting them. They are vulnerable where they are, and my father will have them all killed, all except Nicholas because he will turn him into the monster that he wanted me to be. I don't know if I can prevent that, but I have to try. I am granted a second chance at life, a life with a different view, a different body, and, perhaps, a way to spoil my father's plans without detection. It's not quite the second chance I was hoping for, but if all goes well, I will not only save my children, but I will have a chance to be with Sophia again. I have so much to gain and everything to lose.

My life is now at a lower level, but this opportunity gives me a chance to be with my children like I never could before. Tonight, they are all gathered together.

Lena, the daughter I would have raised on my own if I thought I could have, was raised by Andrea, a much better choice for her and the best mother a girl could have. Andrea was tough, but loving; she never let Lena get out of line. She was the perfect mother for a girl, especially one that could have easily been swayed down a bad path. Andrea was well established, intelligent, and able to give Lena the life I couldn't. Lena is an example of one of my few good decisions.

Lena and her new husband, Brady, sit cuddling together in one chair, reminding everyone they came back from their honeymoon too soon. I sniff him repeatedly, checking him out. He seems to love her deeply and doesn't seem to be bothered by me sitting in between them while I give him a closer look.

"Hey, Jayzon, what is wrong with your dog? Did you train him not to like cops or something?" Brady says, laughing as he tries to kiss Lena around me.

"Do you think Nick would bother to train that dog?! Are you kidding? Unless that dog can spy for him or handle a gun, then he has no time for him. Not liking cops must be a natural instinct, Brady. They do say dogs have good instincts about people." Ryan laughs nodding in Nicholas's direction.

Ryan, my youngest, is growing into such a fine man, and so happily teasing Sam as they talk of their own wedding plans. I have heard them discussing running away in the middle of the night and skipping the large wedding now that they have built their dream home. I imagine it is only a matter of time before they do just that. The way he talks to her, I'm surprised that she isn't pregnant already.

"Come here, Eey. I have to tell you something," Nicky says, grabbing my collar and pulling me onto the floor to show me his new toy. My grandson, Nicky, already showing signs of being just like his father. Even his responsibility of being the older brother mirror Nicholas's relationship with Ryan. Nicky rarely lets Brayden out of his sight. Kayla had to move Nicky's room next to Brayden's just so they could share a door in between, a door that is never closed. Nicky looks after his little brother's every step and never lets him fall. Not that I can blame him, Brayden, looks just like his mother. His angelic face makes you drunk with love. No one denies him much; I even let him chew on my ears whenever he wants. As much as he looks like his mother, he still has the blood of his father. His strength is low from being ill most of the time, but you can see the swirling anger in his eyes if you deny him something he wants. Brayden, however, tends to use his mother's angelic gift to get what he wants, a gift his mother uses quite well, too.

Kayla, I had no idea how strong she was when I pushed Nicholas in her direction. The more she denied him, the happier I became. I watched their relationship grow to something so strong that I am sure no one can break them, not even my father. Kayla is beautiful, intelligent, and a wonderful mother. Most of all, she loves my son like he has never been loved before and like he deserves. She also has moves that hypnotize you. Yes, Nicholas is a lucky man, and it is no wonder he rarely misses an opportunity to get her naked and close to him.

"Eey, go on, move," Nicholas says, pushing me out of Kayla's lap and away from her affections. "That dog is constantly on you." Kayla laughs, calming him with sweet whispers and tender kisses. Nicholas, my son, the strongest of them all. His shoulders carry them, but if not for Kayla, Nicholas wouldn't be the man he is. The two of them need each other more than they even know. My first goal is to make sure *he*, Savage, Asmodeus, my father, does not take Nicholas away, but I'm not sure I can manage that much longer. My father has been constantly sending out spies to draw him in. I find them hovering around the estate and provoking Nicholas to come out to meet them, but he is too smart for their baiting games, something that only increases my father's hunger. I would like to say that no spies have attempted to come into their home, but there is one woman that has already entered the house more than once, and I suspect she works for my father. I'm not sure why I distrust her, but I get a faint scent of desperation and dishonesty every time she steps into the room. Nicholas does not block this spy from what she wants; Kayla does.

Nicholas is strong, intelligent, intuitive, and powerful, and Kayla is the same. Together, they are unbreakable. The goal of my father will be to separate them somehow, and once that happens, the resilient pair will become frail and weak. I just wish I knew how he plans to do it. I assume he will go after Kayla and lure her into fear, and to her death.

My second goal for being here is to make sure my father does not kill Kayla as I know he wants to. She stands between him and my son, and she alone keeps him from becoming filled with anger and destructive beyond control. Nicholas needs her, and she needs him.

My third goal is to insure he never gets to Nicky. The only chance they all have is if Nicky survives. His power is like no other. I didn't even realize what he was capable of until he helped me. He is young but smarter than anyone three times his age.

Everything is quiet tonight, and I enjoy the smiles and laughter until I sense something strange. I instantly run outside to investigate. It's a brisk evening, with the fall air making its way through. There are many scents, but one clues me in to *who* is watching us. It has been a long time since I have seen her, but her scent is distinctive, and I will never forget it. Before I have a chance to check it out, Nicholas steps out beside me, searching the darkness as well. *Does he sense her too?* With a cock of my head, I watch him as he listens and carefully observes the trees' movements. His sudden low growl evokes a trembling in the air and a spine-chilling effect on me.

Nicholas looks down at me and hesitates before speaking, "Do you sense it, too?" I get excited by his acknowledgment of me. He doesn't usually pay me much attention, and he certainly never speaks to me, but tonight, we share a common trait, one I wasn't aware he had. Looking back out at the trees, he stiffens, and I follow his gaze. She is not visible to him or me, but I know she's there. Racing towards the trees, I follow her and back her up to the fence. She turns to me and instantly eyes me down as she always had with foes. I can only assume her attack strategy hasn't changed either. Sure enough, she comes at me in her usual fashion, and I wait for the right moment before slipping her grasp and finding her weak spot. No one knows that spot except her father and her brother. I release my hold on her, allowing her to stand in amazement.

She paces around me in awe as she begins to realize. "Dante?" Galena asks, but she knows the answer. "I am only looking after him, Dante," she says as I growl my disapproval. "You can distrust me if you want, but I was the one that helped you. I talked Father into letting you go and not killing you. Now, I can help your son, too. Protect him from Father and make sure he doesn't fall into trouble he can't escape." I know her, and the only reason she tried to keep Father from killing me was in hopes of protecting her own secrets. I am the only one that knows the secret that Galena would never want our father to know. She approaches me with a smile, carefully reaching out her hand. Looking deep into her eyes, I search for any sign that she might have changed, but before I can decide, I hear Nicholas calling for men as he and Ryan head out towards us. I quickly lunge at Galena, sending her retreating over the estate wall. My sister is too controlled by my father to be fully trusted, but there is still something there that I once knew and loved. My boys head off every possible escape as they meet me in the midst of the trees. Galena is long gone before they can cut her off.

"There is no one here Nick," Ryan says.

"There was. I know it."

"Yeah, you know it. I think you are on edge and jumping at the shadows of the trees."

Nicholas smiles as he looks down at me and brushes his hand over my head, removing a piece of Galena's shirt from my teeth. "Trees don't wear clothes," he says, holding up the fabric to Ryan.

"Wow, it would seem even our dog has a special kind of sense about him," Ryan says rewarding me with a loving rub of my ears.

"A special sense. Funny how that worked out for us," Nicholas says, eyeing me suspiciously. "There is something about you. I don't know what it is, but I am beginning to trust you more with my son, dog... Eey," Nicholas says.

Chapter 7

Kayla

"Nick? Nick!" I yell, a little louder each time until our bedroom door opens and I see his tall, dark form slowly walk in with an admiring smile.

"You called, Princess?" Nick says, leaning down and pressing his warm lips to mine. Feeling his strong hand press sweetly against my cheek, he leans in and hums, "You look better. I was worried about you. You were screaming in your sleep last night. I wrapped you in a blanket and kissed you several times, but nothing seemed to work until I let you sleep on my chest. Not that I minded having you that close to me, but I hate that you are having nightmares." I don't say a word. Not that I have to, he knows the cause of my nightmares and considering the look on his face, he is feeling the guilt already.

Savage's face haunts me every day. That night, oh that night was my worst nightmare. I couldn't do anything for my husband, or my child. All I could see was evil's swirling eyes stealing the breath from my lungs. The more I tried to free myself from him, the more he controlled me. I could hear my mother's voice screaming at me, "*You loser, you weak little nothing. You don't even deserve Nick and your boys.*" In the end, through her laughter and my son's and husband's screams, Savage comes forward and backs me into a corner where I can neither breathe nor escape. I hold onto Nick every night, desperate for him to tell me he has it all figured out and everything is going to be okay. I am beginning to fear that he won't be able to come up with a plan in time.

Nick leans down and gently kisses me. "I decided to let you sleep once you calmed, but you didn't sleep long, Princess," he says as I catch a strange mark on his neck. The mark is almost like a branding into his skin, except it doesn't resemble anything more than a simple blackened circle. I try to pull back his shirt to see it more clearly, but he grabs my hands and holds them with his. "That's nothing. I promise, Princess. It is nothing to be worried about. As you can see, I am fine and still more than strong enough to hold you in my arms and keep you safe." He embraces me fully, proving how wonderfully safe it does feel to be in his arms. "Lay back and rest. The doctor did say you will need some time before you can regain your full strength again. As always, you have been trying to overdo it too soon."

"I'm fine Nick. What I need is to know what happened with Savage?"

"You don't need to worry about that. I am taking care of everything. You just worry about taking care of yourself and our boys."

"Don't do this Nick! Don't shut me out and force me to standby and wait for things to happen while you're out protecting everybody else. I'm strong enough to handle anything, and you know it. Please, let me help you."

"Princess, I know you are quite capable of handling most things, but this time, the situation is not something for you to handle. This time, I need to take care of it on my own. It is beyond you. I fear it is beyond me even, but I have no choice if I want to protect you, protect the boys, and everyone else. Savage is too strong, and until I can figure out a way to beat him, I have to work with him," Nick says, staring at me hard and doing the best he can to convince me there is nothing I can do.

"So are you going to tell me what your plan is? Do you even have a plan? Oh, please Nick, please tell me you have a plan?"

"You know I always have a plan, Princess. Good or bad I always have a plan. I can't explain it right now, so you're just going to have to trust me." I tug my hands from his and quickly pull back his shirt to gaze over the burn marks and bruises on his neck, arms, wrists and chest before looking deep into his eyes and trying to understand what he is doing to himself. He doesn't speak. He doesn't even try to explain. The expression in his eyes tells me all I need to know. He is endangering his life somehow, and I will certainly not agree with whatever his plan is.

"Nick …" I try to speak, but the words just won't come out. No matter how hard I try to confess to him I am scared and, for the first time, fearful that we are going to lose, I can't. I can't force the words from my mouth. I can't do that to him. I can't burden him with that right now. I'm being selfish, hoping he will soothe my confessions with the right words that everything is going to be alright. The more I look into his eyes, the more I realize, he doesn't know, and those words I have been waiting for are not going to come, no matter what I confess. So with the best smile I can form, I simply say, "I love you. I love you so much …" Tears form in my eyes, and he immediately stops me with his comforting hand on my cheek.

"I love you too, very much. What's wrong, Princess? I haven't seen that look in your eyes since … since you were a kid, waking up with nightmares. I don't like to see you like this. Tell me what I can do to fix it?"

"Promise me. Promise me you will always love me and never stop fighting for us? Promise me that, and I promise you I will feel better and not need to know anything else."

"Kayla, don't you understand that my love for you is so embedded in my heart that it doesn't beat without you?" I smile wide, wrapping my arms around him. "You went through a very traumatizing experience, Princess. You were comatose for two days, and I don't understand why you insist on acting like you're able to handle everything that you usually do so soon. You're still weak and tired. You will feel better in a few more days," Nick sighs again, cradling my face in his hands, "Rest, and we will talk more later." A sweet kiss, a tender grasp of my thigh, and he smiles. "Get all the rest you can because I am anxious to prove my love for you, *in my special way*, later tonight." I take hold of him and don't want to let go. *Why wait until tonight?*

"Nick?" I stop kissing and fondling my husband to see Franky peeking through our bedroom door. "Oh, there you are? I managed to find that information on your mother for you. Do you still want to see it?" Franky says with a sweetly innocent smile.

"Yes. Thank you, Franky. Get some rest Princess. I have the boys playing in the office with me, so don't worry about them." Nick kisses me on the head, a g-rated kind of affection that I am not accustom to.

"Are you not feeling well, Kayla?" Franky asks with a concerning tilt of her head.

"I'm fine. Just a little tired is all," I say imagining myself choking her sweet little head off her body, but with a smile, of course.

"Are you sure? If you need me to, I would be happy to look you over and write a prescription if necessary?" she says.

"No thanks. I'm good." I smile back at her as Nick looks back at me with a grin.

"Thank you, Franky. That is very nice of you." Nick says. "I think she just needs a little more rest." *Uh-huh rest ... and my gun.*

"Oh, it is absolutely no problem. Happy to help," she says, holding her hand over her heart. "If you change your mind, I will be downstairs with Nick for another hour, I would think? Wouldn't you Nick?" Nick nods, taking my hand as if he knows I am ready to jump across the bed at her. He excuses them both before I can respond, which is probably best for everyone.

I don't know why that woman bothers me so much, but there is something about her I just don't like. I lie back in bed and actually begin to fall asleep until I feel the bed move. I feel someone slyly climbing into the bed near me. "Don't get excited Kayla. I am not Nick, so you can keep your panties on," Exie, says as she suddenly plops down right against me.

"What are you doing here?"

"I called earlier, and Nick said you were having nightmares all night."

"And you came by to check on me? That is so sweet."

"Hell no! I thought you would be out of it enough so I could steal those shoes I have been asking to borrow for months now," she says, causing me to laugh.

"I should have known," I say as she finally breaks a smile. "So did you see her?"

"Who? Oh, Franky?" I nod impatiently. "Yeah, Nick introduced her to me when I came in. She seems nice." I sit up and glare at her. "I mean… nice for an obviously evil, cum-guzzling, cheap, back- alley slut, and all other horrible things in the world that I am too much of a lady to mention." She looks sideways at me until I back off my sinister glare. "Gees. She dated Nick in high school, so what? He married you."

"He asked her to marry him first."

"No! You don't say. Well, it's settled then. We must kill her," she says sarcastically. "And… Nick is insanely in love with you, and I don't think an old girlfriend is going to change that any,"

"I know, but I get a bad feeling about her. Of all the things Nick told me about her, it seems like she fits them, but she fits them almost too well." Exie rolls her eyes. "Don't roll your eyes at me. The woman acts as if she is reading a script about a woman she has never known. I don't trust her," I snap.

"Then pull out your Kayla investigation glasses and look into what she is telling your clearly vulnerable husband," she huffs with a laugh. But she gives me an idea. I turn towards her and smile wide. "Oh no. No! No! Whatever it is, I am not helping you. I am busy that day and the next. No. No, Kayla!"

Chapter 8

Kayla

Exie's arms are still crossed, but I ignore her disapproval and continue to wait for the right moment to sneak into the medical facility where Nick's mom stays. It may seem stupid and paranoid, but there is something about Franky I don't trust. Exie begins shaking her head as soon as she realizes my determination to go through with this. "Stop shaking your head. You agreed to help me, and besides ... you look absolutely amazing in that outfit. I bet Bo would be on his hands and knees drooling if he saw you right now," I say with a smile.

"Really, you think so?" Exie says, proudly looking down at herself. "Hey, don't change the subject Kayla! I am not at all happy about being tricked into this. You said we were going to do something that was not going to cause us to get arrested. Breaking and entering is against the law I believe."

"We aren't breaking anything. We are walking in and exploring. There is no law against exploring. Besides, Nick pays a lot of money for this place. We should be able to do whatever we want to, when we want to do it. Now, unfold your arms, and let's go." I don't bother to continue trying to convince her, I just go, knowing Exie will never let me go alone. I wait to sneak in through one of the side doors, and just as expected, one of the orderlies steps out for a smoke break which isn't allowed on the premises. He is so determined to hide his habit that he doesn't notice us going into the door he conveniently left propped open.

Once we are in, I take a moment to look around and verify where any possible staff members might be, but the place is nearly empty at this late hour. I can find only one orderly who is too busy playing a game on his iPad to notice us. No matter the skeleton crew, I am still cautious about rounding corners and leading Exie down long halls.

"Do you know where you're going?" Exie whispers to me. *She has no faith in me, as if I would come here without knowing exactly where I am going.* Eddie was able to provide me with everything I need and was happy to do it for me, although I had to swear that I would never tell Nick. I find the door I am looking for and smile wide to the immediate roll of her eyes. "Just hurry up," she barks.

I go through the keys I had one of our men steal for me earlier in the day until one finally works. We hurry in, and I instantly begin searching through the computer to try and find the information I am looking for. Unfortunately, the woman we stole the keys from was smart enough to put a lock on her computer. I quickly take out my phone and dial, "Hi Eddie. Yeah I'm here, but she put a lock on it." Eddie, gave me a gadget to attach via the USB, and once I do, he immediately takes over and breaks in within seconds. I watch proudly as Eddie downloads all the information about this facility for me.

"Kayla, hurry up! I think someone is coming." Exie says in a loud whisper as she peeks through a window in the door.

"Okay Kayla. I got it all. Shut it down and get out of there."

"Thanks Eddie, see you soon. We got what we need Exie let's get out of here," I say, making sure to put everything back the way I found it.

"I think we are too late," Exie replies, and I glance out to see several orderlies gathering around. A quick look around and I decide our best bet is to use the skills we both know well. I mess up our clothes and dishevel our hair before we both nod towards each other, understanding exactly what we are going to do. We sneak out the door and lock it back before I toss the keys into a nearby laundry chute. We walk towards the men, giggling and holding onto each other in a drunken performance.

"Hey! What are you girls doing out of your room?" One yells at us as we just giggle and smile, allowing them near before we rub against them and sigh an erotic need. They don't complain and, as expected, they immediately forget about their jobs. We have two apiece to deal with, but we both manage to hypnotize them with a sway of our hips, a lick of our lips, and an alluring hum that draws them even closer to our admiring hands. We tempt them this way and that, watching as the four men begin to laugh nervously.

"Can I have some water? I am so very hot," I say as Exie twists her fingers into the cleavage of her shirt. They quickly show us to the employee lounge and rush to get us whatever we want while we sneak their keys from their pockets and lock them into the lounge. We wave goodbye, make a quick stop to delete the camera footage at the reception desk, and walk out, tossing their keys near the back door where their chain-smoking friend can eventually find them. We leave out the front door, jump in my car, and are gone within a breath, although our adrenaline high remains long after we escape.

"Damn Kayla. I swear, a few more years of being your friend and I am surely going to have a heart attack," Exie says harshly but eventually smiling when I laugh. "Alright, alright. I will admit, you keep my life interesting, and at times, it's worth being your friend." She smiles, and I know she feels good about her skills for the night.

By the time we get to Eddie, he is already going through the files with Terrence. "Have you found anything?" I ask them.

"Yes and no." Terrence says. "There is actually nothing at all on a Francesca or Franky with any last name anywhere in the files. No work information, no education file, no medical. Nothing. However, they have records of every other worker and patient in the place. Every doctor that works there has a complete career chart, where they worked previously, every school they attended, and all their medical certification numbers. Yet, there isn't one thing about this woman. There doesn't even seem to be anyone that would resemble her under another name. It's strange, Kayla. When we look up Nick's mom's file, it says her doctor is Francesca Conti. She's the only one in the facility with that doctor."

I look over Eddie's shoulder to view the documents he has pulled up and stare at the words "private physician." "She only sees one patient? That can be right. She has a permanent office for one patient?"

"Does Nick pay for that?" Exie asks.

"I don't think they would offer anything like that, even if Nick required it. Nick would surely say something to me about that. I think I need to talk to him about this?" I say, not considering why I would ask such a question.

"He is not going to like how you got this information, or that you are having Franky followed," Exie says to me.

"Well, I don't have to tell him everything. Just that I was worried about his Mother?" Exie shakes her head. "Okay, I will confess that I wanted to know more about Franky, and I didn't want him to know that I am … intimidated by her?"

"You're intimidated by her?" Exie doubles over in laughter. "Okay, good luck with that. I have to get back to the club and close up." Exie waves goodbye while I try to figure out how to talk to Nick about this.

No matter what I come up with, I can't imagine it is going to help me avoid an argument. *Nick, I was worried about your mother and … no that's not ever going to work. Damn it Nick, I have a right to know everything about her! Oh no I am in real trouble.* It would be best to just say it and reflect the issues back on Franky before he has a chance to get angry with me. Although, it can't hurt to tell him in his favorite lingerie. The moment Nick walks in, he looks me over with suspicion. *Damn the underwear was too much.*

"What did you do?" he sighs, expecting trouble already. He knows me too well.

"What? Why are you immediately assuming I did something wrong?" I ask him with attitude, but when he cocks his head and huffs, I know I am not going to convince him of anything other than the trouble I have caused. "Fine, I dug up some information on Franky. Do you know there is no record of her anywhere at that hospital and that the only patient that even has her listed as their doctor is your mother? Why is that, Nick? How can she get away that? She is stalking your mother to get to you." I hold out documents to him that I had printed and look up at him with innocent smiling eyes.

He looks down at my hand, but the moment his eyes start to swirl, I know I am in trouble. "Kayla, what the fuck did you do? Did you break into the hospital and steal her information? What is wrong with you lately? Do you not trust me? I have never in my life known you to be jealous or insecure around anyone. Why are you worried all of a sudden?"

"I'm not. I just don't trust her! There is something about her that isn't right, Nick."

"There is nothing about her, except that she cares for my mother and I used to fuck her! And you hate that I ever had feelings for anyone other than you. Yes, I cared for her deeply, I still care for her, our relationship meant something to me ... *at the time*. Fuck Kayla, that was a long time ago, and those feelings are not even close to the same feelings I have for you."

"I know that. This has nothing to do with jealousy or insecurity. I don't *trust* her. And I can't believe that you do?"

"Don't do that. Don't pretend this is about me. This all about you."

I push my folder into his chest and look up at him with pleading eyes, only he rolls his and tenses his jaw. "Just look them over, and you will see what I am talking about. She was dead Nick, and suddenly she is alive? Why now?" I can tell by the way he is standing in front of me and the expression on his face that he has stopped listening to me. He is so angry with me that he won't even look at me.

"Are you done?" Nick asks, looking away from me. "Can I go now?"

"No, I want you to listen to me!"

"I love you Kayla, but right now, I don't want to even look at you." Nick turns away from me and walks out the door. He has been angry with me before, but he has never been so angry that he had to leave.

Chapter 9

Nick

I had to leave before I said something to her that I would regret. *The last thing I need to deal with, is this! Does she not understand I have enough going on? I am trying to keep my family alive, keep my friends from being tortured, and she is worried about some ex-girlfriend of mine. Is she fucking kidding me? I am fucking electrocuting myself for her! I am not doing it for Franky!*

I drive for hours before I somehow end up at my mother's hospital. The long drive gave me plenty of time to calm down and just enough time to begin to question Kayla's findings myself. Stepping towards Franky's office, I reach for the doorknob before shaking my head and pulling back. This is stupid. Who cares why or where she has been? I walk away but turn around again, walk right into her office, and stare right into her eyes. Her feet are up on her desk, and she is touching up her makeup in a compact that she quickly shoves back in her bag.

"Nick! Oh this is a surprise." She jumps up and runs to me with open arms. "You look so good and smell even better. Oh, if you weren't married the things I would do to you would be against the law." I look down at her awkwardly. "Ummm, I mean … I am just kidding. I had some allergy medicine at lunch. I think it has made me a little loopy."

"How come you only see my mother and no other patients here?"

"What? How could you possibly know that?" she asks, taking a step back from me.

"What happened to my mother's previous doctor? I never thought to ask where he went. He had been here for some time but was far from retirement age. If he did decide to leave or even retire, why didn't I get a letter telling me that? I should have been told who my mother's doctor is don't you think? At the very least, I should have been informed that her physician had changed? Why wasn't I ever told?"

She shakes her head, seeming to search for the right words to say to me. "Nick I'm sorry you were not told about her previous doctor. Believe it or not, I actually heard about his accident through a mutual friend, and I already knew that he was your mother's doctor. I was worried who might be taking over her care so that's when I decided to step in and help."

"When? When did you decide to step in?"

She steps back, huffing at me, "What is this about? Why are you interrogating me? Have I done something wrong to you or to your mother? As far as I know, she is not complaining about me at all, but insisting I stay."

"Kayla went through the hospital files and found no record of you, except, as my mother's physician. That doesn't make any sense, Franky."

"She did what?" I can't believe her! She is something else, Nick. How you can be with someone of such a low caliber, I will never understand. She is absolutely the most …"

"Answer me Franky!" I yell at her.

"I told you Nick. When I found out your mother was here, I wanted to look after her for you. I wanted to do whatever I could for you. The hospital had already hired a replacement physician, but they agreed to let me come in and see the one patient until they needed more help. I am taking a mediocre salary, but it is worth it to help you and your mother. I have become so close to her. I feel like she is my mother. I couldn't possibly allow anyone else to take care of her now." She begins to cry as she turns away from me. "You loved me once Nick, and I wanted so bad to feel that, to be close to you somehow. Not because I wanted you back but simply because that part of my life, my time with you, was some of the best memories I have. All I have are those wonderful memories. My father is gone Nick. I have no one left but you."

"Your father died?' I ask, and she nods with tears in her eyes. I open up my arms, and she immediately dives into them. She begins telling me all about how her father died and left her alone and unsure what to do with her life until one day she found an old picture of us together, a picture that she has hidden in her wallet. I smile as I take the picture from her hand. The day I talked her into skipping school and spending the day with me. The only way she would was if I promised to take her to the zoo. I threw her over my shoulder and acted like I was dragging her there, just in case someone found the picture they could blame me for her skipping school. I have to admit, that was a great day.

"You remember, don't you?" She asks smiling as I do. "That was a wonderful day. I still can't believe you talked me into going to a stinky zoo, but you do have an incredible way of getting me to do whatever you want." She approaches me, caressing my face, and looking into my eyes. I look at her awkwardly, but before I can challenge her memory, she stands up on her toes and steadies herself to kiss me. I quickly turn my head before she reach my lips. She stands back in shock and then smacks me hard across the face. "Fuck you! You said I meant something, but I was nothing to you!"

"I didn't come here to rekindle our old relationship. That relationship is over. I'm in love with Kayla now, truly in love with her. We can be friends, but we can never be anything more." I give her a sideways glare as I rub my stinging face. "I came here to get answers and nothing more. Now tell me, Franky, why are you really here and why is there no record of you anywhere? I just had a friend of mine search through DMV records, real estate sales, car deeds, but there is nothing. There is nothing about you anywhere, not even at the college you say you graduated from," I say, pointing to the framed degree on the wall.

"I can't believe you don't trust me, Nick."

"Answer me then."

"Of course there is no record. Everything is still under the name the FBI gave me."

"Which is?"

"I can't tell you that, not until I have clearance from the FBI. But since you seem so insistent on knowing, I guess I will ask them if it is okay to share that information with you. Until then, I can't give you much more than my word that I am only here for your mother right now. I will admit, I came searching for you, but once I found out you were married, I backed off and found comfort supporting your mother. You do not know how hard that was for me. You don't know how many times I have dreamed about being with you again. I have learned a lot since we were together last. It would be nice to prove to you that I can fuck better than you have ever had," she says, shocking me. "But for now, I have to go. My boyfriend is picking me up, and I am going to spend tonight fucking *him*."

"You want to fuck me, but you have a boyfriend? What is with you? You are not at all like I remember. You're more like that girl I told you not to be. Remember that wannabe girl, the one that you pretended to be that night at the party when I had to rescue from that goon who was all over you? The night you thought it better to wear high heels and a short skirt with lots of makeup and overdone hair," I say pointing out all the things she is wearing now that match that night exactly. "This is not you. I don't know who this girl is, but it isn't anyone I want to associate with."

"I am not a girl anymore Nick. If you would wake up for a second, you might realize that. As far as my relationship, he and I have a special *open* relationship, which works much better than any marriage I have seen. You should try it. When you get tired of being married to a dominating, paranoid, lunatic let me know. Now, if you don't mind, please leave now so I can lock up."

She pushes me out the door with a forceful shove, but I don't go far. I stand outside, waiting until she walks out to meet the car that pulls up. "Franky. Franky. Franky!" I yell over and over until she finally turns. It is like she doesn't even know her own name. Maybe she doesn't. Maybe the life change has taken away every part of the Franky I knew, including her name. Franky shoves her chin in the air at me and gets in the car, despite my attempt to get her to come to me. Before she can shut the car door, I take a second to look in at the man in the driver's seat as he admires himself in his rearview mirror. I step towards them. "I want to talk to you!" I say to the man, racing towards them. He looks at me and laughs. "Don't be scared asshole. I won't hurt you. I just want to talk." He stares directly into my eyes, and I feel my body tighten and my veins begin to heat up as my eyes begin to swirl with control. "Get out of the car," I say, forcefully. His eyes turn black as coal with bright anger shining from the center. The man boldly denies my request, and I step back with a better understanding of Franky's odd behavior. *She must be under another demon's dark spell. I need to free her somehow.* But I don't get a chance to say or do anything before the man turns away and Franky slams the door shut. They speed off, and I can clearly see the plate on the back, the same one I saw before. I assume she met this guy wherever she was hiding out at, but why are they both here, now? No man follows a woman that he is in an open relationship with unless he wants something, and seeing now that he is no ordinary man, he obviously wants something. I hate to admit it, but I think Kayla is right.

Returning home, I ignore Kayla while I look in on the boys and figure out what to say to her. I can't seem to come up with anything by the time I walk into our bedroom, but surprisingly, she rushes to me and wraps her arms around me. Not a typical response from my stubborn wife, but it makes it much easier for me to tell her she is right.

"Nick, I am so sorry. I should have trusted you and left it alone. It doesn't matter who she is or what she is doing, all that matters ..."

I stop her, holding her out in front of me. "You were right, Kayla." She is shocked at first, but it doesn't take long before her cocky smile forms. "Before you glow with pride, it was still wrong what you did. You should have talked to me about it first. That said, I asked Franky, and she doesn't seem to have any answers for me, not yet anyway. On top of that, that boyfriend of hers is similar to me, and I don't mean related. He has a power similar to mine, but he doesn't seem to be nearly as powerful, thankfully. We shouldn't have to worry about him at least."

"How do you know that?"

"Because the coward ran away when I told him to face me. Clearly, if he had an ego, if he thought he could hurt me, he would have stayed and challenged me."

"You challenged someone without knowing who they are? Are you crazy?" She yells at me.

"Calm down. I only wanted to find out who he was, but now, I know that Franky is under this guy's spell. She was easily susceptible to mine, so it would make sense that she would fall for another and explains why she is acting so odd." Kayla rolls her eyes. "What now?"

"I don't think she is under any spell, and besides, spell or no spell, it doesn't explain why she is here."

"No, but I will find out soon. I promise." Kayla paces away from me, and I can already see the wheels spinning in her head. "Kayla, stop. Don't you dare do anything else. You let me handle Franky." She is resistant; I can tell by the way she avoids looking at me. "Kayla."

"Nick, you have so many things to worry about. Why don't you let me handle … her?"

"*Her* name is Franky, and she was an important part of my life. You don't know her. She was very shy and naive. I was her first everything, Kayla. She was very sweet and innocent."

"Well she isn't anymore," Kayla says with an exasperated huff.

I begin to think about that. She really isn't the same person I used to know. "I don't know why she is acting this way. I don't know if it is because of that guy she is seeing or if it is something else entirely. Maybe she is trying to be what she thinks I want or what he wants, she has been known to do that before. "Right now, Franky is the least of our problems. In fact, it is probably best we keep her as far away from us as possible. I don't want my mother involved in this mess anyway. Although, I don't trust that asshole, I do trust Franky with my mother. She has done everything she can to help her." Kayla removes her clothes and climbs into bed, and that damn dog jumps right in with her. "Where the hell did he come from?" Kayla shrugs as she cuddles with him and allows him to curl up right next to her. "Oh no. You get out!" I grab him by his dog collar and pull him off the bed. "Now go back to your bed." I point the way, and the damn dog huffs at me. "Watch it, dog. I can make you sleep outside in a dog house rather than in a nice warm bed indoors," I say, closing the door in his face.

"You are so mean to that dog, sometimes. Why don't you like him?" Kayla asks with her arms folded.

"Because he gets more attention from you than I do." I smile before leaning towards her, waiting for a kiss which she promptly gives me, along with some help removing my clothes.

"Come to bed Nick, and I will give you all the attention you want," she hums, kissing down my chest and finding my erection that is already protruding between us. "Let me show you how sorry I am for being so very naughty today. Let me earn your forgiveness, Nick."

I shouldn't forgive her easily, so I try to hold my tongue while she kisses my inner thigh, but then, she moves toward my dick, and I take hold of the back of her head and watch as my cock gets warmed by her beautiful mouth. I growl my forgiveness to her, only I want more. I want more from her and her body. I move her from my dick and twist her around, taking a bite of her ass before positioning her perfectly in front of me. "Do you really want me to forgive you, Princess?" I whisper against the nape of her neck. "Then let me feel you come on me." I penetrate deep inside her, and then again, harder and harder while rubbing her ass and feeling her become wetter with each stroke. I feel down between her legs and finger the wetness against me until she reaches back and grabs my thigh, screaming out in pleasure. She is exhausted and ready to pass out, but I am not done yet.

"Oh Nick!" she screams while I get mine. I feel my cock as it becomes wrapped in the heated indulgence that begs me to come inside her.

When I am done I wrap my arms around her and hold her against my chest. "You're forgiven, my forever love." I smile.

Chapter 10

Nick

My mind is not exactly on work these days. Of the time I have left, rather the time Savage has allowed me to have left, I am doing everything I can to take care of business before I must leave it behind. Everything seems to be going smoothly, too smoothly. I haven't had issues in weeks, and I usually have issues of some kind every hour. When a new man meets Terrence and me for an exchange at customs, I back up, ready to have him torn apart, but the man handles the routine just as if Nolan was handling it himself.

"Who are you?" I ask.

"My name is Seth. I am your humble servant as directed to be," he says, never bothering to look away from the tops of his shoes. I motion for him to continue while Terrence looks my way with a shrug.

Savage. Damn him. I haven't heard from Nolan Pickard since … since I ran into Adair at the warehouse. Taking out my phone, I dial quickly and wait through several rings before his voicemail picks up. Pickard is my most nervous informant. He rarely waits for a single ring before answering, and now he lets it go to voicemail? My body begins to tense, but there is nothing more I can do at the moment, so I call Dwayne and have him check it out. Within the hour, Dwayne verifies that Pickard died of a heart attack a few days ago. Savage never leaves any stone unturned and certainly never leaves anyone alive that can verify his existence. Pickard would've never said a word; the man was too paranoid to ever say anything. Dwayne says the fear in the man's expression was so extreme that it was etched deep into the flesh on his face. Savage made a promise to me, and now he has broken it.

My fears are set aside as I pull up to Savage's home. Rabbie greets me with a simple nod as I walk up the stairs to the door. There's apparently no surprise that I am here. Savage's smile as I walk in the room is unnerving. "Nicholas, joining me for lunch today?"

"Not exactly. I want to know why you killed Pickard. There was no reason to kill him; he would've never talked."

"I think you'll enjoy this lunch today, Nicholas. I had my favorite chef come by and make it special, just for us," Savage says, ignoring my anger.

"I don't want to have lunch. I want what you promised me! You said you would stay away from my business and leave my people alone."

Savage sits, sighing, "He was trouble. He knew way too much. I refuse to justify my actions to you, Nicholas. I did what I had to do to protect you and protect our family. I don't understand why you can't see that."

"Pickard was way too nervous, too scared, to say a word to anyone. He was no threat to us. If you would have talked to me about it beforehand, I could've explained that to you." My strong stance against him does not go over well.

"I am only going to say this once, so listen to me carefully Nicholas. I take orders from no one. I allow people to live when I want them to live; otherwise, I will deal with them as I see necessary. If they threaten us in any way, they will die. I don't care who they are or who they are to you. Sit down, Nicholas, have some lunch and relax. Don't worry about your man, I have already found you another. Seth is a much better servant for you. He will do as asked without question and will gladly slit his own throat before talking to the police." No matter what I say, he ignores me as if I have no power. And I don't. I have no power, no leverage against him at all.

"I don't know how I can trust you if you don't involve me in your decision making, especially on decisions that involve my business." Rabbie continues trying to give me a napkin and urging me to sit. Fed up with the foolishness, I knock him backwards off his feet. "I don't want to have lunch!"

Savage stands with anger swirling in his eyes, "Nicholas! For the last time, you sit down and you have lunch, quietly and respectfully. Then, we can discuss business. I do not discuss anything based on demands and anger with anyone." He motions for me to sit again as he sits. I do so with so much frustration and anger that I am numb to everything around me. Rabbie is back up, touching me up with a napkin and setting up food and drink in front of me like I never touched him, but the rapidly growing knot on his head and the blood on his arm says otherwise. "Eat Nicholas. Don't waste this great meal because you are angry with me." I pick up a fork and shove food into my mouth, but feel no better about the situation.

"So can we talk now?" I ask him after a few bites.

"Very well," he sighs, "but I have to say, you are quite exhausting. What is it that you want to discuss?"

"I want to discuss what you want from me? What is it that you are planning to have me do?"

"It's simple. I plan on you taking over the position that your father should have taken years ago, my next in command as most would say. You will be in charge of all that is a part of our family."

"And how does my family fit into this plan?" My question seems to catch him off guard. "You can't possibly think I am going to leave them behind?"

"Of course not." He smiles wide. "I welcome dear Kayla and your sons with open arms. They are now as much a part of this family as we are."

"And you will leave my people alone? All the people that work for me will be allowed to handle my business with no problems from you or from anyone that works for you?"

"That works for us, Nicholas. And I guarantee they will have no problems from us for as long as you say they are important to you."

I nod, looking him in the eye and choose to believe him. What choice do I have? We discuss more of what my duties will be and how I will be introduced as his grandson, and heir to everything that is Dennis Savage, or Asmodeus, the head devil in disguise. The opportunity will come with responsibilities that sound ridiculous, but from the serious expression on his face, I assume that ridiculousness is real. "So, I am what… a judge of people's souls?" I laugh.

"Yes, at least of the ones that are presented to our realm. The rest are judged by others in their own realms. Ours happens to be the most powerful and the most unforgiving."

"Wonderful, can't wait," I say, rolling my eyes.

"The sarcasm is not appreciated, Nicholas. You need to take this seriously or risk being challenged by some of the other Lords. Any of them would love to tear our family down and take over. Power is just as desired in our world as it is here."

I stop myself from sighing as he eyes me carefully. He seems to be waiting for me to say something, but I have nothing that doesn't sound sarcastic. *Oh, what the hell.* "Do I get to call you grandpa?" I laugh, but he doesn't. *I guess not.*

Lunch with Savage was bitter, and I'm beginning to understand what role I am going to be taking on when I join him, a role I am not anxious to have. My only way out of all this is to take him out. So again, I sit in the chair, tethered to this machine, waiting to give the signal for Eddie to release the current. I close my eyes and breathe before lifting my hand, signaling go. I feel as if my skin is going to bleed as my heart thumps and begins to speed. The moment my heart starts to rumble at full-speed, the heat begins to transfer energy past the tips of my fingers, beyond the tips of my toes, and on into my bones where the pain seizes me. When it's all over, I look up, eyeing my men as they wait to attack me. They are not anxious, but they do as I ask and come at me with full force. Except now, unlike before, no one can get within three feet of me. I need to find a way to help them more. I need to up the power and push my heart even further, giving them a better chance at fighting me.

When I get home, Brayden demands my attention first, as usual. Even though he resembles his mother, he has similar mannerisms to myself, including speaking only when it's necessary, which is hardly ever. We thought, at first, it was because he has been so sick. It wasn't long before I realized that he is only paying attention, taking in everything around him, and understanding things most children more than three times his age don't understand. While Nicky is strong, intelligent, and more than willing to take on anything twice his size, my warrior, Brayden is my silent assassin. Brayden will study your weaknesses first and then use them against you. Tonight, he seems to be a little feverish and wanting just to be held and comforted. Once I give Brayden his desired attention, Nicky is not far behind, nearly vibrating with anticipation to tell me all about his day. "How was your day, my little man?" I say with a smile, knowing that is exactly what he has been waiting for.

Nicky instantly begins telling me all about what happened at school today: the girls talking to him, some of the boys trying to bully him, and all about how he handled it in the perfect Jayzon manner. "And then Daddy, I just said, you can't make me do anything. I will only do what I want. Then, they left me alone, and this one boy came up to me and said he wants to be my best friend. And I told him if that's what he wants, then that's fine with me. His name is Oscar, he's funny. He told the teacher that he didn't have his homework because he thought the teacher was working too hard and should not have to grade his homework too." Nicky laughs and Brayden follows, seemingly understanding what his brother is trying to say.

"Wow! That sounds like somebody else's best friend, or at least something that he would try to pull." Kayla smirks. I lean back in my chair and smile, refusing to respond. "How is our friend these days?" she asks.

"Well it sounds like Oscar is doing just fine, Princess." Her laugh makes me smile wider, and I can't fight my desire to kiss her. "I just saw him today, he is his usual Eli self."

"That bad huh? I thought he was moving?"

"You know Eli… he changes his mind with the wind most days."

"He changed his mind, or did someone or something change his mind?" Kayla asks while the boys play with their food and pretend they are eating more than they are.

"Boys, stop playing, and eat your food," I say, ignoring Kayla's accusation. Thankfully, she drops it, and we move on with our night in the living area as a family, a normal, loving family.

Nicky drags his game with him as he curls up next to me, and Brayden makes himself comfortable in my lap. Kayla eases in on my other side with a book in hand, and suddenly, I forget who I am and become simply a man. A father. A husband. All that I want to be. Taking in the moment, I smell Kayla's hair, watch Nicky's bright eyes as he laughs, and feel the soft, warm beat of Brayden's heart as he sleeps against my chest. This is who I want to be, what I want forever, to be forever in love.

All of my enjoyment is quickly ruined when Savage calls. You can't ignore him as I have found out; he will find a way to get to you. I leave my family and step outside to take the call. "What do you need? You're interrupting my night, with my family."

"Nicholas, I should tell you that I think our warm greetings could be greatly improved. For now, let's work on introducing you to the right people. I need you to accompany me to a party tomorrow night," he says.

"I don't work for you yet. You said I have time to work on changing over my own business."

"It is just a party, Nicholas, not work. I want to show you off to some friends, you're my grandson. I am proud of you. Allow me a moment of being the proud grandfather? Bring your family, let me show off my great grandson, too."

"Great grandsons... with an "s." I have two sons, remember?"

"Yes, of course. I misspoke; don't hold my aged mind against me. Come on Nicholas, allow me the chance to practice being a grandfather for one night. Allow me this, and I will owe you."

"You will owe me?" I ask to make it clear.

"Yes, yes, whatever you want," he sighs.

"Fine. Where and what time?"

"Wonderful!" he exclaims, joyfully. "I will send a car for you at seven," he says, hanging up almost instantly.

Savage sent some extravagant jewelry over for Kayla to wear tonight and a car to pick us all up by seven. I hate everything about this, but I go anyway, trying to ease any tension between us and maybe gaining some trust with the old man. For some damn reason, I want him to owe me, not that I fully trust that he would ever honor his word. We go through the night with Brayden in my arms and Nicky holding tight to mine and his mother's hands. My grandfather, as I am asked to refer to him, introduces me to one odd being after another. I don't know where these so called people came from, but I hope I don't have to deal with them much, or at all, in the future.

"Nicky, come here," Savage says, holding out his hand to him. Neither Kayla nor I want to let him go; however, he lets us go and walks bravely to Savage, taking his hand. Savage smiles wide and picks him up in his arms. My blood begins to heat up. "And this is my great grandson, Nicky. He is a sure General in the making." I can barely contain myself when Kayla rests her head against me and Brayden presses his little hand on my face with an innocent giggle. As always, Kayla, calms me.

"Nice to meet you, sir." Nicky says, shaking an elderly gentleman's hand and causing everyone to laugh and enjoy the sweet moment. Even my tough as nails grandfather laughs joyfully, and Rabbie nods with a smile towards him.

For a brief moment, I feel good; however, the moment passes, and I sense something else coming our way. I grab Nicky and hand him and

Brayden to Kayla before stepping in front of them and watching everyone around us flee when two men come running at us with dark-age styled blades. They get no closer than another step once I spot them. Down on their knees, they surrender to death, and I take a deep inhale before exhaling even greater.

Savage turns towards me with a slight nod. "They were after me Nicholas. I rarely need the help, but thank you for the support."

When I turn to Kayla and the boys, she is shielding them from the scene and shaking in fear.

"Take your family home, Nicholas, I will take care of everything here," Savage says.

"Is this what I have to look forward to?" I ask.

"Is your way of life any easier? There is always someone who wants to cut you down, and even more so when you are the one closer to the top. You know this as well as I. I believe you have battled before for members of your family … have you not?"

I really don't want to say anything to him, but I reply anyway. "I have, but nothing like this."

"Nothing like what? If someone wants to kill you or your family, does it matter who they are, or where they come from, or even why? I don't think it does, Nicholas because either way, you are going to do all you can to get them first. Just like you have always done."

He stares at me as if he knows every moment of my life and has an argument for anything I might say. One thing I have learned over the years is that some arguments just aren't worth having with people who don't care to understand your point of view. "I am taking my family home now," I say, picking Nicky up and wrapping my arm around Kayla as she carries Brayden and safely leading them to our awaiting car.

The boys, thankfully, saw nothing and are completely unaware of what happened. They both happily fall asleep in their beds. Kayla, however, saw everything, and falls into my arms in hysterical tears.

"I'm sorry Nick. I didn't want you to know how scared I was but …"

I scoop her up, trying to quiet her cries and kiss her tears away. "No one is ever going to hurt you, Princess. Anyone that tries will have to deal with me. No matter where you are, or what I am doing, I will come running to protect you. I will come running for you whenever you need me. Just call my name." I lay her down next to me and wrap my arms around her, promising, to my death, to protect her and our sons.

Chapter 11

Nick

After last night, I feel as though I have no choice but to do everything in my power to become stronger. I sit in my father's chair with the power moved up by ten, not something that anyone else is happy with, but I don't care what they want. I have to be able to protect my family to the best of my abilities, and I am determined to have those abilities heightened as fast as possible.

"Eddie, now," I say, waiting as he silently argues with me. "Now Eddie!" He curses me, but finally does as I ask. The steel pain shooting through me is hard to take without screaming, and before long, I can do nothing but scream. Ryan runs at me in fear, but I fight his attempts to release me until he finally curses at me and stomps away. Once it's over, I demand them to come at me. "Don't hesitate, force me to recover!" Brady slams me backwards and Bo strikes me hard before Dwayne comes at me and grabs me by the collar. He holds me up, ready to slam me on the ground. Hitting the ground hard, I grimace, trying to move before Dwayne can strike me again, but I have nothing left to keep him from doing it.

"Stop! Put him down, Dwayne. Nick, are you out of your damn mind!" Elijah screams before grabbing my shirt and shaking me. "Stop this now Nick! There has to be another way."

"There isn't Eli." I choke out at him.

"How do you know? How do you know there isn't an answer somewhere? Have you been through everything? Have you studied Savage completely, talked to everyone that could possibly have information to help?" I have nothing to say, not that I have any energy to say it even if I did. "You know you haven't! You ran straight for the one answer you had. You haven't checked every solution. I know you are short on time, but you do still have time."

"Do I Eli? Do I still have time to protect my family? How do you know? Because Savage says he is giving me a numbered amount of days? Since when is he to be trusted?" I ask, but he has no response.

"Nick, do you even know what the chair is for, what its purpose is at all? All this information and your Dad never said why. He never explained why he built it? You say it is to make you stronger. Okay, I can see that, but make you stronger for what? For Savage? Or for something else? Maybe it is for something else, and these attempts to push yourself are for nothing. Maybe you have already surpassed what you need? You say your strength is coming from this machine, but I think you are getting stronger just by practicing, just by learning to focus. I don't know why you need this machine. You don't need to torture yourself in order to accomplish what you want," Elijah emphasizes, looking down and into my eyes for the first time in a long time. I am too exhausted to argue with him, so I simply close my eyes and shake my head. "You spent a long time denying who you are Nick. It is only just now that you are facing it head on, so of course you are getting stronger."

I push him away and struggle to my feet to go clean myself up before returning home. I force myself to stand up as straight as I can and use the wall as a prop. Ryan follows me and is there when I stumble exiting the room. He stiffens as he pulls me back up. The look in his eyes is hard to see, but I am doing this for him just as much as the rest of them.

"I'm not going to let you kill yourself Nick, and I am not going to let Savage take you away either."

"You stay away from Savage, Ryan," I cringe, trying my best to not need him to lean on. "You enjoy your life. Start that family you have always wanted and let me worry about Savage."

"I don't remember a time that you ever let me down, Nick, and you better believe that I am not going to ever let you down either. You're my only brother, and together we can solve anything, remember? Together no one can stop us, remember?" he says, reminding me of the time sitting together, goofing off from school, and talking about the life ahead of us.

"How are we ever going to escape being poor, Nick? We are fucked for eternity. We are going to be forever nothing."

"No. No, Ryan we will be something. I know it. Together … no one can stop us as long as we stay together. We are brothers, and we are both smart, and handsome as fuck – I mean just look at us." We would both laugh nodding at our scrawny bodies. *"But most importantly, we are together. We will never turn on each other, and with us together, we can't be defeated … by anyone."*

"Remember Nick? Remember, no one can defeat us when we stick together," Ryan says again.

"We are not kids anymore, Ryan, and this isn't as simple as stealing cars or overcoming poverty."

"No, but do you think my love for my brother, my determination to stand with you, is any less because of the situation?" Ryan asks.

"I don't want anything to happen to you Ryan," I say to his hardened stance in front of me.

"And I don't want anything to happen to you either," he replies. Finally, my legs give, my body fails, and I collapse against him. Ryan holds my shaking body with a strong hold so no one can notice my weakness. "Don't worry, Nick. I got you. Your brother's got you, now and forever."

Ryan takes me home and helps me to the door but knows enough to let me go into my home on my own, no matter how drained I am. Kayla greets me, full of energy, and instantly, my day is behind me, and my wife is all that is on my mind.

"Hello Princess." My hands immediately find their way underneath her clothes and my lips trail down her neck while she warms me up and hums her love for me.

"Did you have a bad day?" she asks.

"No, not at all. It is not over yet, and already, I am here - home with you. That is a good day as far as I'm concerned," I say, but my voice shakes a little. Kayla takes my hand but suddenly looks over me with concern.

"Why are you so weak?" She grabs my clothes and pushes them from side to side, examining my wounds. "Nick, what are you doing to yourself?"

"It's nothing. I just over did it a little bit today. No reason to worry; it's nothing that some rest and my wife can't help with." I wrap my arms around her, but I can still feel the vibration in my touch, and from the look on her face, so can she. "I'm going to go to bed and lay down for a little while. Don't hold up dinner for me, but save me a spot on the sofa before the boys go to bed." Kayla nods and, without a word, helps me up the stairs and to our bed. Kayla's touch has always calmed me, but apparently, she can't rejuvenate me. Or, maybe I did more damage than I thought. Even the pressure of the bed hurts. Once Kayla leaves, I freely cough up blood that I have been hiding from her.

"Daddy?" Nicky says, peeking in from the doorway.

"What do you need son?" I ask him, trying to hide my pain.

"Do you want to see my drawing I did today?"

"I do. Can you show it to me later …" *Oh damn the pain.* I lie back, trying to get the room to stop spinning. I forget about my son until I feel him touch my hand. Taking my hand with his, Nicky curls up next to me and just breathes, in and out, in tune with me. The rhythmic sounds of our breathing cause me to fall asleep and the pain to subside.

My mind drifts for I don't know how long when I hear Kayla calling for me.

"Nick? Nick honey, the boys are going to go to bed soon, and you should probably eat something, too." Kayla looks over me and smiles. "Well you do look better, even your bruises are healing up nicely." I sit up and look over myself. My once damaged body looks nearly untouched. I feel … great. I feel as if I have slept for days. "How do you feel?" Kayla asks.

"I feel fine. I guess the nap was all I needed." I smile at her. "I'll be down in a minute, and yes, I am hungry too. Do you mind making me a plate of food?" I say, getting up and feeling good about my strong legs.

"Not at all. I should warn you though. Nicky has a whole new list of things to tell you about. If you want, I can tell him to keep it to a minimum," Kayla says with a questioning expression as she looks me over herself.

"No, I want to hear all about his day," I say happily.

Kayla nods and disappears downstairs while I continue to check out every part of myself. Reaching, stretching, and punching, I analyze my abilities, and I am wonderfully surprised that my body is better than ever.

Wow. I guess I didn't give Kayla enough time to help me. Now, how do I tell her what she can do for me, or should I not? Should I continue to keep her secret to protect her from Savage, someone that I still don't completely understand? For now, I think it best to keep my secrets to myself and save them from getting out to the wrong people.

Chapter 12

Savage

Nicholas is stronger than I thought. What he did, what he was able to sense before it happened … he is so much like his father.

"Did you see what my grandson was able to do Rabbie?" I say as he sets down a drink for me. "He has the senses of his father, but the strength … oh, he has the strength of his uncle and cousin all rolled in one. He needs us more than ever; he needs me for certain."

"Do you really think he is going to willingly do as you say, especially with that beautiful family of his? They are his priority, not you Father," Galena says, kissing me on the cheek.

"That isn't a problem, not a problem at all. He simply needs to be convinced to leave his family behind." Galena laughs. "You doubt me, my daughter?"

"Never, Father, but this time, I think you may underestimate his bond to them. If he is anything like his father, and as we already know, he is plus some, then he will fight like no other for his family."

"His bond to them is what we will use to convince him to leave them behind. He will come to us, willingly, once he realizes he is what is dangerous to them," I say as Galena expresses a silent agreement in my direction.

Nicholas. I have known he was strong since he was a child. He was so young, and yet, he dismissed my attack on him with little effort, not that I put too much heart into hurting him. He was small at the time; he didn't need much to kill him or so I thought. To have him at my side now would make my army unstoppable. Nicholas scared those assassins right into their death. I savored the look in their eyes as they realized they were done, and I certainly relished the look in Rein's eyes as he watched his men dying on the floor in front of us. His men were scared shitless of Nicholas. My men? Well, they would follow him anywhere, and he would lead them to one takeover after another. My enemies would be on their knees in front of him and giving me whatever I wanted just to have me pull back the reins on him. But how to get control of him?

"How is your relationship with Amery these days, Galena?" I ask with an idea in mind.

She growls, with a turned up lip. "About the same, why?"

"I think we should introduce Amery to Nicholas."

"But Father, if Amery finds out who he is, he will do everything he can to provoke a war with him and try and kill him before he can be of any use to you," Galena says.

"You underestimate him," I say with a low growl. "Amery doesn't stand a chance against Nicholas, not even with his entire army behind him. Nicholas needs the kills. He needs to savor it and desire it. Once he starts, he shouldn't be able to stop if provoked properly, but it all depends on that woman. Kayla has some kind of control on Nicholas, and I need to understand exactly what that is. Let's plan a test run before we set our plan into motion."

"And what kind of test would you like to do, Father?" Galena asks with a doubt in her voice. Her disrespect lately is getting out of control. I give her a pointed glare, and she bows her head in shame as she should. I know exactly what we need to do.

My plan is set into motion and Galena and I set up at an office building with the perfect view. We wait nearly thirty minutes before Kayla walks past us with Nicky and that other one in her arms, and for some reason, that damn dog, too. Nicholas approaches from the opposite direction to greet her with open arms.

"They are a beautiful family," Galena says next to me.

"We are his family. They are nothing but a distraction." I growl towards her. "Where are our men, anyway?"

"They will be here, although sacrificing men is not something I would think you would savor," she huffs back at me. I raise my hand to quiet her down. I don't need her disrespectful attitude simply because she is missing out on an afternoon of fucking that loser of hers.

Nicholas settles down in the park with his family. The four of them laugh and play as they prepare a quiet picnic. The park is away from the city and from anyone who might know them. Something they do often, without anyone knowing, except me. Since discovering him, I have made it my job to know where he is at all times. While lovely Kayla sets up lunch, Nick picks up the smallest one and plays some sort of game that causes him to laugh. My little Nicky tries to join in with that dog that sticks to his side every second. That overprotective dog is going to have to go, too. The moment Nicholas stalls his play time and begins looking around, I move to the edge of my seat and look for our men. I catch sight of them nearly a minute later running into view. My grandson is so perceptive, a skill that cannot be taught.

"Oh Galena watch this. This is going to be so good." Nicholas hands the little one over to Kayla and faces off with one of our men away from his family, one of our best fighters is determined to win, but that determination doesn't do him much good. He tries hard for the whole fifteen seconds that he lasts against my grandson. I see the bloodlust in Nicholas's eyes as our other fighter, our supposed warrior, begins to retreat in fear. All the signs are there: the clenched fists, the heated exhaling breath, and the hungry pursuit of his prey. Nicholas pursues the man into a corner, and the man drops to his knees, begging for his life. I can't hear his begging words, but I can see his fear. Hell, I can sense his fear, and I lick my lips, craving the kill myself. The wait nearly drives me insane when … that woman appears and takes hold of Nicholas. He jerks his head in her direction, and I get excited, hoping for his action that I didn't even think to hope for, but instead, he calms. His fists become unclenched, his breath cools, and his hunger seems to vanish. They send our man running away and return to their sons. Nicholas helps her load them in her car while he follows them closely in his. No one is getting close to them with him around, and Nicholas is never going to know who he truly is with Kayla around him. I glance over at Galena as she tries to pick her jaw up off the floor. "And this is why we always test our theories. That wife of his is a nuisance."

"It is very much like Dante and Sophia. That's incredible that they both were able to find …"

"Do not remind me of that woman!" I yell at her. "I thought we had discussed that before?"

"Sorry, I had forgotten, but you have to admit that is remarkable how much the two situations resemble each other?" she says, ignoring my eyes on her.

"You forgot? Of course you did. The simple things are always hard for you to remember." I stew in my seat trying to decide how to act next. "Kill that man. To explain it better for you, I want you to kill that coward that Nicholas let go. Do you understand me?"

"Yes, but why kill a perfectly good man?"

"Because I said so Galena! Now, go clean that mess up and don't come home until you have taken care of it all." I get in my car without her and have my driver take me home.

Once I am home, I find Rabbie. "If she manages her way home tonight, don't let her in the house. Make her sleep in the servants' quarters." Rabbie nods like the perfect aide that he is. "I'm sick of her questioning me." I swear her name under my breath when Barr approaches me.

"Sir, if you would oblige me, I would be more than willing to take care of this Kayla Jayzon for you. I will have my best men accompany me to make sure the job is done properly," Barr says, my head general so to speak. Barr has been with me for some time and is my most ruthless killer. He enjoys his job more than any, and I hate to deny him his joys.

"When the time is right, I will certainly let you have that pleasure, my Mighty Slayer." I think for a moment. "There is something you can do in the meantime. I need to make sure she is not able to conceive children again. I can't have Nicholas fathering another child by her. I need to make sure she is fully vulnerable and not with child when we kill her."

"It will be done within the day," Barr says respectfully.

As I wait to hear back from Barr, I take up refuge in my study, preparing myself for a delivery of women to please me. I walk towards my balcony doors so I can step out and enjoy the night air when Rabbie runs in the room and promptly steps in front of me, cutting me off, an action that is quite unlike him. I raise my hands trying to understand what his nervous action means when he suddenly points to the door.

"I believe he is trying to tell you that I am at the door demanding to see you. It seemed to make your people nervous, so I showed myself in," Kamini says as she enters my study with her usual overly confident attitude. Rabbie tries to straighten up the room and get rid of anything that might not be fitting for her to see, but I wave him away. I don't care what this bitch sees or thinks of me.

"Kahhhmahhhneee ..." I growl out the sound of her name under my breath, cringing with every syllable that passes my lips. What is it that you want, Kamini?" I ask with a sour tone.

"I want one of your men, and out of respect, I have come to you first. I expect you to hand him over with little fuss," she says, casually, as if she just asked to borrow some sugar.

"Oh dear." I roll my eyes "And which one is it that has disturbed your shrilling and crying world, Kamini?"

"You are so much more charming than your father, Dennis," the wise ass says. "How did he die again? I have heard it was a stab wound of sorts?" As if I would tell her my secrets. The blade of my father is all that can destroy me, and I will not give any hint to it so that someone can strike me down with it as I did him. "Your father thought so much of you. I remember his proud moment introducing you as I believe you are going to be doing for your grandson, Nicholas, is it? It's too bad that his father never got to be introduced. Dante was a handsome man but then, his mother. What was her name ..."

"Sancia. Her name was Sancia," I snap, growing more impatient with her game.

"Oh yes. Sancia, a beautiful woman. She had many suitors until you. Then, suddenly, they all started disappearing. She herself probably would have lived if not for your attention towards her. Your wife was not real happy about her was she? You know, as well as I, that she poisoned her, but I guess that doesn't matter to you. She was nothing but another fuck to you, right Dennis?" I turn back towards her with a snarl and fisted hands. "Go ahead. Do your worst," she hums happily.

"You would like that, wouldn't you? Have your blood on my hands so I can be sentenced to death myself?" She shrugs, angering me even more. I grab her and throw her down on my sofa. Her body tenses while I enjoy the feeling of her body next to me. "You smell even better up close," I breathe against her neck. "You know you want me to fuck you, always have. Say the word, and I will give you what you want, what you have always wanted."

"I would love that Dennis. I would love to be the one to sentence you to be skinned and burned for eternity." She turns her head and faces me with gritted teeth and a witch's smile.

Damn her! I jump up and rush to the other side of the room, trying to calm my emotions before I do something I will regret. I need for her to leave as soon as possible. I'm not sure I can control myself much longer. "What it is you want?" I breathe away from her but watch her every move from the corner of my eye.

She smiles wide as she judges my décor with a shaking of her head and sideways glances. "I want your man Barr. I'm sorry to tell you this. I know he has been a loyal servant to you for a long time now, but you have so many loyal people. I can't imagine losing one is going to be that big of a deal to you." She knows damn well how important Barr is to me. I would be a fool to believe that she is here out of respect for me. She is enjoying seeing my reaction to her request.

"I will need to know why you need him rather than any other scum that roams this world." I glare hard at her.

"Of course. He raped a woman, several by my final count, but what has finally done him in is the last one he raped, and inadvertently killed. She was pregnant at the time. You know that's not allowed, and it always causes The High Council concern. After a witness came forward, we will need Barr to face his judgment. The High Council has ordered his immediate demise."

"I will need proof of this before I can hand over such a dedicated servant of mine. Let me talk to this witness, and verify their truth for myself. If I find this person trustworthy, then I will be more than happy to hand him over."

"Oh Dennis, you know very well that you are not allowed to do that. Of course, I will have to put the request through to the High Council first. They will need to have the request reviewed, and if they find it worthy, then they will send down a notice to hear your pleas. Together, they will review your request, along with all your documentation as to why you should be allowed to speak to the witness, and if they agree then by all means, you may speak to the witness." She smiles happily. "However, all that can be avoided if you happen to die. You can, then, speak to whoever you want without the council's approval." You would have to give up all the extracurricular activities that are not appropriate for a Lord of your level, but if Barr is that important to you, I am sure you won't mind doing that."

"Funny. I assure you I have no evils or inappropriateness in my day to day work. I simply do the job as required, nothing more. I run an honorable business that is like any other common man's self-employment venture. Is it my fault that I am successful at what I do? I would think not."

"You may be able to pass that bullshit onto the High Council, but I know those men committing evils are yours and only abiding by the orders you gave them. I will catch you one day, Dennis, but for now, I want Barr."

"I'm not giving him to you without a direct order from the Council, Kamini."

"I'm not asking. I'm telling you." She snaps her fingers and two of her people struggle to bring in Barr, placing him in front of me.

"Sir, I promise, I have done nothing but …"

"Shut up! Release him now Kamini!" I demand, standing toe to toe with the witch. She smiles at my demand, reminding me that I have no power over her. One day, I will be in control, and I am going to fuck this woman until I tire of her, and then I will tie her to my ceiling, naked, and leave her waiting for my attention. It would be exactly what she deserves.

Her beauty was gifted to her specifically as a trap for men, to draw out their evil and then punish them with the most horrific torture I have ever witnessed. Murderers, rapists, the worst of the worst of men, she was born to right their wrongs the only way you can once they die. Even I cannot watch it. Their torturous screams alone make my ears bleed. The last man I saw had killed several children, raped many more, and committed other atrocities that sentenced him to her draw. She came in as an angel, relaxed him, and then forced a power on him one hundred times worse than the total horrors he inflicted in his life. The sight of it all is useless to me, and I find no enjoyment out of that torture.

"Say goodbye, Dennis," Kamini says, sliding her monogrammed battle gloves onto her hands. There is nothing I can do. This woman is too powerful for me to tangle with right now. I allow her to take Barr and stand stiff and silent as the witch waves goodbye to me.

I doubt the accusations about Barr are true. Barr has no interest in sex or even women for that matter; he does as I ask nothing less and nothing more. I would never jeopardize my best warrior. She knows that, and I know she would never sentence a man to a wrongful death. She will be forced to return him in time; she is taking him to hinder me for some reason. I don't know what she is up to, but I can't do anything about Barr's loss right now. I need to concentrate on getting Nicholas home so we can begin the war against our enemies. *How best to do that?* He is so love struck and drowning in family affairs that it is impossible to get him to believe in anything else outside of them. That fucking woman of his! I want her neck broken in front of me. I want her body ripped from this world and her child to become mine. I must find a way to kill her. A thought comes to mind in my rage, a thought to use Nicholas's love against him and force him to seek my help. For them. For her. To help protect them all.

All I need to do first is peak Amery's interest in Nicholas. I send word to the High Council that Nicholas is under my protection and is not allowed to be approached by any other Lord for their armies. The notice will cause an instant interest among all the Lords but even more so to Amery, who believes it is his own duty to make sure every Lord follows the rules. He has become a pain in my ass ever since he took over his father's realm. Now, I am going to bait Amery into a war he can't win.

Chapter 13

Nick

I try to finish up some business, but suddenly have a craving for my wife. I look in on her where she is deeply enjoying her shower. I love watching her shower; it makes my dick hurt to see her swaying hips and hear her humming moans. Her motions would send any man into a sexual frenzy. Wetting my lips, I make a desiring sound to gain her attention. Kayla glances over her shoulder at me and winks, causing us both to laugh. Oh I am going to have to *fuck her now*. I start to get undressed when I trip over the dog, who is also deeply enjoying watching her. *What the hell is up with this dog?* "Hey!" I yell, and the dog jumps and runs out of the room. Kayla looks at me with a frustrated expression. "The damn dog is sitting here staring at you."

"He's a dog, Nick. What's he going to do, take pictures?"

"I don't know, but it is strange don't you think?" I ask her, and she shrugs. "Kayla, the dog was just staring at you naked."

"He does it all the time. I assume he must be in awe of the shower. He does like water; he gets into the pool all the time and plays."

I huff, "I don't think it's the shower he is in awe of."

Kayla protrudes her bottom lip, mocking me. "Oh baby, then maybe you should have a talk with him. Let him know there will be no more puppy treats if he keeps staring at your wife in the shower." She laughs hard.

I strip my pants off, allowing my erection to breathe proudly. "Ha, Ha," I say, stepping into the shower with her, causing her to back up against the wall. "Don't mock me and think you are going to get away with that. Come here, beautiful." She steps into my awaiting arms where I warm her with all I have as a man.

I play with my wife and then clean us both up before I step out of the shower and find that damn dog again, lying at Kayla's feet while she combs out her wet hair, naked. "Maybe you should put some clothes on?"

Kayla looks back at me in confusion. "Who should? Me?" She looks down at the dog and begins laughing. "Oh Nick, he is just a dog, only a dog who happens to enjoy my attention. I am the one who feeds him after all."

"And haven't you fed him enough already tonight?" My wife is so desirable to me. She can erase my thoughts in an instant by simply moving her body or whispering to me, and she knows it. I stand, watching her until I realize … "Damn it Kayla! The dog. I want him out of our room, and keep him out of our room," I snarl, trying to hide my smile when she begins laughing. At least she respects me enough to put on her robe before sweetly escorting the dog out of our room.

She thinks she is funny, but there is something about that dog. *I swear there is.*

My frustrations and pride force me to ignore her as she comes to bed, sliding off her robe behind her to expose her naked body to me. I try to pretend I don't notice while reading my reports, but she knows better. From her toes up to her bare legs and across her stomach, my gaze wanders easily up to her full breasts that bounce freely to the pulsations in my dick. Kayla smiles, leaning in to kiss me while her hand dives under the sheet to stroke my dick. "You seem to be hard again, Baby. Is there something I can do to help you with that?" Suddenly, all the frustrations disappear, and my dick enjoys the loving respect of my wife's mouth.

"You are going to force me to …"

"Force you to what?" she asks, sitting up and wiping her lips with a smile. I sharply smile back before taking her hands and lifting her to where I want her. My dick knows where to go. I don't have to give it any direction; it finds the soft wet place that sends her moaning backwards and me ramming forward.

"You know, Princess, if you wanted to fuck, all you had to do was ask, but I did enjoy the prep work," I say, twisting her into a better position so I can suck on her breasts and squeeze her ass deeper into my hips. My dick is full and ready to explode when she grips me tight and begins to rub her hips against me even more. Kayla's lips pinken, becoming fuller and wetter, causing me to want even more. I watch her, feel her come on me, and instantly explode into her with everything I have. I growl my appreciation as I lie her down into the soft bedding. Her angelic image, shining brightly in front of me, is more amazing every day. "I would be lost without you, Kayla."

There is something wrong, I have felt it all day, and it is just getting stronger as the day goes on. I continue to search within the shadows for something, or maybe someone, but so far… nothing. I know I am making everyone uneasy, but I bring everyone in and keep them close as we finish out the day. As we make one last stop, the feeling grows stronger, and I demand everyone to be on guard. I search the shadows hard, cursing every movement within. Ryan looks at me and then all around us before looking back at me again with a puzzled expression. "What the hell are we looking for?" I hold up my hand and listen. "I don't … fuck!"

They come at us with a walk to destroy, and I am their main goal. They walk up on my bodyguards and throw them aside with ease. There are many and one steps up to challenge me personally with a hardened duty within his black eyes. I square my body towards his and feel my hands tense, with fire building inside of them. I know I can take this man, but my overeager brother decides to go at him first. Ryan makes his way into their path. "Ryan no!" I yell at him, but it is too late. They already realize, and now he has become a target too. There is a leader among them, directing them from here to there and focusing their full force on Ryan and my guards. Now, do I rescue my brother or continue to protect my more vulnerable guards' backs? Ryan is handling his own, but he is wearing out quickly. The sound of his breaking point sends me searching and watching him fall. A low growl rumbles from my throat and emerges as a death threat to them all. The once mighty and strong stand back in fear, and are ready to retreat just by the feeling of my eyes on them. I remove the attackers from my brother's back easily which causes the others to step back, and most to run. Their leader loses his smile. I step towards him and bare down my focus. He takes a breath and fights with only a few at his side. He is a warrior for sure but not one that is strong enough to take me on face to face. When the dust clears, my men look upon me in awe, and my brother steps up to stand at my side.

I believe it is over, but then I look up to the roof of the building in front of me and see one more, a spectator. My swirling eyes meet his, and I can do nothing to detour him. We are of the same body shape, but when he stands into the light, it is clear he comes from another family. His sandy blond hair and his bright eyes begin to swirl gray, warning me to stay away. A curl of my lip sets my intensity into motion, and I match his resilient warning with no fear.

The man smiles. "Perhaps another time, Nicholas. I am apparently not properly prepared for you. One day though. One day I will give you a shot at me," he says as I near.

He leaves, and I look over at my brother as he wipes the blood from his chin. "I had them, you know," he says. I growl at him, shaking my head. "What is your problem?"

"Did I not tell you to keep a low profile? I told you to make sure you don't stand out and make yourself known. You just became a target, Ryan!"

"Fuck you, Nick!" I can handle them as well as you. If you would just teach me what you know already then I could help you even more. Hell, I was handling them all tonight without you. If you would have given me a chance, I would have finished it, too. They don't scare me."

"It's not them that I am worried about," I say as he huffs and tries to walk away from me. I grab him and pull him back. "Ryan, if Savage finds out about you ..." Ryan jerks his arm away from me.

"I got it Nick, but maybe you should start realizing I am not a kid anymore and can handle myself," he says, reminding me of a conversation I had with his mother once.

Ryan's mother asked me to look after him because she knew as well I did that he is stubborn and determined to be at my side, not following behind me. Ryan looks at me now as he has always done, strong and determined to prove he is just as a capable. "Little King, that's what the name Ryan means," I say to him as he settles his brave chest down. "That's why your mother named you that. She thought you were going to be something special. She knew, as well as I do now, that you are something special, and you deserve my protection. I am nothing more than a King's protector, Ryan. Now let me do my job as I promised your mother."

Chapter 14

Nick

Kayla insists on us going out to this charity event she has been planning for months. It is a good cause, and good publicity for our family detours people from the rumors of us being criminals. After all, "philanthropist" is a much better title than "criminal. It's good for our expanding children's gym business and our boys, too. Kayla says it gives them something to be proud of and talk about with their friends. Of course, she asks to go to this event without knowing the conflict I faced the night before. The only way to convince her to stay home is to tell her, and that is something I am not willing to do. I don't want her to be in fear any more than she already is. So while she enjoys the night, I keep my eyes on everyone around her. I am tense and ready to pounce on anyone that looks the least bit out of line. Sure enough, a man sneaks in, eyeing Kayla directly. I move in on him, break him, and send him tumbling back out the door where Dwayne takes care of him for me. There are a few more that make their way in from one place or another, and each time, I have to casually scramble to get rid of them. What concerns me is every one of them is focused on getting to her, and none bother to search for me. Someone is out to get to me by killing her, and that makes me even more nervous. As the night winds down, I am more than ready to go when Kayla leaves my side to go to the bathroom, but as I wait for her, I notice her being escorted outside to the alleyway. I am on my feet and out that door in a heartbeat, ready to attack, ready to kill, only when I get there, I see the group laughing and pulling party supplies out of the back of a van. I spot Kayla laughing too as she helps another woman light candles on a cake she is removing from the car. I walk up to her side and sigh.

"Nick, what's wrong?" Kayla asks.

"You said you were going to the bathroom?"

"I said that to everyone so no one would suspect the cake we got for Nancy. She organized all this, and today is her birthday. I thought we should reward her with something." She looks over me and my tense posture before ushering Janice inside. "Thank you, Janice. Go ahead and start without me. I will be in a minute."

I smile with an apologetic expression until she is gone. Then, I turn back to my wife. "Kayla, you know I don't like you disappearing from my sight these days. Not even for a few minutes."

"Nick, you have been a ball of stress all night. What's wrong? There is something that you are not telling me." She reads me better than anyone.

"I have a bad feeling, and I am just on edge about it," I say, not appreciating her doubtful expression. "This is not the safest event venue, and that makes me worry a little more than usual." Before I can say another word, I feel a metal object being pushed into my ribs.

"Okay mister, I don't want to hurt you or your lady friend, so just give me your money and that jewelry she has on, and nobody gets hurt," a man says, poking me in the back with what I assume is a gun. *I knew it!* I must have missed him coming on me because of Kayla distracting me. *Damn it!* I tense, meeting Kayla's eyes.

"Nick, no!" she yells at me, shaking her head.

I turn to the man, grab him by the collar, and pick him up off the ground to eye him perfectly. "Oh shit! Never mind. Keep your money! In fact take mine," he yells as a rumbling growl erupts from my chest.

"Nick, no don't kill him. He is a friend of mine!" Kayla yells out.

"Oh, please Nick, please! I can't die today. My Momma will kill me," he cries out, annoyingly. He opens his eyes and looks into mine. "Oh what the fuck is up with your eyes? Am I going to hell? Please Nick, please. I didn't mean any harm. I just wanted to get my Momma a gift for her birthday," he whines before looking back at Kayla for help.

"He is harmless, Nick." Kayla lifts his hand with the gun in it. "See it isn't even a real gun. Just a water pistol." The man holds it up nodding before shooting water at me and pissing me off even more. "Oh don't do that, Ro. Nick, please. He really is harmless, please let him go. I am sure he will never do anything like this again, will you Ro?" Kayla grasps my hands around his neck and tries to ease me off of him.

"No, I will never, ever do it again, Nick," the man says with a rickety voice.

"Stop whining. You're annoying me," I say to him.

"Oh," he gulps, looking back up at me with a forced smile, shaking to the point that he begins to cause my whole body to vibrate.

"Stop that shaking," I say to him, but all he does is close his eyes and shake even harder. I ease up some, and he looks up at me with hopeful eyes. "I can't kill you when you shake like that. It is distracting," I say to him.

"What? No," he says. "I mean, please don't hurt me. I tell you what. I can get you a great new watch or tickets to the game or, or, or I know! Great seats for you and the lovely lady to the Ice Capades?" he says, opening his coat to show all kinds of used crap.

"You stole all that stuff?" I ask him.

"No, I found it," he says, trying to justify to me while still trying to touch the ground with his toes. "You see this here watch? I will sell it to you for the bargain price of $250." Narrowing my eyes, I begin to concentrate. "No, I mean … 200? No, my bad, my bad. It's yours, Nick. Merry Christmas! Happy Birthday! And a special Valentine's wish to you and your lovely lady," he says with a gleaming smile. Kayla laughs suddenly. I have to glare at her to get her to stop.

"I don't want the damn watch," I say.

"No? Okay, how about …" He begins searching frantically through his coat while his feet dangle freely. "You know this would be much easier if you could put me on the ground." I lower him, and he brushes himself off and then tries to run, not that he gets anywhere with me holding onto him.

"Why can I not kill him?" I ask Kayla. "He is very annoying."

"Because he is a friend of mine an old, very good friend of mine. Ro, this is my husband Nick. Nick this is Ro, otherwise known as Roland Roosevelt. Ro's a pain in the ass? Sure, but he's harmless." She hugs him, wrapping her arms around him as tight as he does her until he looks over at me. He then removes his arms away from her with a wide smile. "He is someone that I shared a lot with," she says as I begin to remember him myself.

Before Kayla came back to me, I found out about a man who took her in and protected her from some of the dirt bags she dealt with at that disgusting club she worked at. I sent his mother money to let her stay with them as long as she promised to never say anything. She was a nice lady and wouldn't take my money, at least not from the man that I sent to her. She thought he was up to no good and was expecting something from Kayla. She beat him with a broom until he left, with my money and all. I felt much better about Kayla's life after that. She finally found someone I could trust to help her in the right direction. Unfortunately, Kayla was too determined to seek revenge on me and left that good home behind for Pagelle.

"How have you been Ro?" Kayla says.

"Oh, you know, keeping up the business and taking care of Momma. She misses you by the way. You should stop by for Sunday dinner at least once in a while. What about you?" He stands out in front of her to look her over. "Wow! Girl you are looking, so damn good. I knew you could look good, but I had no idea. Rich looks good on you! And married to tall, dark, and scary over here!? You seem to be doing well."

"And I have two sons," Kayla says proudly.

"Two! No? Really? Oh Momma is going to be so excited. Did you name one after me? Little Ro-Ro?" He laughs. They exchange numbers, and after a few minutes of catching up, Ro feels the need to get back to work. "Nice to meet you Scary Nick, but I have to get back to work."

"Don't you think there is a better job for you? This one is liable to get you killed."

"Killed? Me? No way, I stealth in and out before anyone can make a move."

"Stealth? I guess you weren't using those skills on me?" I say, causing him to huff with a scrunch of his eyebrows.

"I am a little off tonight. I have a cold. But when I am in good health … you would be amazed. You would say, 'Where did that man go? He is like a ghost sneaking in and out of here. I wish I was like him,'" he says with a smile until he looks up at me shaking my head. "Well maybe you wouldn't."

"No, I wouldn't, but instead of sending you out to inflict your stealth skills on others, why don't you come with us, and I can help you get a more suitable career," I say.

"Really, that's very nice, but I am more of an entrepreneur type. I prefer not to work for anyone, but thanks anyway Nick. I must get going. I got other business to take care of before the night is over," Ro says, kissing Kayla on the cheek and straightening out his hat before quickly heading into the dark night. "Stealth!" We suddenly hear him yell.

"Yeah, stealth but not silent. He's going to get hurt or arrested within the hour," I say, shaking my head.

"Don't worry about Ro. He always manages to find a way. Now, let's get you home so you can rest those tense, big, strong muscles of yours." She smiles with a sweet laugh.

"Go in and say your goodbyes, Princess, so I can take you home and show you my big strong muscles. I need to relieve my tension as you pointed out," I say, kissing her plump lips.

Chapter 15

Savage

This facility smells. Before I am able to walk in too far, a lady rushes up to me in a panic.

"Sir, you can't come in here without prior authorization."

"I can do whatever I want," I say calmly before staring her down. She nods and backs down. "Show me to Mrs. Gillian Jayzon's room please." She nods again and rushes in front of me to do just as I asked.

I open the door to her room and walk into the modest surroundings with a sigh. It looks similar to the home Nicholas grew up in, disturbingly so. The place is disgusting for no reason. Nicholas can surely afford to give his mother better, she must not want it.

"Who are you?" Gillian asks, looking at me in fear.

I hold out my hand with a smile, "No need to be scared, my dear. I am a friend."

"A friend of Dante's? He isn't home right now," she says oddly. *Oh yeah, she's crazy. I almost forgot.*

"Ah, yes, I know. I spoke to him earlier. He assured me that you could help me though."

"Oh, okay. Can I get you something to eat or drink?" she says, offering me a seat.

"No, thank you …" *The very idea of eating or drinking anything from this place is stomach churning.* The woman continues to move around the room, cleaning and straightening the same damn things over and over again. "Gillian, I need to ask you an important question. Can you please sit for a moment?" She ignores my question and continues on with no concern for my rapidly growing impatience. I decide the best thing to do is to take her hand and show her where to sit. "Tell me, Gillian. Do you have any children?" She looks at me with wide eyes. "I assure you, I am only asking for your family's safety." She shakes her head. Taking a deep breath, I calm and gaze deep into her eyes. "Gillian, tell me, how many children do you have?"

"No I don't have any," she says with sadness.

"You do too, Gillian. Now stop pouting."

"Well, only Nicholas. Dante says he is special, and there is no need to try for another. He was a handsome baby." I smile and nod in agreement. "But Dante said someone was going to come for him and take him away. Still, he would not let me have another, so I have no children that are my own to keep." How Dante put up with such drama I will never know.

"What else did Dante tell you? Did he mention who would be coming for Nicholas?"

"No, he only said he was evil and would kill us both if we tried to deny him what he wants," she says, troubled by the idea. It's true though.

"And so Dante has no more children with anyone else?" She hesitates and begins cleaning again. Before I can ask again, her door opens.

"Oh Franky, where is Dante? We have company, and he should be here to entertain him. You know I am not good with such things," Gillian quickly rambles on at her physician.

"He is out still, Gillian. He will be back later. Now, please sit and talk to the nice man. You don't want to be rude do you?" She sits her down next to me. "Gillian, tell us about the other women that Dante is friends with? Tell us about the one you talked to me about before, the beautiful one that Nicholas loved to be around. Didn't she have a son too?"

"Did Nicholas enjoy her home because of her, or was it that he was friends with her son?" I ask her.

"Both I imagine. She was very nice. I went to retrieve Nicholas from her one time, but he was asleep. She said he was sick and needed to rest. Her son slept nearby. He was much smaller than my ... Nicholas."

"Smaller? Younger you mean?" I ask.

"He had this tattered bear that he slept with. I wanted him to be mine. No one was coming after him, and he was sweet, and I know I could have taken care of him. Dante would be proud of the way I would take care of him."

"How do you know no one was coming after that boy?" I ask her, taking her hand so she will focus on the questions I need answered.

"Dante was making sure of it. He had a plan. Dante always has a plan." I smile with her. "There was this one time ..."

"Gillian, about the small child with the bear, what was his name?" She shakes her head. "What was his mother's name?"

She thinks for some time, and I am afraid her mind is wandering off beyond my question. "Rianne. Yes, Rianne Milio."

I smile wide. "Thank you Gillian." I feel satisfied but wonder if there is more. "Is that the only other woman Dante was friends with? Did you ever visit another or did Nicholas ever talk about another playmate of his that he was especially close to?"

"Dante has many friends, female especially. He is wanted by many women, but he always comes home to me. They can pretend all they want, but he is still my husband."

"Yes, yes Gillian, he is. You are the one he cares for above them all, even that woman you can't stand," I say, assuming there has to be at least one she couldn't stand. Sure enough, her eyes begin to squint as her lips tense.

"I really didn't like her at all. I told Dante she didn't bother me, but I lied. She was very pushy, and her daughter was even worse. This one time she brought her daughter over with her, and I caught her trying to rock my son to sleep. Nicholas was so small then, and that little girl was not much older. I was so angry that I smacked her. I didn't mean to, but she could have dropped him taking him out of his crib. That woman came at me, but I didn't care. I didn't like her being there anyway. Dante calmed her down and told me to apologize to her and her daughter and he would make sure they never came over again. I apologized, but I really didn't mean to hurt the little girl. I told Dante that, and he said he understood. Dante kept his promise though, and I never saw that woman again until I stopped into a store to buy a new dress. Can you believe that woman owned the store?! I tried to leave, but all she wanted to do was discuss Dante."

"What about Dante?" I ask her.

"Hmm, I don't remember. She was very frustrating, and I just wanted her to go away and leave me alone."

"You *do* remember, Gillian. Now, tell Mr. Savage what happened with the woman."

"Why should I? It is none of his business," Gillian snaps.

"Now, you know I love you and want the best for you, and you want the best for me too, right?" Gillian nods to her supposed doctor. "You want to be with Dante, and I want to be with Nick. Mr. Savage has promised to make sure all that happens for us. We can both be happy but only if we help give him the answers he needs."

"Just ask Dante. He remembers things better than I, or ask Nicholas. He was there at the shop, too."

"Nicholas was at the shop?" I ask her. "Why?"

"He was talking to that woman's daughter. I'm tired. I need to go to bed now. I have to get up early for work in the morning."

I'll be damned! This crazy ass woman is going to drive *me* to insanity. "Fine. Go to bed. Ria see me outside before I leave," I say, exiting quickly before I break this woman's neck in frustration.

"Sir, your anger nearly gave you away."

"Gave me away? To that insanity in there? Don't insult me. That woman is no threat to me. And don't you dare correct me ever again," I say to her pale-faced expression. "If you want my grandson then I expect you to do whatever it takes to please me. I also expect that you will stop fucking that reprehensible Marius Cane. For as long as I live, I will never understand that man's draw."

"But ..."

"But nothing! You do as I say and only as I say. No one else. If you continue with that man, then you will never feel my grandson's flesh inside you, and you will never bare his children. I will not have any part of him tainted. Do you understand me, Ria?"

"Yes," she mutters quietly.

I leave her behind and return home to meet up with Galena, who is clearly still angry with me for forcing her to sleep in the servants' house for a week. I don't know why she bothers; her silence is something to be celebrated, not feared.

"I want you to find a woman for me. She owned a clothing store and was sleeping with your brother before Nicholas was born. I have a feeling she had a daughter that is also my granddaughter. I want her found, and I want to verify for myself if she is worthy."

"And if she is not you will kill a full grown woman who is no threat to you? Just let her be," Galena says to me boldly. I grab her throat and squeeze until her tongue shows.

"I am getting so tired of your mouth! Speak to me that way again, and I will cut your tongue out. Now, go do as I ask."

Everyone that I can't account for is a threat to me. Anyone that wanders freely with my family blood becomes a target to be used against me, used to drain my energy, to drain my power, and I can't have my weakest blood relatives easily available to my enemies. It is bad enough that they are watching Nicholas. I don't need them seeking out any others. I need to advance my strategies and force Nicholas home now.

Chapter 16

Nick

I am sound asleep with Kayla in my arms when my mother calls me in the middle of the night, whispering. I can barely understand her, and I have to sit up and ask her again and again why she is calling me. She never calls me unless she is looking for my Dad; she still thinks he is always with me. I assume that is what she is doing now, but she never mentions my father's name.

"Nicholas, there are some people here, and I don't know them."

"What? Where are you?" I ask still in a sleepy daze.

"I am at home, under my bed. These people came in and started going through all my things. They threw stuff everywhere. It will take me forever to clean this up. Tell your father to come home immediately before they mess up anything else. He is going to be so angry when he sees this."

"Kayla, stay here and lock down the house. Don't let anyone in until I get back." I don't even bother hanging up before jumping out of bed. I call in a team of my men to meet me at my mother's care facility. No one is to make a move until I get there. When I pull up to the facility, I meet up with my men and quickly talk them through the plan I came up with on my way here. My mother is no longer answering her phone, and when I enter the facility, I find no one manning the receptionist area or any of the nurse's stations. Further into the facility, I find some men dragging my mother out a back door. I have never seen these people before, and I don't waste time getting to know them. I beat them down and retrieve my mother. Another group comes up from behind me, but my men have my back, and they have little trouble dealing with these people. We begin to get things back under control when I am distracted by an image out of the corner of my eye, "Kayla?" I stop in mid-fight and chase after my wife as she runs away. Only by the time I catch up to her, I discover that she is not my wife after all. "Who are you?" I grip the woman harder, but she does nothing but stare at me. "I said who are you?" She struggles to get away from me, so I take hold of her neck and ask again. "Who are you?" She grips my hand on her throat and fights for breath when she looks up at me with innocent eyes, and suddenly, I see Kayla. I gasp, releasing her instantly, and before I have a chance to make sense of it all, the woman is gone. My heart speeds, but my mother's cries change my concentration. I rush back to her as men attack her, beating her with all they have. Rushing to get to her, I take hold of one after the other and rip them apart. My mother lies on the ground, bleeding and crying, with little ability to move at all. The scene breaks my heart, and I feel a horrible guilt weigh me down. "Mom, let me help you back to your room." I pick her up, carry her to the nearest bed, and immediately seek out someone to take care of her. I find Franky passed out on the floor bleeding herself. "Franky? Are you okay? Franky?" I check her over carefully and try to revive her until she finally opens her eyes.

"Nick? Oh Nick, these people they took your mother!" Franky says, getting up and struggling to find her way out the door.

"Don't worry. I got her, but she is hurt and needs a doctor. Can you help her?" Franky instantly begins to cry and tell me she is sorry and that she tried to stop them, but she couldn't handle them all on her own. She has no idea how they got in or past security, but I do. Her panicked rambling means she is clearly in no shape to help my mother; she obviously needs help herself. A few quick calls and both Franky and my mother are rushed to the nearest hospital.

My anxiety increases as time goes by, and I still have no word on my mother. To make things worse, not long after we arrive, Savage shows up with a concerned expression. "What are you doing here?" I ask him.

"I heard what happened. Contrary to what you may believe, I am very concerned about you Nicholas, especially after what happened the other night. So I have some of my people watching out for you. How is the rest of your family?"

"They are fine. I just talked to Kayla, my … one of my best men is with them," I say, stopping myself from calling Ryan out as my brother.

"Are you sure? These people are not ones to give up easily, and they are certainly not ones that your usual guards can handle. They won't stop until they have you vulnerable. They are testing you to figure out how to kill you, and you are making it easy for them. They don't realize who you are. If you would do what I told you to do, then you wouldn't have to worry about your family." He stops briefly to look over at Franky as she approaches me with a weak smile. "Or your girlfriends," he hums with a questioning expression.

I snap my head back in his direction. "She is only a friend that got caught up in this mess because of me."

"Nick, I am so sorry …" she cries, crashing into my chest.

I shake my head, trying to console her without encouraging any further judgment from Savage. "Don't worry about it. It wasn't your fault. I am going to take care of it. I think it is best I move my mother out of the facility for everyone's safety."

"No, you can't do that. She is happy where she is. She doesn't handle change well, Nick. She is just starting to make progress. You can't to take her away now," Franky snaps back at me.

"I don't have a choice Franky! She is badly hurt. She wouldn't handle another attack. I am not even sure she is going to make it through this one!"

"Nicholas, I think all this disagreement could be handled simply by you joining me sooner than anticipated. I can teach you what you need to know to protect your family. In the meantime, I am happy to help you move your mother safely to your home and hire this beautiful young lady full time to be your mother's personal physician." A quick glance in Franky's direction, and I can already see a smile beginning to form. I guess she is agreeable to that idea, but I am not sure I am.

"I don't think that is a good idea," I say, shaking my head.

"Why not?" Franky asks.

"Because I don't think it is a good idea to have my ex-girlfriend living in my house with my wife," I say to her with a hard glare. Surely she remembers our last argument that Kayla caused by investigating Franky. There is no way those two can stand to be in the same house together now.

"Oh, now I remember! Yes, Franky. My, how you have grown into a beautiful woman," Savage says. "It is too bad you two lost each other so early in your relationship," he continues with a smile until I glare at him.

I turn back towards Franky, "It is a bad idea, and there is no way Kayla ..."

"Why, is she threatened by me?" she asks, and I instantly laugh.

"Kayla? Threatened? That is hilarious. You don't want to mess with my wife, Franky, and that is why I don't want you there."

"You're scared of her?" Franky asks as Savage now laughs.

"Don't you have somewhere else to be?" I ask him.

"Nicholas, this is foolish. Let me help you, and then we can help each other. Your family will be safe with Nicky and … your other trustful guards. I can have one of my men come in and watch over them, too. However, I think you should have this young woman move in with your family since she has obviously been labeled as a target for them as well. They are all safer together under one roof, and more easily protected."

"Why would Franky be a target?" I ask.

"She is connected to you, and you are here with her. That alone tells them that she obviously means something to you. All that they want is to take from you until you break and show yourself to be vulnerable."

"Who are they?" I ask since he seems to know.

"Our family's enemies. Since Adair's departure, they see me as being weakened, and they think it is a good time to strike me. However, my connection with you has them worried. So, they are out to destroy any possible allies I might have, but they are starting to realize you are more than just an ally."

I can't listen to him anymore. "Just shut up please! I can't deal with this right now."

"It is your decision, but I warn you, they will not stop. You need me, Nicholas, your family needs my help," he says, causing me to feel as if I have just been punched hard in the gut.

I don't bother arguing with Savage any further. My main focus now is my mother and getting her better. Kayla kindly doesn't argue with me when I tell her I am moving my mother, along with her physician into our home.

Within a day after arriving at my home, my mother falls into a coma and stays there for days. I stay at her side the entire time. I keep everyone out of her room except for her caretakers, but somehow, Eey wanders in unnoticed. I didn't even notice him until I feel him at my feet. I open my tired eyes as he lays his head on my mother's hand. I don't know if he is concerned about me or her, but the damn dog does seem to care. For some reason, no matter his reason, it makes me feel better. My mother looks weaker every day, and I begin to believe that the pain of losing her is better than the pain she is going through. Kayla checks on me periodically, sharing a kiss and a loving touch, all I need from her, and she doesn't hold back giving me more when she sees that I need it. I even cradle Brayden in my arms and read to him until he falls asleep. Nicky always tries to be patient and wait his turn with me. Kayla says he pretends to be me some days when he is playing; she says he thinks of me as stronger and better than any superhero there is. He wants to be just like his father, Kayla says. So how can I deny him when he looks up at me with a pitiful expression from my mother's doorway? "Come here, son," I say, motioning to him. Nicky instantly runs to me and climbs into my lap to hug me and give his grandmother a kiss on the cheek.

"Feel better, Gillian," he says sweetly. He doesn't say much else; he just holds onto me and lets me feel some peace for a few moments. Even Franky gives me peace and does her best not to cause any issues with Kayla, at least none that either of them bother to tell me about.

My mother seemed to be getting worse, and I nearly give up on speaking to her ever again when her eyes open. She seems confused and scared when I take her hand to reassure her. "Mom? Mom, I'm sorry. I'm so sorry that you were cursed with me. I'm so sorry that my father walked into your life," I say to my frail mother. Her eyes are still swollen, her body still broken, but her eyes focus on me for the first time.

"Nicholas, why are you rambling apologies?" She squeezes my hand weakly. "You obviously don't know much about my life before your father, otherwise you wouldn't be so apologetic now." She coughs roughly, and I try to hush her, but she waves me off in frustration. "Your father saved me from the neglect and abuse I was enduring from my parents. I had never known love until him."

"That was love?" I huff.

"It was more love than I had ever known which is probably why I didn't know how to love you. Honestly, I was afraid to. To find love and to lose it is pain I didn't want to know. It is easier to pretend that there is no love at all." She starts coughing horribly, so I get up to get her some water. Franky walks in and smiles.

"You are awake. Good. I hope you are not tiring her out talking too much Nick? She needs her rest." Franky checks her tubes while my mother eyes her funny. "Maybe you should go get some rest, Nick. I'll sit with your mother for a while." My mother grips my hand, triggering a smile to form on my face. She obviously doesn't want me to leave, so I look up at Franky and shake my head. "Okay, well do you mind if I join you two. What are we talking about?"

"None of your business," my mother says sharply.

"Mom."

"I want to only talk to you, not her. Why is she here anyway?" my mother complains.

"She is here to help you." My mother tenses, looking away from us both. "Franky, go ahead and go. Thanks for the offer, but I am fine here by myself."

Franky reluctantly leaves as my mother watches her exit, wide-eyed. "I need to tell you something," she whispers.

"It's okay, you just rest, Mom."

"No, I need to tell you now before it's too late. A man came the other day to see me and your father."

"What man?"

"I don't remember. He was an attractive man. A friend of your father's, but he acted strangely. He kept calling everyone by the wrong name." I shake my head, knowing her delusions cannot be trusted. "Listen, she is not who she says she is. She is an alien, and that man had her take over Franky's body to kill me. I just know it. Don't let her near me or anyone else we know." I shake my head. "I'm telling you Nicholas. She is a spy. I bet she wants my company's secrets."

"Okay Mom, I'll look into it," I sigh, trying to get her to calm down.

"And there is something else ..." she pauses and starts to cry. "I messed up. I know it. I just know I messed up terribly. I'm sorry. Tell Dante I'm sorry."

"It's okay Mom. No one is angry at you."

"You will be when you find out what I did. I didn't mean to, but your father was right. I told ..." she says, beginning to choke again. I try water, but her throat begins to swell. I scream for help while she grips my shirt to stay with her. "He knows about them." She whispers through her tightening throat.

"Who knows? Knows about who?" I ask she fights to stay with me, but the nurse jerks her away to try and open up her throat. It only takes forty-five seconds, forty-five seconds for my mother to go from breathing to death. The apologies come immediately from her caretaker, but all I want is to be left alone. Everyone does as I ask, except Franky who tries to console me.

"Leave me alone, Franky."

"Nick, you shouldn't be alone right now." She wraps her arms around me and kisses my cheek when I suddenly tremble and feel a warm calming feeling come over me. I slip out of Franky's arms and find Kayla in the doorway, waiting for me with open arms.

Chapter 17

Ryan

Our new house was just completed a few months ago, and Sam has been working nonstop to make it perfect. I gave her free reign to do as she wishes along with some experts to help her shop for just the right things, anything to keep from having to be part of the decision making process and to keep that beautiful smile on her face. Every night when I get home, I find her and pick her up so she can tightly wrap her arms around me and kiss me the way she wants to, and tonight is no different. I walk up behind her knowing she knows I am there, and kiss her neck. She turns and jumps into my arms, entwining me in her arms and legs with the excitement I love feeling from her.

"I thought you would never come home," she says, kissing me ecstatically.

"Silly, I am home at the same time every night, and you know it. Do you think I'd spend even one unnecessary second away from you? Crazy girl, I can't wait to have these arms around me, those lips on mine, or these great legs around my hips." I laugh, carrying her to our new bed. "I certainly wouldn't want to miss an opportunity to get you naked and in bed."

"All you care about is sex," she sighs with a smile.

"No, that's not true. All I care about is you. It just so happens that having sex with you brings you even closer to me, and I love having you as close to me as possible. Not to mention, it feels really nice, too," I say, taking hold of her lips with mine.

"It's that good huh?" she whispers

"You're that beautiful. I can't believe that I get to stare at such a beautiful woman every day," I say, making my way in between her legs and letting my erection out of my pants to breathe.

"You know what would make me smile?" she says suddenly. "I would gladly give up on that puppy I have been bugging you about if you let me have something else," she says as I groan my happiness against her bare breasts. "I would like to have a baby with you. You're the love of my life, Ryan, and I can't think of anyone else I would want to do this with."

She has been hinting her desire to be a mother for some time, but until Savage is gone, I worry about what a child of mine would be subjected to. My brother is going through hell right now, and Kayla the same. I don't want that for Sam. "Don't you want that big wedding that you have been working on for months first?" I ask, trying to divert her to another subject.

"I would, but you keep putting the date off because of work, so screw it. Let's run away tonight. Let's get married and get pregnant all at the same time," she pleads with me.

"Baby, I will give you whatever you want, but let me talk to Nick first." Her smile instantly fades. "Only to let him know that we are leaving tomorrow night for a few days. I will take you wherever you want to go for however long you want to go. No need to pack too much clothing though..." I take in one lip after the other in between mine, "you won't be needing anything but me to keep you warm. We can have room service and sex for days."

"Alright!" she says, happily jumping on me and ripping off the rest of her clothes. I love the way she feels down my chest. She knows every spot on my body that makes me squirm. I reward her thoroughness by spinning her back onto the bed and sliding my growing respect deep inside of her. Her wetness envelops my cock so warmly that I groan my excitement. Her breasts bounce against my lips, and her legs wrap tighter around my waist while my dick swells deep inside of her. My movements inside her are smooth and precise, provoking a whimper from her lips to mine. Sam grips my arms and lets her head fall back, moaning and climaxing to ecstasy before her exhaling breath releases her gorgeous smile. I come hard and with energy to spare that I use to cover her naked body with zealous kisses.

Sam hums her enjoyment of my touch with her eyes closed and her head rests comfortably back onto her pillow. "Ryan, what if I asked you to never leave me, to never stop touching me?" she asks, reaching out for my hand.

I take her tender hand in mind, and reply, "Well then, my love, I would say you have a dutiful shadow for life."

She smiles, feeling my face for mine, and continues, "And what if I asked you to run away with me and hide from the world. What if I wanted you all to myself forever?" I delicately kiss her before running my hand through her hair.

."I wouldn't bother packing before I swept you off your feet and carried you far away from here to your angel's castle in the clouds, away from it all and away from the judging eyes of everyone who would doubt my dedication to you," I say, enjoying her giggling joy.

"Really? A castle? And why do I need such extravagance when I cannot see it?"

"Oh, my love, don't you know, as your consummate shadow, it would be my pleasure to lend you my eyes so you could see all the beauty and wonderful luxuries I would build for you, find for you, and attain for you. There would be no end to proving my love for you."

"Well then, my dutiful shadow, if there is no end to proving your love, does that mean there is no end to your love for me?"

I lean in close to her, wrapping my arms around her and making sure my strong hands reassure her that I am here by her side forever, before whispering, "Sam, my love, there is not a champion warrior brave enough to destroy my love for you. There is not a drug strong enough to cure my love for you, and there certainly is no place far enough for you to run that would keep my heart from ever giving up searching for you. Forever, my love. Forever, I will love you and only you."

"You will never have to worry about running after me because, like you, I am your humble shadow and your forever pride-filled light that will shine brightly upon you day and night. No woman deserves a man like you," she says, sinking deep into my arms with a soft sigh.

"Wrong, my bright shadow ... you are more than deserving." Her eyes open, and her smile spreads across her face. For a moment, I believe she can see me fully. Her blindness has never bothered me, but sometimes, I wish she could see how happy she makes me.

Sam makes a wonderful meal and has me look at a million different baby furniture pieces for the house on the internet, forcing me to describe them all to her while she sits in my lap and lays her head on my shoulder. I hate shopping for furniture, but I love every second of this. It is amazing how much my day can stress me out, but the moment I have this woman next to me, everything becomes perfect. After the hundredth crib, I shut the computer down and take Sam to bed. "It's time to sleep my Shadow. We can design our future children's rooms tomorrow if you want."

Sam falls asleep in my arms, and I fall asleep breathing her sweet scent in, but I awake abruptly in the middle of the night with an odd feeling. I sit up straight in bed, listening and waiting. Sam wakes and begins to become frightened as she grips me for answers. "Stay here. In fact …" I take her by the hand and hide her in the bathroom with a gun. She does better than most, and I would rather her shoot me than risk her life. I step through the house quietly, watching the darkness. I see a blur cross the window outside, so I run to chase it down. The blond haired man runs through the yard and into the trees, and I follow. He turns on a dime and smiles at me, his eyes swirling with anticipation.

"I have seen you before, on the rooftop, wanting to kill my brother," I say to him, preparing for any attack he may have in mind.

"Your brother, huh. I guess that's why," he says, backing off slowly from me.

"That's why what?" I yell at him.

"That's why Dennis wants you dead. If I were you, I would be running and not bothering with me," he says calmly.

"Who are you?" I ask, looking him over quickly to find anything that might clue me in to who he is.

"A friend if you want it or an enemy if you prefer to come at me now."

"I prefer you leave my family alone!" I stand my ground, ready to attack.

"Your family came after mine first." He stands straight up as if he hears something I don't. "He really wants you dead doesn't he?" I have no idea what he is talking about. "Run young one, run far and hide before it is too late. I would stay away from your house, too because it is about to go up in flames."

I turn and watch my house blow up into the air, brightening the night sky in full glow. "No!" I scream and run towards the house. "Sam!" Before I can reach the house, it explodes again. I fight to get inside, but Nick comes from out of nowhere and holds me back. "Let go of me! Sam is in there!" I scream at him.

"It's too late Ryan. It's too late. She's gone." Nick yells back at me, holding me tight while Eli jumps in and holds me down, too.

"Sam!" I cry out to her over and over, but the flames overtake everything. "Sam!" Nick grips me tight to his chest until he sees attackers coming. While he goes after them, I fight to get to my flaming house and to her.

"Ryan, she's gone. She is gone, Ryan. There is nothing you can do now," Elijah says, grabbing hold of me and forcing me to the ground again. I fight him, screaming out for her. I plead with the night that she, somehow, left the house before it was too late. Elijah grips me tighter and holds me, and all I can do is cry and wish I was dead.

Nick returns and drops to his knees in front of me. "I'm so sorry. I tried to warn you, but you wouldn't answer your phone." I fall against his chest with nothing left.

"I should have been with her. I should have died instead. I …"

"No. No, I should have protected you both better. It was my job. It is my fault Ryan, not yours. They were after you because of me," Nick says, but all I can feel is the pain of losing her.

Nick takes me to his home where Kayla awaits. I didn't allow anyone to console me on the way here. I didn't want anyone to touch me or talk to me at all. I just wanted to be left alone, but somehow, the moment I see Kayla with tears already in her eyes, I welcome her arms around me and release screams and tears that I didn't even know I had inside me. She lies on the floor with me and holds me, listening to my cries and crying even more along with me.

Chapter 18

Nick

As I watch my brother fall apart and struggle with his broken heart, I recall the moments prior to me calling Sam, prior to her dying so horribly in that explosion. I knew something was wrong, I just didn't know what:

Elijah is kind enough to meet me at an out of the way place.

"You called?" he immediately says with an attitude.

"Yes, I need to make sure you watch out for Ryan. He is out of control and reckless with me around. I can't imagine how he will be when I am not."

"Are you planning on leaving us?"

"You know damn well that I don't know what is going to happen," I say to him.

"Damn it Nick! You know you have to let him grow up at some point and make his own mistakes. Not everyone and their actions are your responsibility." He curses me, and everything around us, knowing I am not listening to him.

"Normal mistakes I don't mind, but the mistakes he is making will cost him his life if he is not careful. All I want is for you to make sure he stays under the radar when I am gone, and you better fucking make sure he gets the hell out of here if …" Elijah sighs and looks away from me

"I can only imagine how sick Ryan is hearing your constant requests to desert you when you merge over to the dark side. I don't know why you think I can get all these people out of the city and make sure they stay away. I only have two hands, and it will take more than that just to keep your wife in check. I don't want to even think about your brother."

"Well, you're lucky that Brady is seeing to Lena or I would ask you to deal with her, too. Brothers for life, remember Eli?"

"Yeah, but you know I originally made that deal because I thought we were talking about women. I only agreed because I wanted to make sure you stayed away from the women I wanted to fuck first. Now, it's turning into this whole life and death bullshit."

I laugh at him and his scrunched expression, "You're the one that wanted a family. I have one if you will just take it." He walks away from me. "My wife and kids mean everything to me, and I know you will die to protect them as I would you."

"Ahhh damn! You had to pull the, *I would die for you* card. Nicky, fuck, at least say something that I can yell at you for, not this crap that makes me feel like shit. You could have at least trained that wife of yours first. Damn Nicky, I thought we were friends?" He says with a smile. Before I can respond, I get a bad feeling rushing through me. "What's wrong?"

"Ryan. Ryan!" I quickly dial his number and repeat, but the fucker doesn't pick up. Sam does.

"Nick, something is wrong. Ryan is after someone, and I don't know where he is. Please come quickly," Sam says in a panic.

"I'm on my way. Don't worry." I speed through the streets until I come up on his house. Elijah pulls in right after and jumps out of the car, trying to keep up with me until the house begins to explode. Fire shoots out from every window and begins to blaze through the roof. "Ryan!" I scream. And then I hear him. I look over and see him running toward the house screaming for Sam. "Ryan!" I scream again, running after him. It takes Elijah and I both to tackle him and keep him from running back into the house.

"Saaaaammmmm! No!" he screams in terror, fighting us with everything he has to get to her. "God no! Sam!" His screams begin to turn into terrorized cries, and my heart breaks for him. There is nothing left in him, so when attackers come for him, I go after them. They didn't expect me, and I show no mercy tonight. I break one neck after the other, and the necks I can't reach, I grasp their hearts and squeeze instead. Not one gets away from me, and not one is left to tell me why. My emotions get the better of me, and all I want is to kill more. So, I wait, searching for them, calling out to them. "Come on you cowards! I know you're there. You want me right?! Come and get me." All I hear is silence, and soon, I no longer feel their presence. I return to my distraught brother, feeling his pain deep in my heart. I fall to my knees in front of him, wanting forgiveness but accepting anything he can give me at the moment. I can do nothing to calm him or take away his pain. All I can do is listen to his cries and hate myself for being grateful that it wasn't Kayla.

Dwayne, Reginald, Eddie, Terrence, and even Bo all come to help search the area for any clues as to who did this. It takes all of us to get Ryan to leave his charred home and into a car so I can take him to my home where Kayla handles the rest. She falls to the floor with him in her arms and cries right along with him, and along with Elijah, me, and everyone else within ear shot. No one is dry-eyed tonight. Ryan's pain cuts us all. My wife holds my brother tonight while I hold my sons.

There is a place in between my indecision, in between staying with my family or going with Evil. It is the only place I feel comfortable. Not choosing is easier than choosing. After pacing for some time with Kayla watching every step I make, I go to my father's hideaway. Now, I understand why he spent so much time here. This is the only place I can think these days. The quiet is short-lived. A car pulls up outside, and someone makes themselves right at home. I leave the back bedroom while someone starts up the power in the chair. *What the fuck!* I run in to see Ryan strapping himself into the chair and readying himself to push the button on his own.

"No! Ryan, no!" I scream, running for him. Thankfully, the surge causes him to drop the device, and I am able to turn it off before he takes on too much. "Are you insane?" I ask before realizing he is in pain and weakened by the voltage that is still causing his body to jerk. I remove him from the chair and help him to a more comfortable place. "What are you doing, Ryan?"

"I want to kill them. I have no reason to stand back and let you take all this on. I should be the one. You have a family, Nick. I have…" Ryan says to me through his gritted teeth.

"You have everything. Don't you ignore the fact that my family is your family. Losing you is not going to be any easier for them. I don't have a choice, Ryan. Savage wants me, not you. You going rogue will only cause our family to lose us both. They will be left, vulnerable and subjected to God knows what before they are killed. Do you really want that?" He pushes me away angrily and staggers back to his feet. "I know how you feel, but you have to be cautious and think clearly before you make any decisions. Everyone is going to depend on you. You are the only one that can protect them, and you know it."

Ryan slams his fist through the wall and screams in frustration, "I hate them! I want …"

"To kill them, yes I know. I want nothing less myself, but in order to do that, we must first figure out who they are and how best to destroy them. How to destroy them so that it hurts."

"I want it to hurt. I want it to be so painful that they will beg for death," he says, and I nod. "What's your plan then? Are you going to continue with this chair yourself and battle Savage?"

"I don't know who the greater enemy is anymore. Now it seems we have others coming after us. We may need Savage. He has offered to bring me in sooner so we can battle our enemy together. With him, they don't stand a chance," I say, avoiding his eyes on me.

"With him, you don't stand a chance, Nick," Ryan says.

"I don't trust him, but I do know he won't hurt me. He needs me for some reason. I don't know why yet, but I am sure I will find out soon enough. Until that time, we can use him to help get rid of our mutual enemies."

"He needs you to be his personal killer. He wants to turn you into him, an unfeeling monster." Ryan kicks the chair in front of him and sends it flying into the wall, causing it to break into pieces. "What makes you think he won't want to kill me? If he doesn't know about me yet, he surely will find out now."

Chapter 19

Ryan

I wish I had the strength to put everything behind me. I wish I could move on, find a way to help Nick and Kayla and get Savage, but every time I try, I think of Sam. I think of my mother and my father. I can't imagine what I would do if I lost my brother, or hell, if I lost Kayla and the boys, too. I think I would prefer to just join Savage and be numb to the world. Hell, if he decided he would rather kill me, I don't think I would fight him. All I want to do is lie in bed and never wake up, but I promised my mother I would live my life to its fullest and never, ever give up on it. I promised her I would fight every day just like she did. I wonder if my fight will do any more than her fight did for her?

"Ryan?" Franky slowly peeks through my door, allowing a bright light to sharply break up the darkness within my room. "Would it be okay if I came in to talk to you for a moment?" I nod, but I am not real interested in encouraging too much conversation. She comes in and, thankfully, shuts the door behind her. "I know you are having a hard time right now, but I thought maybe I could help. I am a good listener, and I am a doctor. I have been trained to do many things that might help you."

"I don't need a doctor, Franky. What I need is my home back, with my fiancé in it."

"I understand, maybe for now I can just lie here beside you and take your mind off things." She immediately finds her way under my covers so she can lay her head on my bare chest. "Now this is much better. Wow… do you have a trainer like Nick?" She feels up my chest and my arms.

"Franky, what do you want?" I say, pushing her hands away from me.

"I don't mean any harm. I am only trying to take your mind off things. A little flirting never hurt anybody. I promise I won't seduce you. Although, I guess you would be much better at that than I, seeing how you are a Savage."

"If anything, I am a Jayzon, but I go by my mother's name, Milio. I am not a Savage," I snap at her.

"Okay, calm down." She is quiet for a few minutes, and I have to admit, having her lying against me reminds me of Sam. She always stayed close to me all night, she never wanted to wake up and not have me there. I learned that the hard way. I snuck out while she was asleep one night when I had forgotten to pick up something for Nick and I knew he would be all over me come morning if he found out. I wasn't gone long but long enough. I came home to her crying and calling out for me. She panicked because of a nightmare, and when she couldn't find me, she became disoriented and lost her phone to call me. I heard her yelling for me as soon I pulled up to the house. I ran in, thinking someone was hurting her, but it was only her own fear that had her scared. I didn't realize that bastard she was seeing before me would purposely leave her alone and move everything around on his way out to try and teach her to be independent. Who the fuck does that? Who treats a blind woman like she is a joke, like she is some kind of game to be played with? When I ran inside, I found her on the floor, searching for her phone that she had dropped. As soon as she heard my voice, she reached out for me and didn't let go. I felt like a complete ass. I held her all night, trying to comfort her. The only way I could get her to smile again was to promise her a dog. She hadn't had one since she was rescued from the fire at her parents' house; she wasn't able to keep him, and that dickhead wouldn't let her have one when she moved in with him because he was allergic. I feel terrible for leaving her that night. The fear in her face crushed me, and I couldn't do enough to make it up to her. And that was just leaving her without letting her know. Letting her be trapped in an explosion, in our burning home, I don't know how she could ever forgive me.

My calm silence seems to have given Franky reason to believe I want her to stay. She begins trying to entice me, but I stop her hand before it gets too far. I don't bother to say a word to her. My growl is enough to give her the point. She backs off, with apologies.

"Sorry, you are hard to resist, you know. A girl can get carried away."

"Go get carried away with someone else! As far as I am concerned, I am still engaged to another woman." Franky nods, smiling.

"You know I could help you be with her again."

I sit away from her, instantly, and reply, "What? What is wrong with you?"

"No, I don't mean kill yourself. I mean I could sort of hypnotize you and let you go back to being with her. You can use me as her during your hypnosis. You will think you are with her, you will feel her, smell her, and you will believe you are with her. It will be a chance to be with her again. Maybe say goodbye in a better way." She takes my hands with a smile. The idea of being with Sam again is tempting, beyond tempting actually, but maybe I should let her go and not continue to try and hold on to a ghost. The debate in my head bounces around for a while until I shake it all off.

"Thanks for the offer, Franky, but I don't think it is a good idea," I say to her. "If you don't mind, I would like to be alone now." She gets out of my bed but continues to rub her hands along my chest.

"Sure. I understand, but if you change your mind, let me know," she says, leaning in and kissing my cheek. I close my eyes, and for a brief moment, I feel like Sam is here. I open my eyes quickly to verify, but all I see is Franky, smiling at me as she exits my room. *Strange, very strange.*

Chapter 20

Nick

Ryan was right. The only way I know how to ensure his safety right now is to make sure Savage understands his value. I arrange for a meeting with Savage and bring Ryan along with me. Ryan is tense the moment we walk into the house and seems to dislike the interior décor as much as I do.

"I feel like everything in this room is alive and watching me. I have never been more creeped out in my life," Ryan says, sticking to me closer than usual.

"Come in and have a seat," Savage says, waving us into his office. "To what do I owe the pleasure of this meeting, Nicholas?"

"I wanted you to meet my brother, Ryan," I say with shaky hands. Savage glances at Ryan, and I see the bloodlust in his eyes. "He is my father's son, and I would do anything for him. I would die for him and him for me," I say, breaking the concentration on my brother.

"Close are you? Why are you telling me this now? Why not continue to keep your secrets from me?" he asks, setting back in his chair and seemingly willing to listen to me.

"Someone is after him and clearly knows of him. They blew up his house and killed his fiancé. His survival is crucial to me; he is a part of me, and I won't stand by and watch his life be threatened by anyone."

Savage sits forward, and replies, "What do you mean?" I silently sit back in my chair, unafraid of his hardened glare. "You think coming here and facing off with me is going to convince me to spare his life?"

"With him watching over my family, then I don't have to worry so much about them and can concentrate more on my duties, to this family," I bargain.

He sighs deeply before standing and pacing in front of us. He suddenly grabs Ryan and jerks him out of his seat. I quickly take action and grab him, "Calm down Nicholas, I am not going to hurt him. I am only testing him." Savage looks into Ryan's eyes as Ryan fights to push him off of him. "This one has potential actually," he says, seeming surprised. I ease back as he eases off Ryan. "I am not sure why you would hide him from me, Nicholas. There is strength in him, an unwavering strength within him." He releases him with a smile. "I am surprised you haven't noticed that your brother is just as strong as you. Sad that he has wasted all this time, and hasn't realized his potential yet. Release that protective bubble you have put him in Nicholas, and you might be surprised." He looks upon Ryan with a hunger, and now I have no fear of him killing him but taking him for his own use. "Have you killed before, Ryan?" he asks, looking away from me.

"Yes," Ryan says calmly.

"Not with a gun, with your bare hands with the fire inside you. As a part of this family, your hunger is satisfied when you take a life with that power within you," Savage says with a glare that craves the information he wants to hear.

Ryan glances my way as he sits up straight and turns his focus on Savage. "I have killed in many ways, and I will kill however I need to in order to protect my family and the men that follow me."

"You are with family now, my son. I assure you; you are welcomed to claim your birth right as much as Nicholas is." Ryan doesn't answer, and Savage doesn't push him, for now. He simply laughs to himself as if he expected the response. "Ryan, do you understand who our family is and what our responsibility is to this world? What your future could hold?" He asks him but doesn't give him much of a chance to respond before he goes into details of the realm our family sees to and the other Lords who oversee the other realms. I told Ryan some, but now, he knows exactly who he is. The expression on his face mirrors mine when I found out.

Our meeting has taken an unexpected turn, and one that has me wondering about my brother. Maybe I have been overly protective of him and missed all the potential he possesses. Savage invites us to his study where we are instantly greeted by naked women who have no shame or boundaries. Savage freely lets the women take his cock out and grasp it with their moistened lips.

"Feel free to help yourself to one. I have kept them busy for a few days to help ease some recent stress I have been having. Some bitch is causing issues for me, and I am trying to handle the situation diplomatically, which takes a lot of patience on my part."

"I didn't know you handled things diplomatically," I say, pushing a woman away from my crotch and fighting through the bouncing breasts in my face. "I think we are going to go," I say in frustration.

"Why? Stay. Have a fuck, or two. Rabbie has planned an amazing dinner for later. What about you, Ryan, surely you would like to relieve some stress?"

"No, this is … I don't know what the fuck this is. But I am not interested," Ryan says, pulling a woman's hand out of his pants and dodging the others. "I think I'm ready to go, too."

"They are here to please, not cause you more stress. Take one home if you are shy about fucking in front of me."

"Nope. We are going to go but thanks anyway," I say, exiting with Ryan as Savage stands and positions himself behind a woman bent over a chair. I slam the door shut before we both are scarred any more than we already are by his apparent abilities.

"He will be in there for days sometimes," a woman says from behind us. "It's absolutely disgusting, but it does ease his stress and make him more tolerable." Ryan and I stare at her in amazement. She looks just like Lena. "So, you are my nephews? I am your father's half-sister, Galena."

I take her hand and greet her as warmly as I can, despite my shock. "It's nice to meet you. Do you live here too?"

"Unfortunately. Father doesn't want me too far away from him. He likes his family close. He is very protective, as you are finding out, I'm sure. Dinner is going to be ready soon. Won't you stay and enjoy it with him?"

"With him? You are not eating?" Ryan asks.

"No, dinner is only for Father and his guests. I am not real anxious to be a part of that anyway," she says.

"So come have dinner with us?" Ryan says, shockingly. "Yes please, come with us. We can introduce you to Kayla, Nick's wife, his two sons, and some friends of ours. Dinner can be a big event sometimes, but it's always fun." Galena smiles but seems to be ready to say no when I understand why Ryan is inviting her.

"Come, please. My two boys will climb all over you. They love new people, but I assure you, they will make you laugh. Kayla has put together a great dinner for everyone. It's a great family night for us, I promise you. It's not like anyone is going to miss you here." Galena glances at Savage's study door and rolls her eyes.

"I would love to have dinner with you and your family," she says with a light smile.

"Our family," I emphasize, causing a wider smile to form across her face.

I try to warn Kayla ahead of time with a quick text.

Nick: *Have a large dinner prepared and invite everyone you can. Except Lena and Brady, and leave Franky out of it, too.*

I don't have time to verify if she received the message before we walk in the door with Galena. I feel much better when Kayla greets me with a reassuring kiss. I introduce her to Galena, and she in turn introduces Nicky and Brayden. Nicky, of course, runs right up to her and shakes her hand before asking if she wants to see his latest artwork. She happily agrees to do just that, giving me a chance to talk to Kayla alone. She has invited everyone and made sure Lena and Brady stay away. Franky is sent out with some guards to retrieve some more of her things while Elijah heard *family dinner* and decided he wasn't about to come anywhere near something that sounded too much like, "A dull night with a big collections of boring fucks," as he said unapologetically. Dwayne shows up though in his finest, gigantic, sweater, which makes us all laugh at the site of the odd look on him. "What are you wearing?' I laugh at him in private.

"What? Kayla said dress for a family dinner. This is what I wear to a family dinner." I laugh, shaking my head. "Fuck you, Nick. This food better be good."

Exie comes with Bo, while Terrence shows up and immediately takes a liking to Galena. He is smooth and doesn't hold back on his flirtations ever. Terrence has no doubts in his appeal to women. I have seen him walk up to the most beautiful woman in the room, kiss her hand, and then walk away with her following shortly thereafter. Women love a man with confidence. Well, confidence *and* money.

"You know, I find older women extremely sexy," Terrence says with a charming smile.

Galena smiles at him and lures him in with a whisper and a deadly smile that throws him completely off his game. "You are certainly related," Kayla whispers to me. I laugh, gripping her hand.

Brayden suddenly laughs out loud and reaches out to touch Galena. Her expression is shock, and her mind seems to wander off to somewhere none of us understand. "Galena, are you okay?" Kayla asks.

"Oh yes, sorry. He is so adorable and so friendly for such a small child. I had heard he was sickly, but he certainly seems brave," she says, breathing again.

"He thinks your Aunt Lena. You look just like her," Nicky says innocently as he tries to secretly pass food to the dog under the table. All eyes focus on her as she looks up at me.

"I guess we all have a twin somewhere. If it grants me more attention from this cutie then I don't mind it at all," Galena says, playing with Brayden and causing him to laugh even more. Before the end of the night, Brayden has charmed his way into her arms, and she doesn't seem to want to let him go. Kayla allows her to sing him to sleep and put him to bed later in the night. "Thank you for allowing me time with him," she says to us as she prepares to leave. "He is a charming child. They both are. I would have liked to have spent more time with Nicky, but his dog doesn't seem to like me getting anywhere near him."

"You are good with children, and as far as Eey, he is overly protective of Nick. Rightfully so I suppose. He did save Eey's life. You are welcome to come over and play with them anytime you want. They do seem to love having you here. We all do, and I am sure Eey will warm up to you eventually," Kayla says to her while leaning in against my side.

"I would love to. Typically, animals like me, so I hope Eey will learn to trust me more, and I certainly love children. You know I had a baby once but … she died," she says sadly.

"I'm so sorry," Kayla says, unsure of how to react to her confession.

"Oh, don't worry. It was years ago, but thank you. It was very nice to be here tonight." Galena smiles with sadness in her eyes, and suddenly, I realize how pained her life has been. Eey looks up at her and whimpers. She doesn't fear him like Savage does. Instead, she runs her hand through his fur and closes her eyes with a hum. "Your questions about Father were good ones, but they won't help you against him. I can't help you against him. Your best bet is just to abide by his rules the best you can and keep out of his way." I step towards her.

"There has to be a way. If you know anything, please tell us. Help us, and we can help you," I say, gripping her hand.

"Nicholas, you are so much like your father, always looking for better. I miss him. Do you really think my father would trust me with such valuable information? I'm just his daughter, not his son … or his grandson," she says, kissing my cheek and saying her goodbyes to everyone else. Kayla leans on me and wraps her arms around me.

"Do you think she will tell Savage about Lena?" Kayla asks.

"I don't know for sure, but something tells me she isn't anxious to have another daughter killed, especially her brother's."

"Do you think he killed her baby, Nick?"

"I know he did. I saw it in her eyes." If I had any hope of having a strong ally that is already on the inside of Savage's tight knit clan, it clearly got busted by the weakness in my Aunt's eyes. Galena is too scared to help us. Savage has taken too much from her and has left nothing but a mindless minion.

After a night of talking with Galena, I decide to go back to my father's notes and papers, to look for more on his sister. Maybe there is something I am missing about her. Maybe there is a way to awaken her soul, awaken the strong woman she talked about once being at dinner.

Galena and my father wrote to each other often, but it stopped for no reason at all before I was born. My father moved from a decent neighborhood to the rat hole that I grew up in. A place, as Galena wrote, "Our father would never go to such a disgusting place." She wrote this when telling my father about a drug dealing gang she was ordered to deal with on her own because it wasn't a place her father was going to be caught dead in. My father took the hint that wasn't given on purpose. I spend hours scanning notes between my father and my mother, all of which amounts to nothing. There are more notes about my growing up and the signs that my power was increasing by the day, faster than my father expected it to. He had ideas of leaving me with Elijah's father and even Lena's mother, but neither were options that would hide me enough from my grandfather. If Savage hadn't sent Saldean to kill my father, he might have been sidetracked enough for my father to find the right hiding place for me. Instead, he was forced to become my personal bodyguard for life, at least his life.

My eyes grow heavy until I find a notebook that is buried deep inside an old bag. The black bag, with the name "Simone's Garage" across it, contains pictures with dates, places, and names. Simone's Garage? Ah no! I pull out one picture after another of a woman with my father and some of them together at Simone's Garage. I can't believe this. "Sophia, nice to meet you. Your nephew has been a pain my ass since the day I met him. Fuck." The beautiful woman rests against my father's chest is in every picture thereafter. The pictures show my father with a look that I never saw on him, happily in love. The notebook verifies his love for her. He nearly goes insane desiring her, up to the point of feeling her naked body for the first time. He writes of every intimate detail, even the first time he came inside of her, but it is her orgasm, he writes, that changed him forever. It is what follows that causes me to pause.

My desire to kill is gone. My power feels even stronger, and my mind, for the first time, feels clear and wide open. I used to desire nothing but to please my father. Now, when I look at him, I see a killer. No, a murderer. He threatened me wanting me to stay away from her but; I wouldn't give up love for him. I told him that. I told him I wouldn't follow him blindly any longer and that I have a mind of my own. I can form my own army, my own business, and with the protection of the other Lords, I could defeat him. I assumed he understood and would back off. I assumed wrong. When he showed up at her door, I dared him to kill me, but it wasn't me he was after. I sensed his desire for her the moment I looked into his eyes. He wants her for himself but prefers her death more. There were men creeping around her house while he tried to distract me. I was too smart for that, or so I thought. I stood in front of her and fought them all: one, two, three or more at a time. With each kill, I became hungrier for another. It was like a disease was awakened in me. I craved it, I enjoyed it, and I became so overwhelmed with the poisonous craving that I killed my own love. Sophia was gone before I could say goodbye. I woke up with her twisted body still reaching for me to spare her, but I didn't realize it was her. If only I realized it was her and my child. I killed them. My poisonous blood killed them.

He won. He got what he wanted and what he believes is better; he got me to acknowledge what I am. The devil inside of me cannot be killed. The killer always remains within me. It desires to be fed, and I fed it with the only love I have ever known. I begged him to kill me, and he screamed for me to take back my role in the family. He turned my brother against me, so I turned to my sister, and with her help, I ran. Her funeral was terrible to see. Her family was as distraught as I was. Most of them believed that she had a heart attack, but her brother approached me and said he didn't believe that. He planned to devote his life to finding her killer, and he begged me to help him. It was my hands that killed her, but it was my father's blood that cursed me to do so. I have to find a way to kill my father, and so I agreed to help him if he would help me. That bond cursed his life and his wife's too. The only person that can cause my father's demise and seek revenge for all the lives he has destroyed is me.

My father's words send chills down my spine, considering what I might become, who might suffer because of me.

Chapter 21

Ryan

Every morning I wake up, and for a brief moment, I believe everything is just as it was. Sam is with me in our home and we are back trying to decide between getting married at a Vegas drive-thru or having a lavish wedding in front of all of our family friends. And what I would give to look at more drapery fabrics right now. Somehow, I manage to get out of bed again today. I am not sure how, but my nephews help me forget my troubles some of the time, Kayla picks on me enough to help me get through some more, and Nick gives me work to do to help me make it through the rest of my day and back to bed. The trouble is when I am back in bed, I'm back to the quiet darkness where I have nothing but my thoughts and memories. I can barely tolerate it and end up having to get up and find something to do, something to take my mind off of things. With everyone else in bed, I turn on the television, pace the floor, throw a ball against the wall, stare out the window, check the security cameras, and then she walks in.

"You miss her that much?" Franky asks. I nod. "You don't have to torture yourself, you know." She walks up to me and sighs, "I can help you feel better. Come on, Ryan. Let's try it. It doesn't hurt to try," she says, lifting her hand up to softly cover my face. "Just breathe and think of a better place, of a better time, and let me do the rest." I close my eyes and let go. I let go of it all and do just as she says, and when I open my eyes, I see Sam. I can feel her, smell her, taste her … I remove my clothes and hers before picking her up and forcing her against the wall. My cock slides in easily, and I feel her tense and moan with excitement.

Something feels wrong, but every time I open my eyes, I see her, and I want so badly for it to be her. "I love you Sam," I say, holding her up and not stopping for one second. No matter her moans, or her breathless pleas for more control, I do as I want to her. Lifting her legs higher and kissing her lips, I move inside of her hard, demanding her full attention. Something about this experience makes me angry, and I have to turn her around, bend her over, and fuck my anger out. Her orgasms do nothing to deter me. I don't stop until I finish, until I come. Then, I pull out and step away from her, closing my eyes and opening them only to see Franky. *What just happened?*

"Hi Nick," Franky says, causing me to spin around on my heels towards him. Nick steps into the room and quickly exits again.

Fuck! I fist my hands into my eyes. What I have done?

"Why do you look so upset?" Franky grabs my arms. "It's okay Ryan, you needed that, and I have to say, it was amazing." She caresses my dick with a purr. "Really amazing."

I push her hands away from me. "Stop Franky! Stop touching me." She won't leave me alone; she just keeps coming, kissing me and touching me and whispering to me until I feel I am with Sam again. My mind is spinning, and I am not sure what is happening. Before I know it, we are kissing again, and I am taking her to my bed to fuck her again.

Franky becomes a habit, a drug I can't let go of. I crave her constantly, and I get angry if she denies me for even a second. I demand for her to be Sam and to do the things she would do. Franky does exactly what I tell her every time, and I never bother to ask why. I don't want to know why this woman is seeking me out, or what she has to gain from this other than getting fucked. Nick never bothers to say a word to me about what he saw. I know he and Kayla are not happy about me and Franky, but I don't care. He would understand if he lost Kayla.

Franky sits up on my chest and looks down at me. "You know, Nick told me all about what Dennis ... I mean, who Savage is. He confided it all to me, and I have been helping come up with even more information. It is all quite exciting, I must say. And now, here you are, another found ... Prince I guess you could say. All that time you both spent in poverty, and the whole time, you were actually more important than anyone around you." She just keeps talking, and all I want her to do is shut up and let me go to sleep. "Do you think if Dennis is able to get you your own realm and have the Council recognize you as a Lord, would you take it?"

"I don't even know what you are talking about," I say, frustrated that she keeps talking.

"Oh, well, think of it as a chance to set the punishment for those who are deserving of it. You would be in charge of sentencing all those who committed horrible things. You would make the decision to inflict true justice," she says.

"That sounds like a heavy burden. Not sure I am the best one to decide anything like that considering I will probably be that person receiving true justice one day."

"Oh Ryan," Franky says. "You are nowhere near the evil I have seen. You are not perfect, but who is? Besides, wouldn't you feel better if you could right the wrongs in a way? There has to be someone you can think of that you wish you could be in charge of or could have been in charge of their true justice?" she says, and instantly, many names and faces begin to appear in my head, specifically that fuck Sam was engaged to at one time. The coward didn't give me a chance to inflict any pain on him before he killed himself. The idea of being the one to sentence him for eternity brings a smile to my face. "See... I knew it. I knew you could do it after all. I think you would be perfect." She lies her head back down on my chest. "Yes, I can definitely see you as a Lord, and as a Savage, you would have your pick of realms. Just like Nick, you have so much potential," Franky says, rubbing her hand against my chest with a deep moan.

"You sure do know a lot about this. I am surprised Nick would confide all this to you."

"Why not? We have known each other for a long time, and he knows I find all this fascinating. I have been helping him do research ever since he found out that his mother has been sharing valuable information with me."

"Nick's mother told you all about Savage?"

"His mother and I talked a lot, and though I thought she was delusional when she talked of Nick's father and Savage, it turns out she wasn't as delusional as I thought. Some of it stills seems unbelievable, but with what we have confirmed, who knows what could be true."

I glance over at her with a strange feeling coming over me. There is something about her that doesn't fit. "You know, most normal people would run away from us if they knew any of this to be true. Hell, Nick and I both would like to run away from it. Why are you running towards it?"

She sits up and gently caresses my face before replying, "Sometimes, you just feel that you belong, and I feel I belong here, with you. I think I was meant to be here to help you. Help you find your love. Help you find your bright shadow again," she says, pushing me to crave Sam. My head becomes dizzy, but I smile wide when Sam finds her way back into my arms and allows me to tell our story again.

"I love you so much, Sam."

"And I love you," she whispers back.

Chapter 22

Nick

Ryan opens his bedroom door, and Franky walks right in, the two of them together does not make me happy in the least. I don't understand what he is doing, but if she is able to keep him from doing something crazy, then maybe it is a good thing. *Maybe.* I begin to wonder about what my mother said and decide the best thing for me to do is to investigate Franky a little further and her friend, the man she continuously sneaks off with. I have one of my men search out information on her father's death and see if there is anything that will help me understand where she has been. Surely he was buried wherever she was. Until I find out more about her, I will honor Ryan's request for Franky to continue staying here a little longer, despite my mother being gone and she having no reason to be around here anymore. I haven't talked to Kayla about it, but I am sure it will come up soon. For now, I avoid the conversation and the trouble by paying attention to Kayla and giving her no reason to think of anything else but me.

I fall asleep with Kayla in my arms, but it isn't long before my peaceful sleep is interrupted. I don't know what it is exactly, but I sit up in bed and listen carefully. Kayla takes a hold of my arm with a look of concern. "Get the boys and stay with them in the safe room," I say to her before cautiously moving down the stairs. I listen and focus. Instantly, a man appears out of nowhere and another and another. I quickly realize that fighting these men off is not going to happen the usual way. No, these intruders are part of an army that has prepared to fight me. My stance needs to change in order to protect my family, and it does so quickly. I don't bother speaking. I simply make my displeasure known from the depth of my core.

"Look boys. This dumbass is going to fight us off in his boxers," the bold moron laughs but still avoids my eyes. "What? You couldn't at least find some pants stud?" I don't speak. "What was that? Did you say something?" he says, nearing me with a single step and a defensive eye, but no more. "Okay, I see you want to listen. So listen here. If you go quietly, we will make it painless for you and your whole family. Otherwise, we will have to force you to hear them scream to their deaths. You won't possibly be able to save them all." He steps forward again as his friends take a strong stance near him. "So, what's it going to be stud? And please, don't make this any harder than it has to be. You work for Savage, and we just can't take any chances that you might make him any stronger than he already is."

"You don't think I can take you all on and save my entire family at the same time? You don't know me that well do you?" I growl, causing the whole group to step backwards at once. I take one step forward, and they back up five. My body is so tense that I can feel nothing but fire burning from my heart to the tips of my fingers. They quickly scramble and decide to attack me all at once. That might have been their best chance to get me, but it wasn't their best decision. These are no ordinary intruders. They don't attack me with guns or fists but with a force like I have never seen before, an attack that is pointed as if they are searching for a weak spot in my body. Despite their precise attack, I still feel their breaths fade as I flex and kill. One after the other, they die at my feet. I demand them to surrender, yet they keep coming and coming, and I keep killing. Their faces become blended and nonexistent to me. I stop asking who they are, who they work for, and begin to enjoy the slaughter. I have never felt so strong and so powerful. The rush of adrenaline causes such a great satisfaction within me, I don't want to stop.

"Nick! Nick …" Kayla's voice begins to surround me. *I won't let them get to her or my boys.* The sound of my wife's voice only makes me more determined to kill. I believe them to be all gone when I feel another presence at my back. I spin around, grab them, and lick my lips, waiting for their beating heart to burst.

"Nick!" Ryan screams at me as he grabs my hand and tries to force my release. He manages to loosen my grip, but I don't understand why he fights me. "Nick you are going to kill her!" Ryan strikes me and strikes me again until I let go and turn to him, enraged.

"What are you doing?" I yell at him. He ignores me and leans down to the person at my feet. "Kayla!" Ryan yells before breathing into her mouth to try and revive her. *No. NO. I did not do that?* Ryan screams at me to help him, to help her, but I am still tense with anger, and I am afraid to touch her. "Nick!" he yells again, pulling me down to my knees. I lay my hands on my wife, and instantly begin trying to breathe life back into her. "I'm sorry. Please Kayla, I'm sorry," I cry to her. I try again to revive her while Ryan calls for help. *Oh God, please …*

"Mommy!" Nicky screams, racing towards his mother. I tell him to stay back, but he doesn't listen. He calls to her and wraps his little arms around her neck. "Mommy. What happened, Mommy? Wake up Mommy.

Wake up!" my son cries, ignoring my attempts to revive her. I grip my face with my bloody hands and pray for this nightmare to be over.

The sudden gasp of breath from the air causes us all to stop breathing. I look down and watch her eyes open. "Oh my God, Kayla." I lean down and kiss her. "I love you," I say, smiling down at her. She wraps an arm around Nicky and kisses him weakly but looks at me with fear.

Ryan rushes over and helps her sit up. "Are you okay?!? Can you breathe?" he asks her. She nods. I want to touch her, to hold her, but somehow I think that would only make things worse. "Nick, I think you should help her to bed and let her rest until the doctor can get here." Kayla's lip immediately begins to quiver as she takes his hand over mine. "Okay, I'll take you. Nick, you stay here and … and calm down." I nod and fall into my hands, not understanding what happened. Franky leans down and put her arms around me.

"It's okay, Nick. Everyone is okay now."

"I nearly killed my own wife," I say, pushing her away from me. *Why would she want to be near me? Did she not see what just happened?*

"She got in the way. She should have given you a chance to calm first. It's dark, you were surrounded by attackers. It wasn't your fault. You were amazing. Absolutely amazing."

"I'm a monster."

"No, you're not …" she says against my ear, rubbing her hands on my bare chest.

"Franky, I am covered in blood. I just nearly killed my wife. Please stay away from me," I urge.

"I don't mind, and you're in pain. Let me comfort you." She kisses my cheek. "You need to relax. Take a hot shower, clean up, and calm down."

"Kayla's in bed. I don't want to disturb her right now. I can't imagine she wants me anywhere near her."

"You have more than one shower, don't you? Use mine. It will help you feel better before you approach Kayla again," Franky says, taking my hands.

I finally agree to step into a hot shower, but before I do, I stare at myself in the mirror, looking over the bloody monster staring back at me. The shower eases my pain some and my nerves, but I don't know that anything can fix my marriage right now. I step out of the shower and wrap a towel around my waist, breathing a little easier but exhausted. "Thanks for letting me use your shower," I say to Franky before noticing her naked body across the bed. She tries to entice me before running between me and the door. "Get out of the way, Franky. I don't know what is wrong with you, but you are not the girl I used to know."

"You're right. I'm a woman now. A woman that can ease your pain."

"You should know better than anyone that acting this way doesn't do anything for me. You should know that. The Franky I knew would know that," I say, silencing her enough to move out my way.

I step towards our bedroom and hesitate before going in when Ryan opens the door. "She's fine, Nick. Come on in." He takes hold of my arm and pulls me in. "She wants to see you, so go in."

I walk into the room, and she immediately looks up at me. The fear is gone from her eyes, but I don't know if it has left her completely. "Kayla, are you okay? I'm so sorry, I … I don't know why I … I," I break down, trying to hide my tears.

She rushes to me and grabs my hands from my face. "Nick, stop. That wasn't you. I know it wasn't, but somehow, we have to figure out how to control that."

"I don't know if it can be controlled. Princess, this is … I craved it. I craved the killing. I couldn't see you. All I could see was your beating heart, and I wanted to stop it. I heard you, but I couldn't see you. The effect you have on me takes too long …" I stop myself and look away from her. If she knew she could calm me, she would endanger herself over and over to help me, until I killed her. I could never live with that.

"What effect?"

"Nothing, I just meant my love for you. It took too long for me to realize it."

"There are no more men to fight tonight. Ryan is going to stay on watch, so you can sleep. Come to bed, and show me that love you have for me, please." I reluctantly agree to crawl into bed next to her, but the moment I feel her body next to me, I feel her calm wash over me. I cradle her in my arms and kiss her all over with tears in my eyes. The thought of losing her pains me to my core.

Chapter 23

Nick

Savage seems to be more excited every time I come to his home. It makes me crazy to think he is happy that I am here, so much so that I can't control myself. "Did you send them to my home?!" I scream at him.

Suddenly, he looks surprised, not the usual man of complete control. "What are you talking about? Who came to your home, Nicholas?"

"Don't play stupid with me. You know damn well who I am talking about! Who are they? They are not normal. They have an ability about them, but it isn't like ..."

"They knew how to defend themselves against your attack? They avoided looking into your eyes? They threatened you to try and draw you to them?" I stare at him, trying to decide if I believe him or not. Savage turns from me, humming his interest in my details. "You are lucky, Nicholas. You are lucky they didn't understand your strength or your weaknesses. You shouldn't have been there. You have no idea what you are doing against them." He doesn't bother to verify his questions as he simmers. "Those bastards will fry!" he suddenly screams, throwing his fists down on the desk in front of him.

"Who? Who were they?" I demand.

"You need to move in here now, Nicholas. I can't protect you all the time, and I can't have you wandering out there without knowing what you need to know to protect yourself."

"No, I can't leave my family. They were going to kill them, too! I don't even like leaving them behind now except I have Ryan to protect them."

"Your family will be fine, much better off without you there actually. If you leave them behind, then that will show our enemies that they mean nothing to you, and if they mean nothing, then there is no reason to bother with them. Ryan is plenty capable of detouring them. Not to mention, that boy of yours is plenty strong enough to handle those morons they sent last night. The real trouble wouldn't come after you at your home, not without knowing who you truly are. However, they will now. Now that they know you are my grandson, and they surely know that now, no one else could have survived an attack like that. You have to leave and move in here where it is safe."

"Who were they?"

"They are your competitors, other families looking to take over. Families of ... similar backgrounds to yours," he says as I grab my head and cringe. "Don't be dramatic, Nicholas. That is one of the many things I like about you, the no drama. Your cousin was full of it, constant drama. Drove me insane. I didn't think he would ever get the courage to actually take you on."

"You encouraged him? You encouraged him to try and kill me knowing ..."

"Knowing that you would kill him? Of course I did, especially when my suspicion confirmed that you killed his father and not your own father as we had originally suspected. I haven't seen that kind of strength and power in ... oh so long. I thought Adair's father was incredibly powerful. I thought he was the one, but then, *you*. I sent him to kill your father, and I was angry when I was wrong, but I wasn't wrong. I just didn't have all the information. When I saw you, I knew you were special. I just didn't know how much. I allowed Dante to live merely to protect you. I kept an eye on you of course, but I couldn't get too close or our enemies would have surely killed you." He laughs suddenly. "Well, they would have tried I guess. Little did I know that you were strong enough at six to take on a whole army by yourself. I wish I had; I could have trained you and prepared you already, rather than waiting until now."

"My family. I have to get back to them. They need me. You have all this to protect you, and they have nothing. My brother isn't strong enough. He can't do it by himself."

Savage exhales, exhaustively, "Nicholas, you need to stay here and train with me, there is no more time for this. If you stay here, we can speed up your training and have you ready to protect your family properly that much sooner. Ryan will be fine. I will send the right men to your home to help him. I assure you, they will be fine. As I said before, their interest is you, and if they can't get to you through them, then they will not bother with them. You have to show no interest in them and leave them, only for now. Once we have our enemies beaten, then you can embrace your family again and live in peace. We can all live in peace. They are after you, not your family, Nicholas. Don't give them any power to bring you down. You have a lot to learn before the war begins, and you can't do that by visiting me at lunch," he says, slamming his fists down in front of me.

"War what war?" I ask, taken aback by this new knowledge.

"The war between the families. Everyone wants to be in control. It is a burden at times, but it has been our family's duty since the beginning, and there is no way in hell I am letting those bastards change that now. Oh have they tried, and now, they think they have these young ones who have new ideas and new strategies. The very idea makes me angry beyond words. Not to worry though, they have their young, and I have mine," he says, grabbing my face and looking upon me with pride. "Don't worry Nicholas. Your family will be fine as long as we win."

"As long as we win? What happens if we lose?"

"Well they will kill us all and all of your offspring, and of course, I am sure that stubborn ass wife yours since she will surely do everything she can to protect her children. They won't be kind either; they will torture your poor Kayla until they are assured there are no more of us. I have to say, their torture methods have become inventive. She will wish she was dead. They once ..." He continues on telling me of their meticulous torture methods and how much the love of my life will be tortured for being with me and having my children. I saw it in their eyes last night, and as much as I wanted to disbelieve everything he is saying, I felt it then and know it to be true. The agony is interrupted by my grandfather taking hold of my shoulders and looking me over with concern. "We will stop them. Don't worry, Ma Joie," he says as if he couldn't be prouder to call me his own. "Together, Nicholas, we will protect *our* family. Our family. Trust me. They will never be able to harm your young ones or your beautiful wife. They will all be safe from their harm. All you have to do is trust me, fight with me, and push them back into hell where they belong. Don't let them win and cause so much suffering to the ones you love so deeply." He continues on, until tears emerge from the depths of my heart.

"I would die for them," I whisper, painfully acknowledging my deepest love for them.

"Of course you would, Ma Joie, but better to fight *for* them," my grandfather says, embracing me like his own and giving me another reason to stand and fight *with* him.

Chapter 24

Kayla

"Where is Daddy going Mommy?" Nicky asks, resting his head against my side.

I run my fingers through his hair, trying to put him at ease. I can always tell when Nicky and his father are upset about something. "He is going to go work out some details for work, honey. He will be back soon."

"I wouldn't be so sure," Franky says, entering the room with an odd demeanor about her. I instantly take a stand in front of my son. "No, I wouldn't expect to him to ever come back."

"What is wrong with you?" I ask calmly.

"Nick, is not for you. Don't you know that by now? He isn't a Daddy or a husband type man. He is much more than that. He *deserves* much more than that. If he is anything, he is a Prince, and you're a peasant. You should let him go, and you should be with someone of your own type. Someone of your own level. Nick is special, and you … and you are not." She steps forward with a strange expression and a twist of her hand.

"No!" Nicky suddenly yells and forces his way back in front of me. The woman falls back in shock. "Leave my Mommy alone!" I stand in shock, watching my son put up a fight against her for what seemed to be a simple step forward. He, however, saw something else. Franky steps back and leaves, not only the room but the house, too. Nicky turns to look at me. "Are you okay, Mommy?" I nod and instantly feel the need to wrap my arms around him and hold him tight to me.

"I love you, Nicky, but please be careful. Don't risk ..." The words to tell him not to do anything to protect me are pointless; he has too much of his father in him, clearly. I wish Brayden was strong enough to ... "Brayden?" Taking Nicky by the hand, I rush to check on my sleeping son and am relieved to find him safe but not looking well. I pick Brayden up and instantly notice his fever. "Oh no! What's wrong baby?" He is whimpering but barely able to cry he is so weak.

"Do you want me to call Lionel to take us to the doctor?" Nicky asks, sweetly. I nod, and he does without question. He also calls his father and demands that he meet us at the doctor. "Daddy says he will meet us the hospital, Mommy."

Brayden cries and cries, and my heart breaks, wanting to fix it for him. The doctors have poked and prodded him with everything possible, and they all keep looking at me with concern. "You're going to be fine. I know it," I whisper to him as I kiss his head.

"How is he?" Nick asks from the doorway of the hospital room.

"He is sick, and no one seems to know why," I say, fighting the tears. Nick approaches with his arms out, and I fall deep within them, allowing him to comfort me and Brayden at the same time.

Nick takes Brayden from my arms and kisses his head before holding him to his chest. "It's okay baby, Daddy's here." Nicky approaches, takes hold of Brayden's tiny hand, and smiles up at his father. We all fall asleep together on a tiny sofa, Nick holding us all until the doctor comes in. The doctor looks over Brayden once again, but this time, he tells us he is fine. He is fine? Suddenly, he is just fine? The fever is gone. He stopped coughing, and he is sleeping soundly. Maybe he wasn't as sick as I thought. Maybe it was me that needed the comfort, the reassurance that Nick would come back to us.

With Brayden feeling better, I climb into bed with Nick and cozy up to him even closer than usual. I have a terrible feeling that he is leaving soon, and I can't seem to shake the feeling. I force myself up and look down into his eyes.

He looks on me with shock, "Are you alright?"

"Don't leave. Whatever it is that you are thinking, you're wrong. You're better off here with us." Nick sits up and away from me.

"I haven't decided anything, and how you know what I am thinking is a little scary."

I feel up his arm and kiss his neck, "Nick, we are not a family without you. We are not whole without you. I cannot breathe without you."

"Kayla, I love you more than anything in this world, you and the boys are everything to me, but I am not about to think selfishly and risk your lives for mine. I am not worth saving compared to you, Princess." I try to speak, but he stops me with his fingers pressed lightly to my lips. "There is more danger than I realized, and I think the best thing for me to do is fight off the danger in the way that I believe benefits you all the best." I shake my head. "You don't understand Kayla. You don't understand at all, and I don't want you to. I want you to have that life you wanted, the one with the beautiful happy family. That's the life you deserve to have, the happiness you have long deserved. You have been through so much, and I am not going to prevent you from that happiness." Nick presses his full sweet lips to mine and takes my body on a journey with his. He envelops me with his warmth and covers me with kisses until I feel him inside me, filling me up tight with every inch of him. I gasp, gripping his strong arms while he looks down at me with desire, tenderness, and love. For once, I allow him to take me over, and I dive deep into his swirling eyes, deep into the waves of emotion and pleasure that instantly set me adrift into the clouds of bliss. From my toes to the tips of my fingers, he controls me. I have denied myself this experience, to be controlled by him, to feel the erotic pleasure that is him, the vibrating pulses that flow through him. It shakes every part of me into an uncontrollable orgasm and forces me into a drunken high. I desperately reach out, trying to hold onto him, to keep my body from floating away from his. Nick takes in my lips roughly before whispering, "I will love you forever, and forever you will be the only one to own my heart."

I don't bother to question. I only give him all of me, including my own heart. I return to him from my high and orgasm again. Only this time, I align with Nick's powerful rush. I am able to enjoy him coming inside me while feeling his energy intensify his smooth stamina.

Nick sleeps quietly while I grip him closer to me. I fear him leaving, and throughout the night, something inside me begins to change. I begin to fear and want to hide. My dreams crush me every time I close my eyes.

By the next morning, I see Nick coming towards me with a look I know well from him. He takes my hand and brings me into his office where Elijah already awaits. I nod Elijah's way, and he returns the favor. Neither of us wastes time with much more. He wants to talk about something he knows I will not like. I stand strong and cross my arms, waiting for him. "Now what is that look for?"

"Well, I don't know yet; however, I am sure you do," I say, avoiding looking up at him.

"Kayla," he sighs deeply.

"Nick," I say sharply.

"Please don't do this. I have thought about this and ran every possibility through my head, and this is the best one for all of us."

"Is it? Best for all of us?" I ask.

"Yes. I am going to go and stay with Savage and work my way into his favor. In the process, I'll pretend I have no ties to anyone else, which should steer any possible trouble from you and the boys. I will still be able to work on my father's notes, and in the meantime, work with Savage to become stronger too."

"You mean work with him so he can change you into him and leave your family vulnerable to be killed so he can have you all to himself when we are gone," I cry to him.

"Kayla! That is not going to happen!"

"Bullshit it's not! That man is ruthless, and now you believe he has your best interest at heart? Are you suddenly some kind of fool, Nick?" Nick takes hold of me, his eyes swirling as he looks down into mine. "Remember, baby, you have no power over me. Be angry with me if you must, but you better believe I am not going to simply let you walk out of our lives without a fight," I say, desperately trying to hold onto any strength I might have.

"I am not walking out of your lives. I am trying to protect you until I can get our lives back to … to normal," he says, walking away from me like he doesn't even believe it possible.

"Nick, I believe you can do anything, but I think, sometimes, you take on issues by yourself when you don't have to. Baby, please let me help you. Talk to me and tell me what you are thinking and doing. I can help you." I approach him and smile, but he doesn't smile back.

"Princess, I want nothing more than to tell you everything, but I also want to protect you from a world that you shouldn't have to deal with. If you would leave with the boys and find a life that makes you happy, I would …"

"Are you fucking kidding me?!! Listen here, Nicholas Jayzon," I say, poking his chest. "You better fucking believe I am not going to be happy without my husband and the father of my children. You promised me the perfect life when we got married, and you are not going to deny me that life. That means you are going to be in it. So help me if you …"

"Alright! Damn you! You stubborn ass mule," Nick snaps at me but allows me to collapse into his arms.

"I told you," Elijah says, getting up and making himself a drink.

"Shut up, Eli," Nick sighs.

"This asshole wanted you and the boys to leave with me tonight," Elijah says, relaxing on the couch with a large smile. Nick eyes him harshly.

"Oh, don't bother trying to destroy him with your demon eyes. I already caught on to your plan. You have tried it before, Nick!" I yell at him.

"Well, my beautiful, frustrating wife, I guess hiding things from you is futile. Yes, I wanted you to leave and hide." Nick fumes for a few seconds before turning back to me and my crossed arms. "It's not like you and Eli don't have something for each other." Elijah stares at him in shock, but I step towards Nick and look him dead in the eyes.

"Excuse me? Have I *ever* been unfaithful to you?" He doesn't respond but stands stubbornly strong against me. "You're right. I think Eli is hot."

"You do?" Elijah suddenly chimes in.

"Shut up, Eli," I say, continuing to facing off with my husband. "I tell you what, Nick. I will leave with him. I will fuck him every day and every night. I will let him suck on my tits and taste my pussy, and we will have more children together, all the while forgetting all about you," I say, watching Nick steam while Elijah slips into a dreamy eyed fantasy. "Is that what you want Nick? For your family to run away and forget all about you? Because I will if that's what you want. I only want to make you happy, Baby. Hell, let me prove to you how happy I want to make you." I approach Elijah and kiss him deeply. Nick grabs my arm and pulls me off of him.

"Are you done?" he hisses, his entire body tense. He lets me go and walks away, fisting his hands. I gently touch him and he relaxes to look back at me. "Are you done with your tantrum? I am trying to explain to you why I am doing this, and if you will give me a minute, I can explain everything I am thinking." Nick glances at Elijah's overly smiling face and growls.

"Your fights are awesome," Elijah says, sitting back in his seat and taking a drink.

"Kayla, there are more people out there who are against me, against who I am, and they want to destroy me anyway they can. The only one who can help me get them is Savage. In the meantime, I can get closer to him and find his weaknesses. Once he helps me, then I can destroy him, too." Nick takes hold of my arms and nudges me to look up at him. "Princess, please understand. I know it isn't going to be easy, but there is nothing you can do to help in this. I have to go at this alone, and I don't want you and the boys anywhere near."

"How do you know I can't help you?" I ask.

"Kayla! Listen to me! Did you see what happened the other night when I killed those intruders? I nearly killed you. I had no control over myself, and I don't want that to happen again. What if it had been Nicky or Brayden? What if Ryan hadn't been able to stop me? I wouldn't be able to live with myself if I hurt you or the boys." Nick softens while I begin to question.

"Intruders? Is that what they were? Is it that simple, Nick?"

"No, it isn't simple at all. There are no easy answers, only trouble no matter which way we go. No matter what we decide," he says, looking defeated already.

"It's *we* now? You are going to listen to what I want now?"

"Do you ever give me a choice, Kayla?"

"No. I am glad you have finally learned that. Now, tell me what you know and be careful, My Love. Don't leave anything out or there will be hell to pay." I smile and sit down next to Elijah who is enjoying the show immensely. I give him a sideways glance, but it doesn't seem to lessen his amusement. Nick takes his time beginning but eventually tells me that he didn't even recognize me and that he became so empowered by killing that he craved even more. When he wrapped his hands around my throat, he thirsted for the feeling of my pulse stopping beneath his fingers until he realized it was me. Nick stops suddenly as if he wants to tell me something, but he continues, confessing to visiting with Savage and discussing their partnership in defeating what Savage calls, "his born enemies." There are eight others with power, but only one can come close to Savage's power, Rein. He will do anything to keep Savage from growing anymore; however, he is too skilled and intelligent to outright take on Savage by himself.

Instead, he has convinced one of the others, if not more, to do it for him. Their first attack was obviously to take out Nick, since he seems to be of interest to Savage. And now they know that Nick is no ordinary interest. Savage feels that Nick should join him now and separate himself from the rest of us in order to protect us. Savage and his crew, along with Nick, will fight off our latest enemies. Once they have fought off the takeover attempt and proven their power, Nick's power especially, then Nick can come home and reclaim his family. "So, you say Savage said all this? And why should we believe that he is out for our own good?"

"That's what I asked." Elijah says with a wide smile.

"I know. I don't particularly trust him either, but I am not sure we have a choice right now. I don't know these … whatever they are, and I have no idea what they are capable of. That first team was a feeler team, to see how easy it would be to take me out. And since I somehow let one get away, they are more than aware of my abilities now. Plus, Savage says he will teach me more, and that can only help our ultimate cause in getting him," Nick says with an encouraging tone.

"I don't like any plan that has you leaving your family," I say.

"Kayla, I promise you, I will come back."

"Come back as what, Nick?" I don't bother waiting for an answer. I know even he doesn't know. I didn't mean to say that to him. I know how torn up he is about it. I quickly change my mood and approach his stiff back with a soft hand. "I'm sorry. I didn't mean that. I hate the thought of you not being with us, and I hate not being there for you. Nick, please look at me. I love you too much to simply agree to a plan that we don't have all the information for, and don't tell me that you do, either. Your fear of hurting us is clouding your judgment, My Love." He cringes and sighs, obviously searching for a way to argue with me, but after a few seconds of fuming curses, he calms.

Nick suddenly looks down and embraces me. "I will find out more then, Princess, and I won't make a move without your approval."

Chapter 25

Nick

I promised Kayla I wouldn't leave her again, and she is holding me to that right now. I am scared to leave my family yet scared to be around them, so I spend most of my time at my father's hideaway. This place calms me for some reason, but I also can get in more treatments on my father's machine. I am hoping that, if nothing else, it will give me more control over my emotions. I have asked Eddie to up the intensity, double the usual, and today, I let everyone know I am going to go even further so they can be prepared. I don't want anyone taking it easy on me, no matter what. Ryan has already made it known that he is not happy with my decision, but he isn't here to stop me this time. Elijah isn't offering any assistance on the matter either, giving Bo and Brady reason enough to back off as well. The rest are busy handling work. There just isn't enough to make it worth my while. Damn them. I will just figure it out on my own. I will do it without them and force myself to recover and fight another way. I set the intensity myself and setup a motivator opposite me. I have sixty seconds to recover or I will get shocked again. I start the machine and sit down in the chair as I wait for it to warm up. Closing my eyes, I breathe in deeply and then …

nothing. The first thing I see when I open my eyes is Kayla, holding the override button.

"What the hell is wrong with you? This is what you have been doing? Killing yourself?" she says to me.

"I'm not killing myself. It makes me stronger," I say to her.

"Oh really? Because you look like shit. I knew something was wrong, the bruises and the dark circles under your eyes." Before I can get up and argue with her, she hovers over me, looking me in the eyes. "Nick, stop. Stop doing this. It is making you sick. Everyone can see it but you. If what you need is to go and do this thing with Savage, then do it. I don't want to lose you. I won't lose you. So go, but you better damn well believe that I will come after you if you don't come back to me when you should."

She is so frustrating at times. No matter what I say or do, she just won't give up on me. "I have nothing but dark clouds hovering over me, Kayla, and those clouds are going to stay with me for the rest of my life. Why would you ever want to live with that? You should just let me go and be happy." Kayla grabs my collar and forces me to look into her eyes.

"You listen to me, Nicholas Jayzon. I love you! I married you. I had your children. All because I love you. If hell rains down on you, I will stand next to you holding the fucking umbrella over your head. We are in this together, and we will spend *forever* knowing we are meant to be ... that we are meant to be together. Do you understand me?"

I cannot help but smile as tired as I am, "Yes Ma'am, I understand you perfectly. I need to do this Kayla, and you need to trust me to handle it." She nods but doesn't agree vocally.

I promised Kayla that I would protect her and the boys, and I don't think having me in our home is in their best interest at this point. I am becoming a killer, a killer that's out of control. How can I protect them when I am the one they should fear the most? The answer is simple. I can't. The only answer is for me to leave them with someone who can, several someone's, until I can figure out how to be the man, the husband, and the father they deserve. My family is everything to me, and even though she agreed, I knew she wouldn't let me go when it came down to the time for me to leave. I pack a small bag including pictures of my boys, Kayla, and a small shell ring I keep for good luck, Kayla doesn't even know that I still have it. I kiss them all goodbye and walk quietly out the door. Determination will bring me back to them, and my love for them will keep me determined.

Savage is waiting for me at the door when I arrive. His beaming expression tells me everything I need to know about his happiness to see me. I'm not in the mood to be congratulated or welcomed.

"I am ready to go to my room. Then I will go workout and train with whoever you think best, but I don't want to talk to anyone. I don't want to be welcomed or made to feel I belong here," I say, trying to avoid looking at his happiness. Savage's smile changes slightly as he graciously points the way. Rabbie helps me get settled in my new room and provides whatever I want. Rabbie never looks directly at me or says a word. The only instruction I get is from Savage who insists that I join him for breakfast the next morning since I seem so determined to spend my first day away from him.

By the end of my first day I am exhausted, but I can't sleep. All I can do is think of my family and how I can get back to them. By the time the sun comes up, I am wide awake and ready to get this day over with. I manage to find my way to breakfast, not that I am hungry for food.

"Good morning, Nicholas. Are you ready to begin your real training?"

"I am, more than ever." My grandfather leads me to a large room where I come face to face with Galena. She stands tall and lean with her long dark hair tied tight behind her. She is of excellent proportions, of course, but it is her eyes that catch me off guard. With a smile, a golden spark ignites within her eyes just before swirling fire begins to form.

"Nicholas, meet Galena, your father's half-sister and your Aunt," he says. Apparently Galena never told him that we have met already. I don't know why, but I assume she has a good reason, so I go along with it.

She leans into me with an awkward hug. "I certainly don't look old enough to be your aunt. Do I?" Shaking my head, I look at her with a questioning expression, but I keep my mouth shut. "Your father was my brother. I looked up to him. I loved him so much. The day he died was heartbreaking for me, but I certainly understand." She grasps my face with tenderness. "You poor dear, you must have been so scared, not understanding a thing about yourself. Your father, I loved him dearly, but his stubbornness always got in the way of his best judgment," she says as I back away from her tenderness. "Well, you look so much like him Nicholas. I am so happy to finally get a chance to spoil you like I should have gotten to do when you were younger."

"Trust me, Nicholas, Galena will drive you crazy doting on you like you're her child," Savage says.

"I don't need to be doted on. I am not a child anymore. I thought I was here to learn, not for a family reunion?" I say, backing away from them both. "I don't want to be here any longer than I have to be."

"Very well. Let's gets started then. There is one more person you need to meet though, Nicholas." I look over and see a large man coming towards us with nothing close to a smile. "Delin, my personal assassin. He can kill anything without hesitation." The man grabs two swords and begins twirling them like they are as light as feathers and no more dangerous. His ruthlessness is obvious, and I have no interest in getting anywhere near him. Delin turns and begins tossing the swords towards Savage, following with knives. Savage moves from one place to the next, knocking them down and away from him. *He's fast for an old man.* "Weapons. You don't need any weapons, Nicholas. You have all you need to defend yourself. Now, let me show you how to control your ability. How to predict what your enemy will do before he actually does it. How to move swiftly through the most ruthless attack," he says, stepping up and squaring his shoulders with mine. "Are you ready, Nicholas, to become who you were born to be?"

I breathe in deeply and look him in the eyes, "Yes."

Chapter 26

Kayla

I rush out of my room and down the stairs ready to scream, but the moment I come face to face with Ryan, I know. "He's gone Kayla," Ryan says. I slam into his chest, furious, but the tears fight their way through anyway. "I am sorry, but he felt he had no choice, and for once, I think I have to agree with him." I shake my head, but Ryan holds me tight. "Those people are after something, and Savage is the only one that can help. He knows about me now and is supportive of helping us. As much as I distrust him, right now, we need him."

I look up at him in shock, "You talked to Savage?"

"I met him with Nick, and he agreed that I am more than capable of watching over you all, while Nick …"

"While Nick seeks the revenge that you want so badly."

"And that you want, too. Don't deny it. I heard you say the same things I did about wanting to destroy Sam's killers. Besides, with Nick on the inside, we can be assured of Savage's every move. He can learn more this way, Kayla, more than we could have ever learned in that shelter that our father built." I pull away from him, shaking my head when I see that woman come down the stairs. I look back at Ryan, and he instantly begins to squirm.

"Why are you still here? I thought you were supposed to leave yesterday?" I snap at her.

"Kayla, Nick still wants her protected, too. She was attacked because of her connection to him. Until he feels she can be safe on her own, she needs my protection as well. I can't watch everyone from their own homes, so I need everyone to stay in one place."

"I don't need you to watch me!" I yell back at him. Ryan comes back and wraps his arms around me.

"Kayla, don't express your anger here. Let's do it in a more private place. No one here is the cause of this." I push away from Ryan and go towards Franky.

As I pass Franky on the stairs, she, for some reason, feels the need to open her mouth. "Good morning, Kayla. It is so nice of you and Nick to allow me to stay with you." Something about her sugary sweetness makes me ill.

"You're welcome, please make yourself at home. Excuse me, I need to go check on my sons," I say, forcing a smile to appease Ryan's glaring eyes.

"Oh, no need to worry about them, Kayla. I checked on them myself a few minutes ago. I made them breakfast. I made breakfast for everyone, actually," she says, smiling wide. I glance towards Ryan as he shrugs. She walks down towards Ryan and grazes her hand across his chest. "I am sure you need a good meal to start the day, Ryan, especially with all the protecting you are going to be doing." Franky goes to the kitchen while Ryan pleads with me to make peace.

"I won't be a total bitch to her, but don't expect much more. And you stay away from her," I say to him.

"Excuse me?"

"Suddenly, she is sleeping in your room and flirting? This is not a good time for you, and she thinks you need that from her? She is using you for some reason, and you are too caught up in your broken heart to see it. Don't fall for it, Ryan."

"It is actually kind of nice to have someone who is friendly around here. You know, someone who is not always telling me to what to do. I will do as I please, and I will fuck who I want. I am here to help you and the boys. I am not here, however, for you to judge and take your frustrations out on," he says, shutting me up instantly. "Come on, breakfast smells good, and you will eat it and be pleasant about it. Otherwise, I will lock you in your room for the remainder of my time here," he says with a typical Jayzon-strong stance.

Elijah walks through the door with his usual annoyed attitude.

"Don't look at me that way," I say to him.

"What did I do? I just got here. You called, and I am here. Why? I don't know because you weren't exactly nice about it. *Eli, get your ass over here.* You know, Kayla, you could really use some brushing up on that sweet talk I hear you are so good at."

"I need you to help me, please. You owe me," I say, smiling forcefully.

"I do? Since when?" I grab him and pull him into Nick's office. "Baby, if you are going to grab me like that, at least moan a little bit."

"Eli that woman is here."

"What woman?"

"Franky!"

"Still? Alright, so? What do you want me to do about it?"

"I want you to get Nick back."

"How the hell do you expect me to do that?" I look down at the floor and have nothing to say to him, no ideas at all. "Oh, well that's a good idea, Kayla."

"I want you to stay here. I know Nick wants you to look after us, and I know you feel obligated to do so no matter how much I get on your nerves. And I feel ... I want ... I want you to stay here with us, too," I say with innocent eyes and a soft touch to his chest.

Elijah is silent for a few minutes before standing back and laughing, "You are something else woman. I have to hand it to you. I almost believed you." I continue to look up at him innocently. "Oh don't give me that face! Getting me to move in here is not going to get Nick to come running back here. He trusts you too much, and worst of all, he trusts me ... *damn him*. So you can stop the act. Good try though."

I try to hold my hurt expression on my face, but another mocking expression from him convinces me that it is no use. We walk back out to the living room when Franky comes in, smiling.

"Elijah, so good to see you again," she says, running up and hugging him. She smiles back at me before nodding my way and running upstairs and out of sight. Elijah watches her curiously.

"What?" I ask. He shakes his head. "No, what? You are curious about something what is it?"

"How do you know that?" He asks looking at me in shock.

"I got paid to know how to read a man, remember?"

"Huh," he says, looking me up and down. "It really wasn't anything. I just don't remember her liking me too much. Really, it wasn't that she didn't like me ... Franky was shy. She barely spoke to me. She wouldn't even make eye contact with me. Now, she is so outgoing. That is some transformation over the years."

"I used to be shy," I say, causing him to laugh. "Shut up! I did! I wouldn't talk to anyone."

"No, you were stubborn and protective of yourself. Franky was different; she was insecure, simple, and not much for the makeup and shoes. And those are some really expensive shoes she has on. I guess she is trying to impress Nick, but it is still interesting how someone can transform over the years."

"Isn't it?" I say, considering the idea.

Elijah stares off, thinking about something before turning back to me. "You know what? I will move in here. Why not? It could be fun. This house is always entertaining, much more so than mine ever is. Now, do I bunk up with you? I should warn you though, I sleep naked, and I am impossible to resist when I am naked." I roll my eyes and walk away from him.

"Oh Kayla, don't deny your love for me," he yells back at me.

Dinner time is interesting, with the crowd that we have now. If nothing else, it distracts me from the absence of Nick for a little while. My sons clearly miss their father, and Ryan is not his usual fun-loving self, the uncle the boys love to hang on. I do my best to fill in, but I know I am not what they really need. When Nicky approaches me to play one of his games, I try to figure it out in my own manner and not how Nick would usually do it.

Nicky looks up at me with a frustrated sigh, "That isn't how Daddy does it, Mommy."

"I bet I know how it works," Elijah says from behind us. He sits down and starts talking to Nicky, and apparently, he does know how the game works. "Your dad and I invented this game."

"You did?" Nicky asks him.

"Yep, we spent hours playing it. I won constantly, but every once in a while, I would let your dad win," Elijah says, and Nicky laughs. "Don't laugh. I am a genius." Nicky laughs again, only louder. "I am starting to get a complex kid," he says with a wink back in my direction. I mouth "thank you," and he nods with a smile.

Chapter 27

Elijah

I don't know what I was thinking moving in. Maybe a part of me really wants to believe this is my family. Kayla is my wife, and little Nick and Brayden are my sons. Nicky certainly has a good life. I don't know why in the hell he would ever give this up. I would fight like hell to keep it, and I hope like hell that's what he is doing. Kayla passes me with a smile and my knees begin to buckle. *Oh what the hell am I doing? I should leave.*

"Eli!" Little Nick runs up on me, carrying his favorite car. "Eli, my car is broken. Will you fix it?" I nod, and he climbs up next to me, watching me as I repair the broken toy.

Before the end of the night, Brayden begins to get tired, crawls into my lap with his blanket, and falls asleep against my chest. Nicky eventually falls asleep next to his mother who is curled up near me, asleep. I pull a blanket down and cover them up. Looking around me, I have to take a second to remember to breathe. *Oh, Dad, if only you could see me now. In this moment right here, right now. This is all I wanted for you, for me.*

"You look good with them," Franky says, looking over us all.

"I look good with my best friend's family. Yeah, I don't think so," I say.

"Well, he's not here anymore, and they are going to need someone. His loss could be your gain?" Franky says with an encouraging expression.

"What are you doing here, Franky?"

"They want me here so I can be protected from those horrible men, too. I have no idea how to defend myself against such ruthless killers."

"The ruthless killers are after Nick and his family, not Nick's dead mother's physician." She looks confused by my words. "I don't think so, Franky. I'm not buying the innocent girl needing protection bullshit. Why are you really here? Why are you encouraging me to steal Nick's family? You have no chance with him anymore. He loves them. He loves her. No one else is going to break that."

"I don't know what you are talking about. I am over Nick. I am perfectly content with my life. My only interest is helping Nick any way I can. Even with his mother gone, I can still help. In fact, Nick is very encouraging about me helping Ryan through his tough time. The poor man has lost his love, Elijah. He needs me." I roll my eyes, laughing at her absurd reasoning. "And what about you Elijah? What are you doing here?" she asks with a sudden attitude. I stand up with Brayden still in my arms, and look down at her.

"I'm here to figure you out, whoever you are." She looks me up and down with a scowl.

"You are a disgusting individual," she says with a snarl.

"See, it's things like that, Franky. I have always been a disgusting individual, everyone who knows me knows that, but you, whoever you are, seem to be shocked by it."

"I don't know what you are talking about. I have changed over the years. Sure, I assumed you had grown up some over those same years. My mistake, I guess. You apparently don't have the ability to progress past a young child's mind."

"Ooh that hurts. Tell me. How does it feel to be in the house of the man you love but not be in his bed? Instead, he puts you in the guest quarters way in the back and away from the family he shares with another woman. How does it feel to walk around seeing pictures of them together, celebrating their happiness and love? You're nothing but a memory, girl, a distant one at that."

She leans in with a tense expression, "I am fine Elijah. How do you feel about it?" She steams, and in that instant, I see it, a flicker of something change about her. It is brief, and I am not even sure she realizes that I saw it.

For now, I back off and let my suspicions rest. "No reason to get bent out of shape Franky. You know me. I just like to mess with people." I laugh it off and watch her stomp away.

"What was that about?" Kayla asks.

"I thought you were asleep." She sits up and cocks her head, waiting for me to answer her question. "I don't know yet, but I will let you know when I do."

Later in the night, I see Franky sneaking into Ryan's room. *Oh gross.* I groan at the horrible images in my head. *Damn you, Nick.* I suck it up for friendship and knock on Ryan's door. He finally opens with a disgusted expression. "Hey sunshine, I think you need to see something I discovered earlier."

"What's that Eli? I am a little busy right now."

"I understand, but it is extremely important I show you right now." He rolls his eyes and follows me out of his room to a private place for us to talk. I smack him in the back of the head as soon as we are alone.

"What the fuck Eli! I swear I will ..." He yells, standing toe to toe with me.

"What is wrong with you? You need to stay away from that woman, not fuck her every night."

"What is with everyone telling me what to do? I can make my own decisions, and if you don't like it, then fuck you" Ryan snaps at me.

"Ooh are we angry now? Good! You're being a jackass. I understand your grief Ryan, but she is using you."

"She is helping me. You don't know what you are talking about. She hypnotizes me, and I get to be with Sam every night. I don't have to miss her so much." Nick was right. He does need someone to keep him from doing something stupid. I feel for him, his broken heart is written all over him.

"She's not helping you, Ryan. She's helping herself. I don't know what she is after, but she is using you to get it, and worst of all, she is using Sam." His hardened expression turns to shock. "You know it. There is something about her that just isn't right, and she just volunteers to pretend to be Sam every night to the point that you fuck her. Who would do that?" He steps away from me, pretending he stopped listening. "You're right. You can make your own decisions. I won't bring it up again, so you go ahead and fuck her. Hell, marry her for all I care. You can pretend she is Sam forever, but at some point, I would think you would realize that she isn't Sam. Then what? Are you going to grieve all over again? You're just prolonging the inevitable. Ryan, Sam is gone, and I guarantee you that woman is not going to ever be able to replace her."

"I am not trying to replace her!"

"Yes, you are! You feel guilty, and if she isn't actually gone then you don't have to feel guilty. I can tell you though, the guilt never goes away, even if it isn't your fault. The best you can do is go on and be the man Sam loved. She wouldn't want it any other way. You are only disgracing her memory this way." He turns to face me, ready to tear me apart. "Fall in love with another woman that is up to her standards, then, you're honoring her. Fucking a woman that isn't even close to who Sam was and pretending she is her, well, I can only imagine how she would feel about that." I shake my head and leave him alone. Ryan passes by me quickly and walks straight into his room. Within a few seconds, Franky is escorted out of his room and the door is shut behind her. I smile wide, much to Franky's displeasure. "Have a good night." I wave happily to her frowning expression before going into my room.

The night air has a sharp chill to it this evening. I have to step back in between the fishermen's storage sheds to escape the blowing wind. The dark night is suddenly broken up by a flash of lights from a car I know well.

"So you were actually able to get away from Grandpapa," I say to Nicky as he walks up with a scowl. "Nice outfit. A gift for a being a good demon boy?"

"I'm not in the mood, Eli. Tell me what you know so far."

"Not much to tell. Everything is going pretty smooth. Not one of your contacts is getting out of line. Terrence has been handling almost everything on his own, and he is getting bored. Majority of your men are spending time playing cars with Little Nick. Work is unusually calm and easy. Ryan is back to sleeping by himself, and Kayla is back to threatening to kill Franky on an hourly basis. Everything is normal." He smiles with a roll of his eyes.

"Speaking of, what about the other trouble I anticipated? I have been waiting to see her banging on Savage's door to yell at me, but she hasn't even tried to call me. Is she planning something, or is she staying steady for now?"

"She is fine, dealing pretty well actually. Now, when you get back, you are going to surely have to do some major groveling. Your boys are good, too. Brayden is super cute. That little one is so lovable that I don't think I am going to be able to sleep without him snuggled on my chest with that little blanket of his. And Little Nick… wow he's a smart kid, and he loves to talk about his day. I think he has a little girlfriend, too," I laugh, smacking Nick on the chest. "He said, 'Eli, I asked her if I could hold her hand and she said yes, so I did.' So, I asked him, 'So what does that mean?' And he said, 'I don't know'." I laugh, motioning how Little Nick shrugged his shoulders. "Every day it is something new with him. I don't know how many girlfriends he's had already. Oh, and Kayla and I watched this kids' movie with them the other day, and Brayden laughed every time Little Nick did. Kayla and I laughed through the whole thing watching them together. I will say, it is tiring, dealing with those kids. We all woke up on the sofa the other day together, even the dog was laying right next to us." I laugh until I see Nick's expression. "What's wrong? You should be happy. This is what you wanted me to do, to make sure they are okay and stay happy. Right?"

"Sure. Happy and *safe*. Are you actually making sure they are safe or are you too busy taking naps with Brayden? Stop fucking around and look after my family. If that is too much for you, then I will find someone else." Nick proceeds to pass me information for Ryan and others before he begins to turn away.

"Before you go, Nicky, someone stopped me before I could get out the door. She wanted me to give you this. I don't know how she knew that I was coming to see you, but I didn't bother denying it. You should know, she isn't sleeping well without you." I hand him the letter Kayla gave to me and walk away.

Chapter 28

Nick

"Nicholas! Concentrate!" Savage yells at me again. "These men will not give you an opportunity to adjust your coat." He steps out from his corner and faces me head on. "Are you bored with the challenges I have set up for you? Maybe you need something a little more." I prepare as he sheds his jacket and comes at me at the same time. His strike on me blows me back like a freight train. I try to get back to my feet, but again, I am whipped onto my back. I can't catch my breath before another blow causes my blood to spray. In minutes, I am laid out with nothing more to give. Savage stands over me with disgust. "I barely broke a sweat, Nicholas. Perhaps you are not as strong as I thought. We are done for the day. Go clean up."

Rabbie helps me up to my room and cleans my wounds before finally leaving me to nurse my ego by myself. The only one that could make me feel better right now is Kayla. I miss her smile, her kiss, and the feeling of her warm body embracing me. I suddenly remember that my wife sent me the perfect letter to put a smile on my face, along with a picture Nicky drew for me, reminding me of everything I am missing. Kayla tries to give me the day to day of what is going on in her letter; it doesn't make me miss them any less, but at least I know they miss me just as much. Now, when I am alone in my obnoxiously decorated room, I can still have my family with me. As soon as I hear Savage coming down the hallway, I jump up and stash my letters and pictures with the rest of my hidden treasures behind the drawer in the chest. When he enters my room, I am laid out with little interest in what he has to say.

"Nicholas, let's go."

"Where are we going?" He rolls his eyes as he waves me to follow him. I am starting to understand where I get my attitude problem from. We get into his car and drive to a dark area of town where he points out a crack house surrounded by gun-toting criminals willing to kill anyone that gets too close to their boss's gold.

"This group has taken it upon themselves to grow in the wrong direction. I have an interest in a company I believe to be an up and coming opportunity. The man who owns the company has recently lost his daughter within this group. They have kidnapped her to encourage him to hand over money they believe he owes them. I don't care about their problems. I care about my investment, and my investment is obviously distraught. He is unable to perform his duties properly and unable to concentrate on the business I have invested in. It does me no good to threaten him if he prefers death than to be without his daughter. I need him to do his work, but until he is relieved of his heartbreak, he is useless to me. I need you to go in there, find her, and bring her to me. Here is a picture of her," he says, waiting for me to simply agree and do as asked without question.

"It's surrounded by people with guns, and you want me to go in there by myself? Do you think they are just going to hand her over to me when I ask nicely?"

He looks over at me with no amusement. "I didn't say ask nicely, nor did I say ask," he says.

I step out of the car, and he leaves me in this mess to figure it out on my own.

"Hey," An older man sitting on his porch says to me as he sits back eating his chips and drinking his beer. "You better run after your friend, cause you don't wanna stay here. A pretty white boy like you won't last five minutes here." He shakes his head at me. "I ain't got no phone, so I can't call the police for ya, not that they would come here anyway." I ignore him and study the area quickly as he continues to judge my stupidity.

I take a deep breath, close my eyes, and go back to the training I have had so far. The old man yells at me again to run, and I open my eyes with a swirling determination. I calmly walk up to the front of the house, and two men run at me with guns in their hands. I stop them both before they are within five feet of me. The smiling faces of the others quickly change to fury. Their fury feeds me, and I focus it all back on them. On their knees, they try to fight me, and on their knees is where they die. I glance back at the old man who has moved his wide eyes and lounge chair further down his driveway with more beer and chips in his hand. The door of the house flies open, and I grab hold of the gun in my face, jerking it forward and forcing the man to fly out onto his head. Imbeciles. To fire a gun here will send us all up in flames. I step into the house, and a man steps out from behind a wall with another gun.

"What the fuck are you doing in here?" he yells at me.

I look up into his eyes, "Quiet, I am trying to think." I say simply as I take out the picture that was given to me. I step over the man's body laid out on the floor as I begin to search for the girl. Women stand naked and high, but I don't find the girl among any of them. I hold up the picture to them, "Where is she?" One girl steps up and points to the back room. I flick my hand, ordering them to leave, and they waste no time doing so. The back room door is shut, and someone on the other side threatens me to stay away. I push my way through the door and grab the neck of the man behind it, ending our fight before it can get started. The girl lies on a bed, tied up and drugged. I release her restraints and throw her over my shoulder. With perfect timing, the leader of the group pulls up in his brand new SUV.

"Who the fuck are you?" he screams, with men following behind him all of whom are pointing guns at me.

"I need your car," I say. He starts to laugh, but before he can deny me again, I grab his neck and squeeze. "I said, I need your car." I breathe against his paling expression. He didn't seem to receptive to the idea, so I toss him and turn towards his men, making it clear what I want and what I expect them to do. Not surprisingly, they do as asked without question. I get in the car with the girl, and we leave the house and the abundantly amused old man enjoying the whole scene from his front yard. The girl is returned to her father along with some new bodyguards. The man is so thankful he kisses my cheek and my hands until Savage stops him. I feel good for a moment as the man cries, holding his daughter. Savage immediately orders the man to get to work before we leave.

As we head back home, I look over at him smiling wide.

"What is wrong with you?" he growls.

"We did a good thing. I feel good about helping that man get his daughter back," I say, despite his disgusted expression.

"We didn't do it for him or her," he says without another word. As soon as we get back home, he leaves me and goes straight to his room. *I guess we are done for the night.*

Today, I get to fight a real rival I am told. Savage awoke this morning with an instinct, so we act on it. He, Galena, and I stand together when an army of men attack us at one of Savage's many exchange sites. They come at us in a trained attack. They know our weaknesses, but they lack the strength to carry out the kill. I feel their breath on my neck, but in the end, I feel their blood on my hands. Each kill feels better than the last, and I gain strength in ways I never thought possible. Savage smiles at me proudly, and I return the favor.

Once their leader is left standing alone, I force him to his knees. "Who told you where we would be?" He laughs, shaking his head. Taking a strong hold of his neck, I growl my impatience, "Who told you where we would be?"

"The same person that told us where we could find your wife tonight. Where we could find her in her new elegant, wisteria purple dress. Where we can easily watch her dance for us and slit her beautifully naked throat." He smiles up at me before I lunge my fist down his throat and stop his heart from beating. I toss him aside, enraged. "They are planning to kill Kayla! You said if I left my family that they would leave them alone."

Savage breathes easily, "Don't worry, Ma Joie. We will make sure no harm will come to her. I will be sure to secure our attendance to the affair tonight, and we can keep a safe watch over her," he says to me. "Don't look shocked. I promised I would make sure no harm would come to the ones you love, and I always stay true to my promises. They want to lure you in. If they see it won't work, that it will only bring out her own guards, then they will give up on that idea." I start to argue, but he hushes me. "Do not worry. We will be there to assist from the shadows. Once they realize she has no draw for you, then they will move on. You would have to expect them to try at least, but remember their goal is still you, Nicholas, not your family. Don't fall for their tricks to get you out in the open. Now, let's get home and prepare for the party."

I am so excited to see Kayla that I don't have time to think about the possibility that she might get hurt until we arrive, and then, I realize there are numerous opportunities for someone to get to her before I can get to them. Savage touches me casually and nods, trying to reassure me. It amazes me that he never worries about a thing. My tux fits perfectly, but I still feel like something is strangling me. The moment Kayla walks in, my heart smiles. She is as beautiful as always. She is so elegant and graceful, it as if she floats on air, and just as our enemy predicted, she is wearing her new wisteria purple dress. They have been watching her closely, too closely for my comfort. Savage touches my arm and directs me to the men surrounding the perimeter. As promised, he has supplied total protection for her. I feel relieved until Elijah walks in with his fitted tux, right behind her. *I assumed she would bring Ryan. Why would she bring Eli? He can't protect her.* Elijah escorts Kayla around the room as if she is his. I move slyly through the room, careful not to be seen but still maintaining an eye on their every move. I watch as Elijah talks to her, as Kayla laughs at him, and touches him sweetly. Her eyes dance as she speaks with him, and he never takes his eyes off of her. I pause the moment he takes her hand and kisses it. I always thought that a woman's beauty is in the smile that she gives you. Kayla's to me was one that has always been indescribable, and hers to him is heartbreaking and hard for me to watch. She nods as he takes her hand and leads her to the dance floor. I focus in on how his lips whisper in her ear, as she rests her head on his shoulder, and how his hand tenderly touches her back and comforts her with every move they make, together. My body awakens with heated flesh and pounding heart, and I barely notice the intruder sneaking in from the side. No, instead, I watch my wife follow my best friend outside into the attached gardens. Their images are concealed slightly by the greenery, but their laughter and whispers are more than loud enough to drive me to madness. *She does love him! I knew it. I bet he isn't even giving her my letters.* Thoughts of them together every night, holding my children and going to bed together, him touching her, kissing her ...

The screams in my head are over taken by the screams from Kayla's mouth. I jump to see Elijah battling several men while guarding Kayla, but he doesn't see the man coming at her from behind with a knife. I race after her, but there is no way I can get there in time. She turns, sees the knife, and screams.

"Kayla!" I yell, knocking out everyone in my path until the man with the knife suddenly falls, cringing, and another man falls behind me. The others are taken out with little melee. Savage walks in with a scowl.

"Clean it up," Savage says to his men. He looks up at me. "You lost your concentration, Nicholas. You almost cost Kayla her life." He turns to Kayla and nods. "Your husband was worried about you, rightfully. You must be more careful about being in public, Kayla darling."

"Who the fuck are you to say what she does!" Elijah yells, stepping in between him and Kayla. I grab hold of him and throw him to the ground.

"He just saved her life that is who he is!" All I feel is rage. "What are you doing bringing her here? What are you doing touching her like that? She is not yours, do you understand me? She is not yours!"

"Nick, Nick!" I hear my name, but it isn't until I feel her touch that I recognize the person speaking to me. Kayla wraps her arms around me and presses her lips to my face. "Nick, let him go. He hasn't done anything wrong. He is your best friend, and he has done nothing but respect that."

Releasing Elijah slowly, I can barely look at him, but stepping I can't help but turn to her and look into Kayla's eyes and tremble.

"I'm sorry. I was nervous for you, and I …" I stand in front of her, looking her over with desire and want rushing through my veins. "You look so beautiful, I … I wanted to be the one with you."

She grasps my face with a smile. "I know, I miss you too." It's easy to forget all my fears when she is with me. Her lips are just as amazing as they are in my dreams, but her smile, as beautiful as she is, her smile is the beauty that sets my head adrift into the clouds.

"I feel like I have been away from you for an eternity," I whisper against her lips.

"Nicholas, we need to go, and your dear Kayla should get safely home as well," Savage says sternly.

I kiss her once more before breathing in and looking back at Elijah. "I'm sorry," I say as he wipes the blood from his chin and nods with controlled anger.

Savage allows me to watch her leave before we return back to his home. It felt so good to hold her again, but now, I ache even more for her.

"Ma Joie, you look so sad. It breaks my heart to see you like this. I think we should move up our plans a little and try and get you back with your family as soon as possible."

"But you said I am not ready yet. You said I still need to train for their most skilled assassins."

"I think you have more of a reason to focus, and we can plan our first attack in a few days and see how you do. You might get a few bruises, but I think you will do better than expected. That beautiful wife of yours gives you renewed energy. I may have to make sure she is available for a kiss before each battle." He smiles, causing me to smile.

Chapter 29

Nick

"Nicholas, today I am going to introduce you properly to the rest of the families. So please dress accordingly. Rabbie will help you," Savage says to me as I sit down for breakfast. I am curious but not necessarily anxious. When I step out of the shower, Rabbie stands, waiting for me with a towel. I am not use to people waiting to dress me, well except Kayla, but she only end up undressing me. I also enjoy her more. This guy is too strange for me to feel comfortable. I have not heard him speak once, and as I watch him arrange my clothes, I catch a glimpse of why. He has no tongue. I can now understand why he never smiles either. He fits me up in a suit that is more of a general's military uniform. The black sophisticated piece fits securely and smooth over my body.

"Was this made for me?" I ask, and he nods. "How? I don't remember giving my measurements." He glances my way, but gives me nothing more. Not that I expected anything different. Once I am dressed, I look over myself in the mirror, and for a moment, I feel … pride. I quickly push that out of my mind. There should be no pride for who I am, what I am.

Savage, dressed in his dark family uniform, leads and has me follow him while Galena is forced to follow me. No matter her length of history in the family, she is always last. I am not sure where we are going, but we arrive at a secluded place by car before we enter a tunnel that dives deep into the earth. We finally step out, and Savage enters with pre-eminence carrying him in. I follow Savages orders to project my family heritage and look powerful, not vulnerable. I do my best, but the odd surroundings and the people staring at us as we walk in catch me off guard. Nonetheless, I try to hold back my amazement of it all and follow orders to stand tall next to Savage's side while Galena remains behind me. Once we enter, everyone makes a nod towards Savage. The first to sit and the most important it would seem, is Savage. He waves his hand, and soon after, he takes his seat. The others follow and the discussion of business begins. I have no interest in their discussions, but I do pay attention to the room and make an assessment of the others. Galena must notice my curiosity and taps my shoulder to point out the first man to our left, a tall athletic-looking man. His concentration on matters seems unbreakable; he hasn't wavered in his stiff posture since he sat down.

"Bade Keel, Lord of the First, he rarely speaks and has little power, so he keeps to himself. He is more of an all-out warrior, a champion warrior actually, and quite admirable in his skills," she moans. "However, he is nothing for us to worry about. Father made him what he is, and his loyalties lie with us for the long haul. Not to mention, he is too self-involved to care about anyone else's issues," she says with what seems to be disappointment in her voice.

"He has no interest in you? Clearly the man is a fool," I say to her instant smile.

"Oh no, Nephew, it isn't me. Unfortunately, I think he would find more interest in you than me." I look back at the Greek god-like man and wonder until he winks at me. The second man looks as if he will turn to dust at any time he is so old. "Daijiro Tallian, Lord of the Second," she sighs, shaking her head. "He is a crotchety old man, but don't be fooled by his feeble appearance. He is stronger than he looks, strong as steel actually. Punch him, and he won't feel it, but you will break into pieces. His body cannot be penetrated with the usual weapon. He must be frozen, frozen solid, and then broken. The man won't even drink ice water out of fear for the possibilities," she laughs, and I smile at her. I immediately sit forward when my eyes move to the next seating area. I recognize him, and I hear Galena sigh. His charm is noticeable, only because he seems to be charmed by his own self. He looks upon others as if he waits for them to admire him, and my aunt, as beautiful as she is, seems to be one of his biggest admirers. "Lord of the Third, Marius Cane," she hums. "Father can't stand him, but I find that he has a lot of potential and a whole lot to offer." I glance her way, but she doesn't even notice me as she is still eyeing at him. "Marius has a lot of followers and a huge army. It is amazing what he can do. Marius is able to provoke greed and hatred between people, blinding them to friendship, loyalty, or even love. He detours people away from what he wants and takes it while they are busy fighting amongst themselves. A master thief you could say. Father would usually find those traits worthy of recognition, but for some reason, he continues to push him to the side. It is disappointing." She inhales and smiles wide again as I move on to the next. "Fagan Aherne, Lord of the Fourth. He is determined to win favor with Father. He has even offered up his daughters for your pleasure." I look back at her as she smiles. "They will be very accommodating to you Nephew. I would consider it if I were you. Audra, Ria, and Catriona. The interesting thing about them is they can make you see things that aren't really there. They can become what you want most, or who you fear the most. They can make you see what they want you to see. You become blind to who they really are until it is too late. The oldest is Audra, and she is … well, let's just say that you don't want to ever see her naturally and certainly not after just eating. She got into a fight with Twila, a wife of one of the other Lords. They were both after Bade, and being the sick bastard that he is, he encouraged the fighting between them. It was a game for him and his men to enjoy. Twila won out, and Audra suffered terrible scars. If she had surrendered quietly, she may have not been scarred so horribly, but Twila had the help of her sister, Mirette, her husband's other wife who struck Audra from behind. She nearly died. If Bade hadn't stepped in, she would have. She is bitter now and shows little happiness for anyone. Her father keeps her home and hidden from everyone. The middle sister, Ria, is the one that is most apt to please, although she is also the most ruthless." The moment Galena mentions her name, I cringe. "She will take whatever she can from you and use her skills to get whatever she wants. She rarely fails. Believe it or not, she is a friend of mine. We have been friends for a long time, actually. I haven't seen her in a while, so I can only imagine what kind of trouble she is getting into. She is also the most beautiful of the three sisters. Every man wants her, and my father has even been tempted to bring her to his bed, but he has held off since she has shown an interest in bedding you."

"Me? How does she know who I am?" I ask.

"Father has been on the lookout for the best mate for you for a long time. Ria not only shows the most potential for strong offspring but also comes with a connection to another Lord, which gives you an even stronger position."

"But I am already married. I am not interested in another wife. I can barely handle the one I got," I joke.

"You can take as many wives or lovers as you want. Ria is more than willing to be behind the scenes." She continues on as if I should have no issue with fucking another woman other than my wife. I wonder if Galena has ever truly been in love. "Now, the youngest sister of the family is Catriona. Cat tends to be a bit bullish and mouthy; she is young and impossible to deal with. She insists on befriending the wrong people. Trust me, Ria is your best option within that family." I glance at Fagan, remembering the woman that I thought was Kayla, and wonder maybe that was the younger sister causing me trouble. I am not so sure this family is one we should trust. I wonder if they are not the ones after my family. Galena leans in and whispers, "Ria has amazing power. She can become anything, anyone. She can become your perfect fantasy." Her wink does nothing to sway me. "Now, their father, Fagan, is even more powerful than his daughters. Father admires his abilities, which is the only reason he listens to him at all. That and Father sleeps with Fagan's new wife on a regular basis. She is also apt to please, in the most sickening of ways. She is a creative fuck from what I hear, which pleases every man that beds her. She is also able to get information about the other Lords since she fucks most of them. She shares the information with father in return for expectations that, one day, she we will be made his wife. The whore has no boundaries." Her expression leads me to believe she doesn't approve so much of her father's exploits. If I had not already seen her cower to him every time he looks her way, I might believe she could be encouraged to help me take him out. She looks up and eyes the next, and he eyes her with just as much ferocity. "Amery Luvis, Lord of the Fifth. The one that killed my mother. He is cocky. His lover, Haile, tempted Father and was disgustingly bragging about his love for her. A disgusting whore that got her due. Father said she was too beautiful for someone not worthy of her, right in front of mother. She refused him, said she wouldn't leave Amery for him. Not that it mattered what she wanted, Father was set to have her brought to him. He was going to fuck her in our home and force her into marriage by getting her pregnant. Do you know what that did to my mother? Father's exploits were always causing controversy in our home, not that he cared. Mother could go mad right in front of him, and he wouldn't give it a second thought. I was sure that was what was going to happen when Haile, sadly, met a tragic end before Father could have her brought to him." Galena smiles wide. "She was found buried deep in cement with her perfect beauty set forever. I, of course, have no idea who would have done such a thing, but Amery swore that Mother and I were the culprits. He got approval from the High Council to go after her, without any of us knowing. He lured her out into public and captured her. He sentenced her to death and tore her head off in front of his massive army, like it was a festive event. I begged Father to make him pay for it, but he says we have to wait until the time is right. The High Council adores Amery at the moment, and we can't risk angering them." She looks me dead in the eye. "It will be your task, Nephew. Amery is out to kill you and your family because he knows that your destiny is to have his head." I eye him and his anger as she whispers his bloodlust for me and my family.

"I know him. I have seen him following me and my men," I say, eyeing him down.

"I am sure you have, and I am sure you will again," Galena says as Amery makes a motion that dismisses us. I instantly begin to feel a twitch within my veins. She begins talking about the Lord of the Sixth, Gideon Stark, an honorable Lord and Savage's most trusted ally apparently. He has strong connections with the High Council and has helped Savage out of trouble more than once; however, his true loyalty lies with his duties as a Lord and will not go against the rules set by the High Council. As a result, we have to be careful what we say around him. No matter what Galena says, I cannot take my focus off Amery until she mentions, "Bastien Trog, Lord of the Seventh." *I know him.* "I believe you two have met. He didn't even know who you were until he tried to double cross you. Father and I enjoyed watching that meeting." I look back at her in shock. "Oh we have been watching you for a long while, Nephew. And your abilities are quite something. You didn't even know who he was, but you put him down with little effort. Scared the shit out of him! One meeting and he tried to best you. The moment he thought he had you, you turned his men against him. I had to hold back my laughter so no one would know we were there. Father was afraid you might need us, but you didn't. How did you know he wasn't trustworthy?" she asks as I recall the meeting early on in the building of my own territory, the building of my business.

I thought I was powerful enough to deal with him, but when one of my informants brought back pictures of him during his day to day, I saw Kayla. It was the first time I knew where she was. She worked at one of his clubs and the more images that entered my head, the more I hated him and the more I wanted him dead. He didn't know her or care to, but everything about him made me angry, and all I could see was him hurting her. I wasn't about to let that happen. It had nothing to do with me or what he thought he could do. The moment I changed the tactic and ordered the attack on him, he attacked me. I felt his sharp assault, even though no one could see it. His problem was that it barely fazed me at that point. My anger built around me like a shield, and I was able to turn to him, grab him by the neck, and smile, saying, "I can kill you so easily right now or you give me what I want." He willingly signed over all of his clubs to me, and as a result, I had Kayla on my payroll from the beginning. I had my eyes on her once again. That satisfaction is the only reason I didn't kill him at that moment. I had found Kayla again and that was all I cared about. I could protect her, see her, and watch out for her. As much as my mind tries to focus, all I can do is go back to those days of watching her struggle to survive and making sure no one could hurt her. I killed many that attempted. She attracted a lot of losers. Some might have had a chance with her, but they never got past me. None of them had any idea of my undying love for her. Kayla became so bold at times because of her supposed luck that I had to laugh. Once, she dared anyone to attack her as she walked down a dark street alone. She was on her way home after someone gave her a tip of a few hundreds for doing nothing more than getting their drink right. She was a perfect target with so much cash, but the moment she was spotted, I grabbed the two men on my own and did them in. She never knew that she had their dying breaths against her back. She had a mission in her mind, and she thought God was on her side. She was ultimately determined to kill me; the one she decided had ruined her life. Maybe I did. Maybe I still do. To me, it doesn't matter. I will never give up trying to make sure she is forever happy. Sometimes, I wonder if she is not some kind of demon that controls me, that makes me love her so much that I can't breathe without thinking of her. Maybe Kayla is the one that helps me breathe period. I miss her so much it hurts.

"Nicholas!" Galena shakes me. "Are you paying attention? You will want to know this." I look her way and focus on the next Lord who looks strangely like, "The Lord of The Eighth, Rein Lorid, the one that looks strangely like Father in almost every way. He tries to outdo him, but he always falls short." He could pass for Savage in almost any light. "Doesn't he make you wonder?" I nod in amazement. "You are not alone. We have all wondered if they are siblings. Father will not say, but obviously they are closer than either will admit. Rein desires Father's power and tries to emulate it at times, which makes Father laugh. Rein, however, does not find any resemblance funny. The fact that Father has bested him at every angle only makes him angry." She laughs, and I begin to drift off and away to my own memories of sibling rivalry.

Savage suddenly glances my way with a stern look and a deep sigh. I eye him impatiently. I do not care for being treated like a child by him. Despite my annoyances, I try to pay more attention to what is being said. The discussions are nothing more than political politeness towards each other, a mere following of obligations and duties spread amongst them. Then, the start of what they call, "The Decision Upon Souls Ceremony." A parade of lifeless people appear in front of us as it is decided what Lord will punish them, or rather torture them, for eternity. The images of pain and screaming by these souls are haunting; however, Savage sits with no emotion, no feeling whatsoever. The leftover souls from the others are brought in front of us, and Savage stands. The first one steps forward as it is made known why he is been brought to the lowest and most powerful level of hell. He killed a child with no remorse. Shot by the child's father in court, he now stands before us, waiting with attitude but not for long. Savage doesn't speak; he simply raises a hand towards the man and instantly sets him to an eternal blaze. His outer layer melts from the heat as he screams in terror and is pushed into a pit with others. There are men, women, and even teenagers brought before us, and all leave with tortured screams the likes I have never heard before and never care to hear again.

I become anxious for it to all be over when Savage looks my way. "I have saved one for you, Nicholas. Enjoy." I look towards his outstretched hand and instantly stand with hunger.

"Billy Earl Maynard, how? I killed him already," I say before I realize where I am.

"Of course you did, but was once enough for you? Considering the pain he caused your wife and her sister as children? Considering the pain he caused many children over his life? The disgust he spread was …" I hold my hand up to him as my jaw begins to vibrate and my hands twitch. There is nothing more he really needs to say. I step in front of Savage with clenched fists and stare down the man that suddenly recognizes me and begins to protest his sentence with vigor. "It is in your blood, Nicholas. Do what feels natural to you. Sentence accordingly." With that, I smile, and with a sharp glare, Maynard begins to tremble so fiercely that his bones crack and his eyes bleed. With his last inhale, his nose seals up and his mouth opens, exhaling screams so sharp that I don't hear a single syllable. I inflict pain on him, an eternal pain one hundred times worse than the worst pain he ever inflicted. I hold my head up high, watching him fall to his marked prison and look up as the other Lords look on with fear. Savage beams from behind me. The feeling rushing through my veins evokes a roar of confidence from deep within my core as I feel a sense of pride for who I am.

I feel so good when we get back home that I almost forget to meet up with Elijah. "What's up with the uniform?" Elijah asks, snarling at my appearance.

"Part of the job," I say, shaking off his attitude towards me.

"Is that so? Is being late part of the job, too?"

"I had a meeting that ran late. Don't fuck with me today; I am in a good mood." His judgment does nothing to change my excitement about the day, but the moment she steps out, I want to do nothing but tell her all about it. "Kayla, oh Princess, if you could have seen me today." I continue to talk about the day and the things I saw and heard and did until her smile disappears. "What's wrong?"

"You're different. You are happy about being with Savage?" she says with a smug attitude.

"I am not with him. I can't believe you would say that to me. Am I supposed to be miserable every day I am away from you? I thought of nothing but you and the boys. I did what I did for *you*! That man suffers for eternity because of you."

"I didn't know convicting someone to eternal damnation was something to be proud of, Nick. It's sad that the world had a man like that in it. It is sad to me that I hear you speak of nothing but destruction of others. Revenge. Revenge for what, Nick? We have a great life. Get out of there and come home." She puts her hands against my face and kisses my lips, and a trembling dizziness takes over me. "Nick? Eli!"

I wake up in Kayla's arms with Elijah hovering over me with concern. "Hey Nicky, how many fingers am I holding up?" he asks showing no hands at all in front of me.

"Fuck you," I say.

"Well, he seems to be himself, but you are not looking too good, Nicky."

"I think we should take him to the hospital," Kayla says, running her fingers through my hair and kissing my cheek.

"No," I say, as I try to sit up. "No, I am not going anywhere. I'm fine. I am sure it is just from all the excitement today." Turning back towards Kayla, I smile and kiss her gently. "It was probably you. You are so beautiful it makes me weak all over. I think you should tone down the sex appeal next time I see you." I laugh, but she still looks at me with concern. "Stop worrying. That's my job. I told you I would take care of you, and I meant it." Taking in her lips, I reassure her once again with a smile. "Forever, Kayla, I am yours and only yours." She smiles, holding tight to me. It takes everything I have to release my grasp of her. Leaving Kayla looking so worried is not easy, but I can't be gone too long, not without being questioned anyway, and I don't want Savage to know that I am still communicating with my family. I don't want anyone to know. I need that edge on him and everyone else. The more he thinks I am separating myself from them, the more comfortable he will get with me and eventually slip up. Not to mention, I am still supposed to pretend not to have any interest in my family, so they can't be used against me.

Chapter 30

Nick

With the promise that I can see my family soon, I pick up the pace and learn everything I can. Galena is kind enough to take me out into the city and help me out during the slow times. "No, Nick, you need to be more patient. Let it come to you, and then control." She eyes an expectant victim, and next thing I know, they are down on their knees, begging to help her with whatever she needs. "See ... simple." She moans as she takes the man's face into her hands. "You are coming home with me." He nods, and I roll my eyes. "There is a beautiful woman for you, Nicholas." I look over at the woman and shake my head at Galena. "She isn't good enough?"

"She isn't my wife. Only Kayla is good enough for me," I say.

"Well, how sweet. It must be wonderful to be so in love, but you know with this position, you are not obligated to one woman. My father has had many women in addition to my mother, and she stood by his side just as confident. I am sure your wife would be willing to do the same considering your powerful position."

I laugh, "You don't know Kayla. Besides, when you have all you need, there is no need for any other." I wink at her, and she smiles.

"You know what? You have inspired me nephew." She kisses my cheek and sends the man on his way.

"You're not keeping him?" I ask, surprised to see her let him go.

"No, I think I will try this dedicated-to-the one-I-love thing. You seem to be very convinced of the idea."

"Oh, you are in love, huh? Who is this wonderfully deserving man?"

"His name is Marius. I have loved him for a long time, and he loves me."

"Marius Cane? The Lord of the Third? The one your father would send you to hell for, before he would ever approve of you being in a relationship with?" I snap at her.

"Yes, but Nicholas, I swear he is a great man. Father's jealousy of him blinds him to his abilities, but I think you could convince him otherwise. If you would only meet him. I am sure you would see his potential as much as I do. Would you like to meet him?"

Reluctantly, I nod, watching as she vibrates with excitement as if she is sixteen and in love for the first time. "I hope he treats you well, or I will have to kick his ass." I smile at her even though I already know he is a dirt bag. She takes my arm with an even larger smile.

Galena doesn't seem to have aged much over the years, in looks or maturity. She still has a hard time handling her emotions. She possesses a naïve innocence about her, she has an almost childish nature. Savage has not allowed her to grow up. Maybe he likes keeping her as his little girl and not a brave woman like she is trying to be for him.

Galena drives me to a place that is out of the way and well-hidden from prying eyes. The estate is impressive and well-guarded. The moment we step out onto the grounds, we are greeted by several house servants who ask us to wait for Marius in a faraway room of the house. Already, I feel as if he is hiding something from us; however, Galena awaits him with no sign of concern. House servants surround us with attention, but I wave them away and wander the estate freely while Galena follows with sighs of frustration. The house is covered in richness and pictures of Marius on most every wall. There is even one large picture of Marius standing naked with a stern, demanding expression. I look Galena's way, and she shrugs.

"He is a proud man," she says.

"Huh. Doesn't look like he has all that much to be proud of," I say to her instant huffing response. Eventually, I find myself wandering into the garage of the home. There are several expensive cars, motorcycles, and every other possible fast toy a man would love to get his hands on. None of them interest me much until I find one that reminds me of another car I had seen once, and so does the out of state license plate. *I knew it was him I saw!* "How do you know him, Galena?"

"What kind of question is that? You know very well how we met. Why?"

"I assume you realize he isn't a one woman man?"

She laughs harshly, "You can tell by his car that he is fucking other women? Really? What? Are there panties on the stick shift, Nicholas?"

"Not exactly, but I have seen him with another woman before."

"Well, it is not as if it is a secret that we both see others, but we are in love and no one else compares to me as far as he is concerned, I assure you."

"Oh, I'm sure." I glance her way but ignore her glare. "Why the out of state license plate? Did he just move here or something?"

"He only stays here for meetings, or business. He usually resides on the opposite side of the country. He prefers the weather," she says.

"You mean he prefers to be somewhere he can be naked all the time and be praised for all his greatness," I mock.

She is not impressed with my display. She grabs my arm and drags me back into the house. "Come on. I am sure once you meet him you will see what I mean." I am instantly guarded as we walk back into the living area, but Galena runs in with excitement. "Galena!" I yell, grabbing hold of her arm to prevent her from getting too far away from me.

"It is okay, Nephew. I am well familiar with this home," she says, smiling wide as she runs towards the man that walks out confidently. Galena pulls away from my grasp and runs into his arms. *Marius Cane.*

He stands stiff as she covers him with affection. "Enough," he says, pushing her off of him. The growl from my lungs must have clearly signaled my disapproval of his rough handling of her. He steps back with a smile and sweetly takes her hand before kissing it. "No worries, Nicholas. She is my light and means everything to me. We argue like any other couple, of course. We have been together for a long time; it is expected for such a long relationship. We have been together ever since she finally saw through that fraud, Keel. How he became a Lord, I will never know." He signals politely to sit with him in an absurdly luxurious room. Servants rush in with food on golden dishes and wine in the finest crystal glasses, while laying a silk napkin on my lap. Marius sits back in his custom seating with a superior smile on his face, and already, I understand why Savage despises this man. "Nicholas, Galena has told me so many great things about you, but I have also done some other inquiring about you on my own. From what I hear, we are very much the same." I raise my eyebrows to his suggestion that we are anything alike. "Yes, we are both highly intelligent, incredibly powerful, and word has it, highly skilled lovers. You could say we are brothers."

"I have a brother, and I assure you that it is not you," I say quickly.

"Don't get me wrong, Nicholas. I mean no harm. I only want to help you understand how great we could be if we worked together. There is so much I could teach you. I could help you improve your skills at every level," Marius says while Galena nauseatingly hangs on his every word.

I fight back my initial impulses and, instead, sit back calmly. "And what is in it for you? All this good will towards me. I can't imagine it comes at no cost."

"The cost is minimal. Nothing more than appreciation. You must know your family's clear power over all the others. If we combine forces, we can take out any of them, and I will be happy to serve our interests from a higher power. I could make a life with Galena here, and …"

"How high of a power?" I ask, knowing already what his desire is.

He smiles wide. "Feel free to make that decision on your own, Nicholas. I am sure you are intelligent enough to know that it is in your best interest to have me next to your side."

"Let's just say I am willing to do this for you. Why are you talking to me and not my grandfather? He is, after all, the one with the power to do this for you." He leans forward with tense lips, waves Galena off him, and sends her to another room.

Once we are alone, his casual attitude becomes more desperate, and he continues, "Galena and I have been together for some time. *He*, for some reason, has never liked me. I am not sure why, but he forbid us to be together and has stricken Galena with infertility until she can prove she has no desire for me. I would love nothing more than to have a child with her, but I can't do that until I have a power of a certain kind. Now with me as a leader …" I stand up, shaking my head, ready to leave. His sudden anger is felt between us both as he rises and eyes me directly. "I suggest you sit, son. You might learn something of value from me." He grabs my arm and jerks me around to face him. Something he should have known not to do.

His grip is feeble compared to my grip on his heart. "Your arrogance is only going to get you killed. I suggest, Old Man, that you stand back, and get out of my way," I say with his army quickly surrounding me and provoking me to want to kill.

"Nicholas, stop! Please!" Galena runs in, pawing at me to release her lover. I let him go, and still steaming, I take a step back from him. "While we are at it, stay away from Franky, too." His initially confused expression tells me a lot. How many women is this man seeing anyway? He doesn't even remember all their names? I leave with a silent Galena in tow.

"No more Galena. I don't want to see him ever again, and I suggest you never see him again either. He is your Achilles Heel, and he will only continue to cause you pain." She doesn't speak but curls over herself in obvious pain. I realize she needs to be comforted now and not by verbal disappointment with her. I lean over to her and wrap my arm around her, something that seems to shock her. "You're too good for him, and he knows it. That's why he treats you so badly. He is trying to convince you that you need him when, in reality, he needs you," I say to her wide eyes. "I won't allow your relationship any more than your father will."

"Or your father. Dante didn't like him either and was just as protective of me as you are. It's nice to have his spirit back within you," Galena says looking over me with a hopeful smile. Right now, I hope I can escape Savage like my father did.

Chapter 31

Kayla

Nick is not Nick, and he certainly didn't look good when he left us. Thankfully, Elijah wasn't in the mood to be his usual smartass self on the way home. I only glanced his way once, but he was clearly deep in thought, and I wasn't going to interrupt that since I wanted to go to my own far off place.

Brayden wakes up from a nightmare as soon as I get home, and it takes me some time to get him back to sleep. I assume everyone else is sound asleep by the time I get ready to go to bed, but I hear Elijah and Ryan talking in Nick's office.

"So, maybe I should handle things from here?" Ryan says.

"Handle it how?" Their silence is troubling. "No, Ryan. You saw what it did to Nicky. That chair will kill you," Elijah fires back.

"It didn't kill him. It won't kill me," Ryan replies.

I rush in and stare Ryan down, "Don't you dare get in that chair!"

"Kayla, I have to. Nick needs my help. That much is clear."

"Why is that clear? He is fine. He is still Nick, and he will find a way to deal with our enemies, kill Savage, and come home." Elijah and

Ryan both roll their eyes at me. "Don't do that. Don't you dare dismiss me."

"Kayla, you saw him. You saw how weak he is. Savage is beating him down, and unless we do something, he isn't going to come back at all. We need to fight these crazy fucks and bring Nicky home before it is too late," Elijah says.

"I need to talk to him. I need to …" I say before Elijah takes hold of me.

"You talked to him. You saw him tonight, Kayla!"

"You saw Nick?" Franky rushes in on us and stares at each of us before focusing on me. "You saw Nick? How is he? Did he say when he would be back?"

"We weren't talking about Nick. We were talking about someone else," Elijah says to her.

"Don't bullshit me. I know you were talking about him. At least tell me that he is okay," she says forcefully to Elijah.

"Go to bed Franky. We will let you know if we hear from Nicky, I promise," Elijah says, waiting until he is sure she has left before closing the door and locking it.

"Why didn't you tell her?" Ryan asks.

"I would prefer to keep all information to as few people as possible for now. Besides, no sense worrying people for no reason." Elijah stands tall and silent for a moment before turning towards us again. "Okay this is what we are going to do …" This is the first time I understand why Nick trusts Elijah so much and why they were so close. They are both similar in their actions and the way they think. Elijah carefully plans out our moves and talks to Ryan and I as if we are his equals, allowing our input to be considered. He is an excellent leader, just like Nick.

After discussing every possible advantage we could take, we decide to finish the discussion tomorrow after we get some rest. I hate going to bed without Nick. I hate being in that bed without him. I prefer to sleep in Nicky's room, so I grab my pillow and head off to his extra bed, but I come face to face with Elijah.

"Where are you going?" he asks, shirtless and with his usually tamed hair hanging down freely around his face.

"I was going to check on Nicky."

"He's fine. I just checked on him and Brayden before I made myself a nightcap."

"A nightcap, really? Is that necessary?" I shake my head at him but find him much closer than before.

"Yes. I can't sleep, and it looks as if you can't either. You don't like your bed Kayla?" I shake my head. "Why?" he asks, looking me over and playing with my hair. "You look tired. You need some sleep. I need you to be well-rested if you are going to help me get your husband back." I look up into his sparkling blue eyes and crash into his chest, searching for that comfort Nick would always provide. Elijah holds me tight and kisses the top of my head. "Don't worry. I'm going to make sure everything works out for all of us." I grip him tighter, fighting my tears, and he picks me up. "Come on, Trouble. You are going to sleep in your bed and get some sleep even if I have to tie you to it." He puts me in bed and lies next to me on top of the covers.

"What are you doing?" I ask him.

"I told you. I am going to make sure you are going to get some sleep, and I think the only way to do that is for there to be a warm body next to you." He smiles. "I promise I will sleep on top of the covers. You can be protectively underneath. Feel free to sleep naked though."

"Eli." I sit up with a huff.

"Calm down, Stress Ball. I'm not going to touch you. I only want to live up to my promise to your husband, nothing more. Believe it or not, you can trust me. Even if you came on to me, I would have to tell you no. Besides, I'm not that kind of man," he says, smiling wide in my face.

"Don't worry. I won't test your loyalty," I say, staring into his calming eyes, knowing he would kiss me right now if I was anyone else. I slide down into my bed and reach out, taking Elijah's hand to his shock. "You can hold my hand but nothing else." True to his word, Elijah never makes a move, but he holds my hand whenever I need him to.

The one thing Savage doesn't expect is for us to attack him. First, we have to decide what we need to takeover. There are no clear options. We have gone over the map and information over and over, and none of us can agree. Then, out of nowhere, our strange dog jumps on to the table and sniffs around before barking.

"What the hell is up with this dog?" Ryan asks, trying to push him away.

I begin to think of what Nick has been saying for months, *there is something strange about this dog*. Nick's intuition has never been wrong. "No wait!" I yell. I look down at the area that Eey has marked with his paw. "I think he knows something?"

"Who? The dog? Are you crazy? There is nothing in that area," Elijah snaps.

"Let's at least check it out," I say but am quickly dismissed and so is Eey. I gaze over at the dog as he puts his paw on my leg. I know he knows something. Nick was right. There is something strange about this dog. No one is going to listen to me, but I bet I can get one or maybe even two to help me check it out.

Secretly, I talk Terrance and Eddy into helping me. I don't think they have any faith in the idea either, but they are willing to oblige me out of respect. Not what I would prefer, but it will do for now.

"Kayla, are you sure we should be doing this?" Terrance asks.

"I have a hunch, and I promise my hunches are usually spot on." I lied. Eddy messes with his equipment, seeing if there is anything out in the middle of this wilderness. "Anything?" I ask hopefully.

"Nothing but some rabbits and some deer. I wish I could say otherwise, but …"

"Just keep looking," I say, sitting back in my seat and ignoring their odd glances towards me. At this point, they already think I am crazy, might as well keeping pushing for results even if it does seem crazy. I did, after all, bring the dog, who is now hanging his head out the window with his tongue flapping in the wind. *They are going to have me committed. I'm sure of it.* Before I give up completely, Eey starts barking wildly, and we all look around trying to see whatever it is he is seeing. "Stop the car Terrance." We pull over and let Eey out who immediately uses the bathroom. *Really?* He looks back at me and wags his tail before barking again. "Great. Good boy," I say with a sigh until he starts running. I look back at Eddy and Terrance before I start running after him. Thankfully, they follow. I can barely keep up with the dog. *Oh I hope he is onto something and we are not chasing after a squirrel.* Eventually, Eey slows down and begins crawling on his belly.

"What is it?" Terrance whispers, trying to catch his breath. I look through the small clearing and see two guards. *There isn't much of anything here to guard.* I turn to Eddy, and he instantly takes out his body heat monitor which suddenly begins reading, right below us. "They are underground." Terrence smiles, looking up at me. "What do we have here?"

We both turn to Eddy as his eyes go wide, and he shrugs his shoulders. "This place is highly protected, so whatever is here means an awful lot to someone," Eddy says.

"What do you want us to do Kayla?" Terrance asks.

"I want you to do what you do. Penetrate the enemy, from the inside out."

Terrence and Eddy spend days scoping it out. Terrence's intelligence is unbelievable and alongside Eddy's technology skills, they are able to find weaknesses in the compound. Terrence smiles wide at me as he lays out the information they gathered.

"This here. This place, Kayla, is Savage's central headquarters. Everything he runs is run from here. All his money is controlled from here; his intelligence system is run from here. Everyone he is watching and keeping tabs on is watched from here. You want to hurt him, and I mean cut his heart out hurt him, then this is the place to do it." Terrence watches as my smile grows.

"Kayla, this isn't going to be easy. Now, Terrence and I have found some weaknesses in their system, but they will only allow us seconds and nothing more. That isn't enough time to get enough men in there to take it over," Eddy says.

"Then, we just get one man in to destroy it completely," I say.

"Kayla … this man is incredibly powerful. There is no telling what we could learn about him if we control the place rather than destroy it. Nick's father gave us some great notes, but it is broken and unconfirmed. This place could fill in those answers we don't know. If there is a way to control and own, rather than to destroy, I think that is our best answer. *If* we can figure out a way to do that." Terrence suggests the impossible, but we have managed the impossible before.

"Alright, then we will do that, and I guess we will need to get some help too." I say watching them both sigh. *Time to share our information.*

The decision to bring in Elijah and Ryan is an easy one, but knowing I am going to catch hell for keeping them out of the loop until now is not going to be enjoyable. Terrence and Eddy go through all their findings before I step up and explain my plan for the takeover. I face Elijah and Ryan with a smile and roll my eyes at their less than thrilled expressions.

"How the hell did Nicky have enough energy to put up with you every day?" Elijah sighs.

"Don't waste your breath, Eli. Kayla always does only what Kayla wants to do, and she doesn't care what anyone else has to say about it," Ryan says. He stands up and looks down at me. "However, this time, I'm glad you did, but stop leaving us out of the loop. You need us, and we may not want to listen, but you know how to force us to so please try that next time. We have been going in circles for days working on these other ideas when we could have concentrated on this the whole time. As far as this takeover, I am going to lead it."

"Why you?" Elijah asks.

"Because I know how to get in unseen," Ryan announces as if we should have already known that. He leans down on the table with both hands, "I know how to do this, and all I need is for you all to trust me."

Chapter 32

Savage

"Alright, Dennis, I am going to be straight with you. I think you are overstepping your ground. I cannot sit by and let you destroy Amery. He had every right to sentence Belinda. We both know she killed Haile without just cause" Gideon says as if I should care what he thinks.

"Haile was a nuisance. She needed to go," I say.

"She wasn't so much of a nuisance when you called for her to entertain you. If she had not of turned you down for Amery, I am sure you would feel differently about her."

"I am growing tired of this conversation, Gideon." I wave my hand for Rabbie to give me a new drink while Gideon sits back and sighs.

"Why did you agree to meet with me if you were not going to be reasonable?" Gideon asks. "I'm sorry, Dennis. I can't support you anymore. Unless you are willing to compromise, I am going to have to side against you." I don't bother to speak until I know for sure he is finished. "Are you listening to me?"

"I'm listening. I'm hearing one of my longtime friends say he is going to side against me."

"You know that's not what I said. Fine, Dennis. What is it that you want? What will end this feud?" Gideon asks finally.

"Oh, good! We are going to get to what I want now. About damn time. Rabbie send for Galena. Gideon, my friend, I think you have been holding your position too long. It is time for you to step down from the Lord of the Sixth and move to ... well just move. I have someone else to take your position."

"Damn it Dennis! You need me to fight the others," he yells.

"No, I don't. Not anymore. Have you met my grandson?"

"I guess you think you can simply replace me with Nicholas?"

"Of course not. That would be a step down for him. Galena will be taking over the sixth until I can clear the eighth position for Nicholas," I say proudly.

"Have you lost your mind?" Gideon stands in a rage. "I refuse to bow down to you. When the High Council hears of your plan, they will force *you* down! You will never regain the ninth again!" he yells as Galena arrives with her men.

"Don't worry, Gideon. The High Council will never know anything other than that you kindly stepped down to allow someone younger and more capable to handle the position. You will be allowed to come back once I take care of the others. For now, you will be in a private prison I have had designed just for you. Get him out of here. It is nearly my dinner time." I don't bother to listen to his huffs or look his way as he glares at me. I wait for him to be gone before sending for Nicholas to have him join me for dinner. He is coming along quite nicely, and I couldn't be more proud.

When Galena returns, I meet her in the study and send Nicholas to handle some light business for me. "Everything go well?"

"It went as expected. Thank you for the opportunity, Father. I promise I won't let you down," Galena says with excitement.

"It is nothing. Just make sure to protect Nicholas. That is your only job right now," I say to her.

"I don't think he is going to join you like you think. He is still connected to his previous life and his family. He fears what they may think of him, if they find out what he does for you. He allows Delin to do most of the killing."

"We are his family now. They are nothing. Outside of young Nicky, the rest mean nothing to me. Although, if we can gain Ryan too, that could assure us pure dominance. You at sixth, Nicholas at eighth, and I could put Ryan at seventh. We already have Keel at first. Marius is of no threat. He is too stupid," I say, glancing her way to force my point. We can bring back Gideon once the others are in place and give him the third as reward for keeping his mouth shut. Once young Nicky is ready, we push Marius down to first, move Keel up to second, and move Nick into fourth. Having complete control, will force the High Council to back off of me, and to stop sending their watch dog, Kamini, out after me."

"Clearly, you have a complete plan, but you still have obstacles to overcome, Father," Galena says, snapping me out of my daydream.

The reality of my world is unsettling. "I want his wife killed and his youngest as soon as it is allowed. I want Nicky placed away from Nicholas until he is able to handle his father." I look Galena over. "You keep him. It will be your opportunity to be a mother. Just make sure you don't get too attached – he is not yours. Once Nicholas is placed in his position, I will take Nicky in and train him. In the meantime, we need to find the perfect mate for Nicholas. I need him to produce another. Fagan's daughter, how she is coming along?"

"She is quite anxious to meet Nicholas from what I understand. Apparently, he has made quite the impression on her," Galena says, not realizing the position I put Ria in hoping she could help rid Kayla from my worries. So far, she has failed.

"I am afraid that she is too weak. Not sure she will do. Gather some other possibilities just in case. My grandson is quite powerful. I don't want him killing the woman as he fucks her, at least not until she bares his child."

"How do you plan to get him to forget his ... forget Kayla and the children he already has? He is quite dedicated to them," she says in confusion.

"With each battle and each kill, he is becoming more and more distant from them. Eventually, he won't be nearly as concerned. It will take time of course, but it will be well worth the trouble," I say excitedly.

"Oh really? He seemed quite excited to tell me about the last birthday party they had for young Brayden today. He seemed to recall every detail with no problem at all, even adding in how wonderful of a mother Kayla is," Galena says with a smile. "He is not forgetting them at all.

Slamming my fists down onto the desk, I stare off, trying to figure out how that could be possible. "He is still seeing her somehow. Get Ria in here!" That woman is not as good of a chameleon as she has led me to believe, and that is grounds for termination.

"I will talk to her, but what can she do to help? Nicholas is not going to accept her unless she is Kayla, and she has already said that he was too powerful for her to be able to hold Kayla's image on him."

"Maybe she can be of use in another way. Nicholas is going to need a distraction. I am obviously going to need to inflict him with the poison, and I can't do that in his sleep. I need him to be awake and strong."

"Are you sure that is a good idea? What if it kills him? You said yourself only the strongest survive it."

"Are you questioning me?" I ask, and she instantly cowers. "There needs to be another attack on Nicholas's home, on his family. They need to go through a terrible tragedy. We will need to be able to show Nicholas his precious Kayla's lifeless body and convince him that there is nothing to go back to. Once he believes that, he will trust us to help him seek revenge for her death, and then, the dragon can take him." Galena looks my way with fear. She does not believe he can survive, but I know my grandson, and he can survive the harshest of treatments. This is for his own good, for our family's own good.

Chapter 33

Galena

"Good morning," Nicholas says to me with a sweet kiss to my cheek. I hate to have to lie to him, but it is best for him. "Is there something wrong?" he asks, looking at me with concern.

"Nephew, you should sit down." I comfort him into a seat. "Something happened last night, and I hate to have to tell you this, but your home was attacked."

"What? Why are you just telling me this now? Why didn't someone wake me? I have to go," he says jumping from his chair and racing toward the door.

"Nicholas no, you can't. The scene is a horrible sight. Father is trying to find out right now if anyone survived." The heartbreak in his eyes hurts me. "We believe your brother managed to escape with young Nicky."

"And Kayla? Brayden?" he asks.

I shake my head, unable to say the words. His expression tears me to pieces. "I can take you to her," I say, wanting to drop to my knees and beg him for forgiveness. He doesn't speak. He just forces me to take him right away. I have our driver ready to go when we step outside, and we rush straight to the hospital. I glance his way during the ride there, and he makes no movements. He is barely breathing.

Nicholas's stiff presence does not change. Even as he walks through the hospital, he seems to be in a daze. When we come upon a nurse alongside Father, he perks up enough to look away from the floor. "Where is she?" Nicholas asks them.

Father pats him on the shoulder with a calming approach. "They tried to revive her, but her injuries were too much to overcome. I am sorry, Nicholas. My men were scattered so much trying to protect your brother and Nicky. Kayla must have been scared and ran off with Brayden, giving them the opportunity they were seeking," Father says to him as he begins to vibrate from fighting the tears filling up in his eyes. "Your friend tried to fight them off for her, but they were too much and were very brutal in their attack. They made sure that she would not be able to recover. The poor young one was taken from her arms and killed in front of her. She refused to run at that point, apparently. She was determined to seek revenge until her last breath. If it is any comfort, she managed to kill several before she died. Your brother and Nicky have been hidden away until we can take care of this. I don't want either to be in the middle of this. Ryan is not ready, and Nicky is way too young."

"I want to see her," Nicholas says to him. I look up in shock, but Father nods and leads him to a room where a body lies with a sheet over it. Nicholas walks up to the side of the bed and breathes in and out several times before taking hold of the sheet and tossing it back to reveal Kayla's lifeless body underneath.

"*No! Kayla! Oh God please!*" His screams force me to run out of the room. Father drags him from the room, trying to comfort him, but I don't know how he could ever be. His pain is so heartbreaking and disastrous that I think it even surprises Father.

"Where is Brayden?" Nicholas asks through his tears.

"Oh Nicholas, you don't want to see him. Besides, they took him to the morgue already," I say quickly.

"He was beaten so badly, Nicholas. It is a terrible sight. You should not see such a thing." I grab my head and cringe, crying myself at my father's words. How could he tell him that? Does he not see what he is doing to him? Does he not care how broken he is? All I can hear is his cries and pleas for the nightmare to be over. As muffled as Nicholas's cries are from his fisted hands that are forced against his face, they still make me want to rip my own body apart, piece by piece, and try and locate the rapidly spreading painful poison taking me over.

With the help of my father's men, we manage to get Nicholas home. He is beyond consolable. I am afraid to approach him, afraid to look at him, but he desires nothing but my embrace to help relieve his pain.

"I'm sorry. I am so sorry," I cry to him, but my words mean something different to me than what he believes them to mean. My father watches me closely, daring me to step beyond his orders. He is not only torturing Nicholas. He is torturing me, forcing me to listen to his cries and screams for his wife and child to be brought to him. The torture continues until Nicholas passes out from exhaustion, but he awakes in confusion and calls out for *her*. I have to explain to him all over again that she is gone. *I hate my very existence.* I am so exhausted and numb by the time Nicholas finally calms that, if he asked me, I would confess everything to him and slit my own throat for him.

When he finally wakes without tears and without a hazy understanding of it all, Nicholas stands and searches the house doggedly until he finds father. "I want to know everything. I want to know who did this. I want them dead," Father eagerly talks to him about the attack and what they found at the scene before reluctantly confessing that he knows who did this. "Who? Tell me who it is now," Nicholas pushes.

"I worry about telling this to you, but I understand how your revenge needs to have a face. Amery Luvis did this," Father says with a wicked smile. "We are already organizing a counter attack on him. I have all the plans laid out in my study. I am going to handle this for you Ma Joie. You should stay here and rest and grieve in peace. I will return once I have avenged our family's loss," Father says.

"*No!* He killed *my* wife and *my* son, and I am going to make sure he, and everyone he knows, dies."

Father waits anxiously as Nicholas storms through the house towards Father's study, demanding to lead the attack himself. Father doesn't even bother putting up a fight. He happily steps aside and allows Nicholas to organize. I begin to tense, desperate to leave, but Father won't let me. The moment the dragon begins to breathe, I hide my eyes. It isn't the bite that bothers me, it's the screaming of agony after.

"*Ahhh!*" Nicholas screams out as he falls to his knees. His shivering torment vibrates the whole room. His tense eyes look up at us in shock as he tries to fight it.

"Don't fight it Nicholas. It will be much easier on you to just let it in," Father says.

I fall to the floor and grab his shoulders, "They aren't dead Nick. Kayla and Brayden are not dead. They are fine. I'm sorry!" I yell to him repeatedly until he finally collapses into a coma.

"Oh Galena, you are so pathetic sometimes. Why did you do that? He is never going to remember what you said to him." Father sighs behind me.

"Maybe not, but I will," I say.

"Now that we have what we need, I am going to see to it that we dispose of Kayla. We can't have her damaging the poison that is now inside him before it has completed its job. He should be well transformed by the Masquerade and ready to be the son I have always wanted at my side." Father breathes in with pride before looking at me again. "I am going to leave it to you to continue to search for this other possible child of Dante's. I assume you can handle that Galena? If she exists, I need her found immediately. I can't have her out there possibly helping Kayla in any way."

"I will find her Father," I say faintly.

"This is a time of celebration, Galena, not sorrow. If you are set on ruining this for me, then stay out of my sight." Father has Nicholas moved to his bed where I see to him until he begins to recover and stay out of the way of Father's great mood. I lean down to his side and press a cool cloth to his feverish head. His eyes flutter, and his hands twitch, all of which are good signs, especially this early on. "You survived. You are so strong. It wouldn't have had to be this way if you hadn't of continued to see her. You have to forget them, especially her. Otherwise, he will do this to you again. Forget her, and you won't have to go through this again. I promise, Nick." I wish I was as strong as him. I wish I was Dante. He would have fought Father for him. He would have fought to the death for his child. He would have expected me to have done the same, but I am not that strong. I am nothing but a coward. A coward who depends on others to save her child. "I will never be a warrior like you, or your father, Nick."

Chapter 34

Galena

Father's orders to find any and all of Dante's offspring are a tremendous. The man rarely left a woman without fucking her. I search every possible place and option there could be, all the while ignoring the one. It would be easy for me to find her. Nicky supplied her name. I know about her mother's store even. Though the information comes easily to me, I find myself avoiding it for some reason. Father would kill me if I lied, if I failed even. Maybe death would be better than life. I spend two weeks going through every other possibility and find no blood relation anywhere. My final day, I turn back to the *one*. I wish she had been harder to find. I wish she was stronger than she is. They have a cozy home and a sweet, loving life. I have to laugh when I find out her husband is none other than the one Nicholas has been so set on protecting all this time. Oh, Nephew, your good deeds could have nearly cost you. It is a good thing Father was too busy concentrating on the one want he had in front of him rather than looking past it to see the obvious potential traitor. I wait by myself outside their home. I don't know why I hesitate. I know what Father would want me to do, but my curiosity has been piqued. When she arrives home, I step out of my car and to their door.

The door flies open, and my jaw locks open. "Hi, can I help you?" Lena asks. I look into her eyes and recognize them immediately as any mother would of her own child. My legs nearly give out from under me.

Taking a breath, I have to look away from her to speak. "I hope so. I have been looking for my cat, and I thought I heard him in your back yard. Would you mind if I took a look?"

"Oh, of course not. Come on in," Lena says, stepping aside to show me to the back door. "Excuse the mess. We are in the midst of remodeling."

"Expanding are you?" I ask, looking over the cozy home with fresh pictures of their wedding.

"Yes, and my husband is determined to make everything perfect, although he spends way too much time on expanding the details and not enough time just getting it done," she says with a laugh.

"Men can be more of a problem than a help sometimes," I laugh with her.

"Don't I know it, but Brady is the best thing that has ever happened to me, so I guess I will put up with his minor faults." She manages to clear a path to let me out the back door. "Okay, here you go. I haven't heard any cat meowing, but there are a lot of places for him to hide out there. We hope to clear that up soon, too." I smile, step outside, and breathe as she rushes back in to answer a ringing phone. She is definitely her. I see myself all over her. I have to kill her now. She is already suspicious of me. I can tell by the way she looks me over. Her senses are good, but her strength is not good enough. Father would never approve of her, and she would be better off with me killing her than Father. He would never forgive me if he found out what I did. Forgive me, Dante, but you know as well as I do that she is better off for me to do it now and spare her the suffering. I turn back to the house and ready myself.

"Lena?" A man calls out suddenly before meeting her with open arms. "Hey, Honey, how was it? I tried to call you from work, but you never answered and then some idiot decided to start trouble in the station. Hundreds of cops and this moron thinks he is going to start throwing punches and just walk out. Absolute insanity ... I would have been much better going with you."

"It's okay! You had to work, and neither of us could wait for us both to have the same day off. Besides, it was great. I'm great, and ..." She smiles wide at him and he returns the favor.

"Yeah, so we are sure now?" he says.

"Yes! We are going to have a baby," Lena says happily.

He lifts her up into his arms and tells her how happy and in love he is. They look so content and excited that I find myself gleefully happy, too.

My mind drifts, and I wonder if this isn't some kind of punishment for me. The day I found out I was pregnant was a happy one. I couldn't wait to tell Marius, but Father found out first and wouldn't allow it. He gave me time to carry the child to full term, but when she was born, he knew immediately she was not good enough for him. I pleaded and pleaded with him not to force me to give up my baby. I loved her from the moment I laid eyes on her. It was all I wanted. I would have done anything, *anything* to keep her. My pleas fell on deaf ears, and there was nothing I could do to convince him. There was no one to help me convince him. Saldean didn't care about anyone by that point, and Dante had gone, but I knew he would fight for her if he knew. I had two days to kill her myself or father would have it done for me. I carried her out one night, wrapped up completely. Thankfully, he assumed and let me be ... just long enough. When I found Dante, I had little time to argue or be assured of his dedication to the secret

I had for him. I just handed him my baby and kissed her goodbye. I never bothered to find out what happened to her. When Father found Dante years later and said there was only a small boy with him, I assumed the worst. I assumed my brother was still angry with me and gave my baby up to save himself. Now, I know better. He didn't kill her. He hid her and made Nicholas believe she was his sister and not my daughter. I look over Lena with pride. She is so beautiful and so… happy. *Thank you, my brother, I owe you. I owe you.*

Father is engrossed in work when I return home. My first instinct is to avoid him and cower off to my room before he can speak to me. Then, I think of Nicholas, Nick and his family, my brother, and of my daughter. To run from him would alert my father, and I would never be able to lie to him. No, it is best to face him and tell him straight to his face. I turn back towards Father and walk up on him with my head held high. "I exhausted every possibility Father, and I found no evidence that Dante has any living children outside of Nicholas or Ryan. There was one other that was a possibility, a daughter, but she was killed some years ago when she got caught in the middle of a gang shootout. Her mother still mourns her obviously, but it is probably for the best as far as we are concerned."

"Very well. Now we can move on to more important matters. Good work, Galena. Return to your usual duties tomorrow."

"Thank you, Father," I say, pausing only briefly to smile my appreciation before retreating to my room with a strange feeling rushing through me, a feeling that causes my head to sit a little higher on my shoulders.

Chapter 35

Ryan

There is nothing in Father's notes that tells me anything more than what I already know, or from what I picked up from watching Adair and Nick. I have spent days going through everything, over and over, and there is nothing here that tells me how to kill Savage. I can't believe that our only choice is that chair. There has to be something else that Dad was expecting to find at some point. The door to Nick's office cracks, and I look up. I don't see anyone until the dog comes around the desk and lays his head on my knee. I rub his ears and smirk at his insistence to receive attention. "For a mutt, you sure do have some answers that the rest of us have not been able to get. So, do you have any for me now? Is there anything out there that I am missing? I toss all of my papers on the floor in front of him. If it's in there, please find it for me because I have no idea what to even look for. I am afraid I wouldn't even know it if I came across it." Eey looks down at them all and wags his tail. "No, I'm not playing with you. Maybe if I get down on your level, I can see things differently?" Lying on the floor, I grab a notebook and go through it as Eey lies down with his head comfortably on my chest. Hours go by and my eyes begin to grow heavy.

As a light whimper echoes within my head, I drift away into a dream.

The room I enter is open, bright, and beautiful, with a beach breeze blowing through. A woman enters with the sun outlining her image, and with her arms outstretched to me, I instantly smile. "Sam? Oh Sam." She enters my arms with so much warmth that I don't want to let go. I don't want to wake up, ever again.

"I can only stay here with you for a short while," she says.

"No, please don't go. I miss you so much. I wish I was dead, so I could be with you again."

"Oh baby, you can't do that. They need you, and you have so much to offer this world. You can do this without me. I know you can."

"I can't do anything without you. I don't want to do anything without you," her soothing scent crushes my heart, and I get down on my knees and plead that she come back to me. "Don't leave me. Take me with you. I will stick a knife through my heart right now to be with you again."

She places her hand on my face and smiles, "You are my everything, and I am your shadow. Remember? I will shine upon you in the sky forever, happily waiting for the day I can kiss you again. I will never let you down, you can be sure of that, just as sure as I am that you will never let me down." My tears flow like never before as I pull myself tighter to her. "It was not your fault, Ryan. Do you hear me? It was not your fault. I love you. I will always love you, and I wouldn't have changed a single thing, not when it comes to you. I would still run for you. I would still chase you down to the ends of the earth, and there wouldn't have been a damn thing you could have done about it," Sam whispers into my ear.

"I am so sorry… I'm so sorry. I should have never left you alone. I should have never … I should have never chased after me. I should have made sure you moved on, stayed away from me, and became happy with someone else, someone more deserving of you, someone that could have kept you safe." I ramble my failures to her while she shakes her head until she quiets me with her fingers to my lips.

"Don't do that. Don't regret knowing me. Don't regret our moments together. I don't."

"Take me with you. Don't leave me here without you, Sam. I would do anything to be with you now," I cry, hiding my tears deep into her hair.

"Don't be foolish and chase after me now when you are so desperately needed where you are. Your family needs you. Your friends need you, and you need to kill Savage. You did everything you could have done. You did everything completely right, but it just happened that it was my time to go. I am needed elsewhere now. I need to help you find what you need," she says, smiling up at me.

"You know what I need to look for?" I ask her.

"I know the blade, the blade with his family crest on it. You will know it as soon as you see it, but it won't be easy to find. Savage is not about to make it easily available to anyone."

Her stunning smile revives my heart but only until I remember that she has to go away. "Will I see you again Sam?" I say, caressing her face and kissing her lips.

"I will always be with you. I will always be there to make sure your handsome ego stays in check." She smiles. embracing me tight ... "I love you forever, Ryan." I breathe my love for her into her vanishing image and fall to my knees, begging to be with her again, somehow.

Unfortunately, I wake without her but feel better for seeing her again.

"Ryan?" Franky comes through the door, already trying to get on the floor with me. I get up as soon as she does. "What is wrong with you?

First, you kick me out of your room for no reason, then you avoid me for days, and now you run from me? Did I do something wrong?"

"No, I just think it is time I grieved on my own. Thank you for your help but …"

"Thank you for your help?" she yells back at me. "Are you serious? All I did for you and you are just going to pretend I don't exist anymore?"

"What do you want me to say, Franky? You're not Sam, and as much as I wish you were, you're not," I say to her steaming face. She doesn't hesitate to smack me across the face, hard.

"You are just like your brother. You take what you want and then leave when you're done. You will regret letting me go. I could have made you very happy."

"You probably should make arrangements to move out, too. I can't hold Kayla off much longer, and since I am such a disappointment to you, I'm sure you don't want to be here around me anymore either," I say to her calmly before sitting down behind the desk, expecting her to leave.

"Ryan, no. I'm sorry. I am just a little upset. I'm scared. I don't want to go back out there on my own," she says, gripping me with a fearful expression. "Please, I don't know what will happened to me on my own."

"You go out all the time on your own, why are you scared now?"

"I go out briefly and unexpectedly. To live on my own day and night, that is more than enough time to give these attackers to kill me."

"You need to move out Franky, you will be fine, I will have guards watch you for a while to make sure. I will give you a couple of weeks to make proper arrangements." I say removing her grip from my arm. "For now I suggest you lay low, from everyone in this house. You haven't made to many friends here since Nick left." She storms out crying and nearly knocking Elijah over on her way out. He doesn't say a word as he walks away with a fresh drink in his hand and smile on his face.

Chapter 36

Ryan

Today, for the first time I am confident and have no concerns about our target. Sam's reassurance gives me every reason to believe that I can do this without issue. Today we hit Savage and hard. We organize four areas, four corners, Elijah, Terrence, and Kayla – despite us all telling her to remain home, Kayla shares her corner along with Reginald though and Dwayne takes on the last corner. Elijah spent most of the day accusing me of goofing off for not offering to control an area; I humor him with a forced smile every time but continue to keep my plan to myself. I leave the rendezvous point only giving Kayla a smile and a Jayzon swagger that she has become accustomed to. Thankfully she doesn't ask but only gives me a roll of her eyes with a simultaneous sigh.

The setup goes smoothly and everyone makes it to their places without any issues. I wait as they all get into position and organize their pounce but before they go too far, I step out into the clearing and walk straight up to the two men guarding the entrance. I can see Elijah out of the corner of my eye swinging his arms and cursing me with every finger and hand gesture he can make in my direction. I hold back my smile and ignore him as I eye down the two men and demand what I want. Once I am in within a few feet of them, they lay down their weapons and open the door for me and my friends. I continue on while the others follow me in. There is no resistance until I get further in and find a bright-eyed man with a snorting problem. He rages at me with a flying kamikaze style attack from above my head. I pull out my gun and shoot him in between his bright raging eyes. *I don't know how to deal with that bullshit yet.* "You should have invested in a gun my friend. They work faster," I say, smiling all as I go deeper and silently order people out. There is information everywhere, but I verify that I have cleared the area before I go looking for the blade. I clear the tunnel from end to end and go back to investigate the different rooms off the main corridor.

"Hey asshole!" Elijah yells, stomping his way towards me. "Do you think you could have filled us in on your plans to invite yourself in? You know, to save us all the planning and the overloading of guns and shit."

"I wasn't sure if it was going to work, and if I had told you, you wouldn't have believed me. Would you?" I ask him.

"No, I guess I wouldn't have. It is a little … well … Hey! Stay out of my head," Elijah snaps. "You can't do that too can you?" he asks, looking me over.

"Maybe." He looks back at me with concern.

"No, you can't. Otherwise, you would know what I am thinking right now."

"You're thinking 'I wish I had a drink before I left the house to come here,' but I don't have to read your mind to know that, Eli."

"Wow, you do read minds. Jackass!"

"I'm the jackass? You should have seen what I got you to do last night. I had to practice on someone, Eli. Don't worry, the only thing you did was strip down to your underwear and walk around quaking like a duck." He looks at me with his jaw dropped to the ground. "I took a few pictures if you want to see later?" I say before breaking into a full smile.

"That's funny, Fucker. Real funny. You wait. Just wait. One day, I'm going to die, and I am going to haunt your ass forever," he says, shaking his finger at me. "Where are you going?" he yells.

"Looking for a reason for this room. There doesn't seem to be anything of real value in here, and there were at least twelve men patrolling this room." As Elijah and I search the room, Kayla walks in and looks us over. "Are you going to yell at me too?" I ask her.

"No, I assumed you were going to do that. That's why I came," Kayla says.

"You knew, too? Why didn't you say something?" Elijah asks her.

"Oh go quack off," she say, winking at me.

"What?" Elijah stands back swearing at us both. "Oh you two are real funny. That better not have happened." Kayla pats him on the chest with a wink before moving me out of the way and looking around. She sits on the floor and crawls to a spot under a desk. Elijah pushes me, and I punch him and receive the same until we both realize Kayla didn't come back. "Where did she go?" he asks as we both lean down and look into a dark hole. "Kayla?" Elijah yells.

"What?" she says, jumping back through the hole and causing us both to fall backwards. "Idiots," she says, shaking her head. "Come on. Stop fucking around."

Following Kayla, I slide through and come to a place where I can stand up and remove her from the front of the pack. She huffs but doesn't put up a fight. She seems happy enough remaining in front of Elijah. This section of the dwelling is dark, unfinished, and gives new meaning to *creepy as fuck*. None of us speak. We barely breathe, it's as if we are afraid to make a noise, to be heard by whatever monster may be creeping behind these walls. There is a sudden shuffle, and I hold back as someone ahead breathes out, and then… nothing. I know someone is there, but they are more silent than we are. Standing tall, I concentrate on listening until I hear the breath again. "Come out and …"

"Come out? You locked me in here! Don't fuck with me anymore Dennis!"

I rush forward and come face to face with a man locked away in a cell. "Who are you?"

"Who are you?" He steps closer and stares into my eyes. "You are a Savage but not one I know," he sings out cocking his head to try and figure it out before he can be told.

"My Father was Dante. I am a Jayzon, not a Savage," I declare.

He sighs, "And may I ask why you have come to visit me today, Mr. Jayzon?"

"Our intention was not to visit you but to invade Savage's stronghold." I look him over as he laughs.

"You mean to tell me you found this place all on your own? Not possible," he laughs.

"We might have had a little help," I say, making sure not to give anything away not that he would believe it if we told him.

"More than a little. Savage himself would have had to of led you here, and since I know that is not possible, then it would have to be someone as close to him as you can get. So who might that be?" He thinks hard. "Galena wouldn't dare betray her father. No one else knows but his children. Saldean is long dead and so is Dante. I doubt Nicholas has been told yet. Hmm… I am curious who could possibly be so brave to betray Dennis this way?"

"Our dog," Elijah chimes in with a goofy smile.

"Your dog?" The man asks.

"Never mind how we found it. Who are you, and what are you doing here? You obviously are not someone he cares for which makes you interesting enough to us," I say

"My name is Gideon Stark. I was Lord of the Sixth. My role over the years has been one of peacekeeper and maintaining honor amongst the Lords. Dennis has been a friend of mine for a while, but now that I disapprove of his plans, he has decided to shut me up until he succeeds in overtaking every realm he can, or rather until he holds a majority and no longer has to listen to anyone. Once he is too powerful to be dealt with, I assume he will let me out, at which time I will be forced to abide by his rules or face execution. I have no idea if I will be able to return as a Lord or as a minion. Galena has taken over my realm, and I assume Dennis has intentions of taking over another realm for his newly found grandson." He pauses, looking us over. "You don't look like an army of any realm; I am still confused on how you found me?"

"We found you by accident. We were hoping that this place would help give us more information about Savage." I pause, wondering if I should tell him our full plans, but something tells me I can trust him. "We are specifically looking for a blade with the family crest on it. Do you know where that is?" I ask. Gideon laughs.

"If it exists, I assure you, no one knows where it is but Dennis. Are we going to continue this tea party or are you going to let me out of here?"

Kayla steps forward and asks, "Is Nick okay?"

"Is he okay? In what way? He is strong and powerful and sure to provide Dennis with a prevailing dynasty. He is nearly unstoppable and one of the reasons I was hoping I could reason with Dennis rather than engage in this war he desires so much. Nicholas's allegiance to his grandfather is unbreakable at this point, and the two will have no problem destroying everything in their path."

"Not possible. Nick would never align with Savage. He hates him," Kayla says forcefully.

The man leans forward and looks her over carefully before asking, "Now, who are you? You are much too desirable to be from the same family."

Elijah steps in front of Kayla and answers, "She is none of your business."

"Well, she is clearly the most powerful one here, and none of you even seem to realize it. My dear, I was instantly weakened by you, and considering your good faith gesture of telling me honestly why you are here, I will tell you that whatever she asks me I would be unable to tell you anything but the truth. I don't know who you are or where you come from, my dear, but I am honored to meet you," he says as Kayla peaks between Elijah and myself.

"Yeah, well, nice try Romeo, but were not buying it," Elijah says.

"If I understand your purpose for being here, then I assure you we are after the same thing. My goal was to get Dennis to stand down against another Lord, but he refused and sent me here to keep me quiet about his plans. Now, I need to rise up against him, but the only way I can do that is to be released from my prison." Elijah and I eye each other, trying to decide what to do. "You will not be able to hold onto this facility much longer. He will fight for it, and you alone will not be able to overpower him. I would think you only have a limited amount of time as it is, so if you please, make a decision quickly. I will sit over here with my reading until you do or until you are forced to join me in here."

"What is your name again?" Kayla asks from under Elijah's arm.

"I already told you, Gideon Stark. I was Lord of the Sixth, now I am simply Gideon, your humble prisoner."

"Where will you go if we let you go?" Kayla asks.

"Good question. I have nowhere that has not been taken over, and I think it would be a good idea if Dennis is not aware of how I escaped, or who released me. If he thinks another Lord, one in particular rescued me, then he will be on edge and it will give me, us, some time to plan. If you will let me come home with you, then I can contact said Lord, and we can band together for our common goal."

Kayla rushes forward, "Our goal is not simply to defeat Savage but kill him and enable my husband to return home."

"Nicholas is your husband?" he asks, and she nods. Suddenly, Gideon's desperation beams back at us with his bright eyes swirling. "You will need my help! And I need yours for sure," he says staring straight at Kayla.

"Release him, and let's get the hell out of here," Kayla demands before walking away.

"Kayla? Kayla, shouldn't we discuss this?" She waves her hand at me and keeps walking." I look to Elijah for some sort of support.

"Don't look at me, no one listens to me, apparently I am only here to be the handsome one." He says honestly.

"What?" I look back at the old man as he smiles at me. I find a way to open the cell and let him out. He graciously walks in front of Elijah and I and seems to be okay for now. "You are not hotter than me." I say to Elijah as we walk back.

"Are you serious, have you seen you and now look at me. Not saying you don't have good points, but me, Son, I got it all." Elijah says nodding happily.

"Shut up Eli." I say, shaking my head when I hear him laugh. *I don't know why I encourage him.*

Chapter 37

Kayla

I decide not to take Gideon and all of our findings home where he can be seen, by Franky in particular. Instead I take advantage of the expansion we are in the midst of doing on Pagelle. Exie won't be happy, but I think the place is perfect to keep our new friend entertained and occupied, not to mention the club can only be accessed from one way right now making it easy for me to put guards on him.

It is prime time right now and Exie is less than thrilled to be a part of another one of my plans. Her perfect Exie expression of disapproval awaits me at the door. "You know I am seriously considering being best friends with someone else. Someone with less drama, possibly a soccer Mom of some sort, someone who drives a minivan and whose biggest worries are whether or not they will have a Fruit Tea or a Frappuccino, not will I break in to this facility to get the information I want, or will I simply torture these people over here until they tell me what I want to know. Hmmm, I think it will be a Frappuccino tonight." Laughing I kiss her cheek with a smile and notice her brief smile before she huffs and walks away.

I motion back behind me and lead the way to the back and around our dancers as they prepare for their next show. "Hello Ryan." Melanie says with a swooning smile as we pass by. She has always had a crush on him. He smiles back but seems to be more interested in Elijah's reaction.

I grab them both by the collars and force them forward. Gideon's wide smile as he bounces his way through is humorous but not needed right now. "Gideon, please."

"What is this place? I like it." He says continuing to dance his way into the back.

"This is where you are going to be staying for a while. I can't imagine anyone looking for you here." I say.

"I'm not staying with you?" Gideon asks.

"I don't think that is a good idea, we are surely being watched by Savage and you will be spotted there pretty quickly. I have made arrangements for you to have a decent setup to sleep and live in for as long as we need. I have security for you and of course there is always entertainment if you like but please keep a low profile and the girls are not to be touched ... *ever.*" I emphasize clearly in his face.

"I understand perfectly." He says stepping back on his heels. "She is scary." Gideon says as Elijah nods theatrically until he catches my raging eyes.

"So what now Gideon, how can you help us?" I ask.

"Well I need to first make a call to a friend, a Lord, Lord of the Fifth, his name is Amery Luvis." Gideon says.

Chapter 38

Kayla

I woke up from a terrible dream and am too afraid to go back to asleep. When I go downstairs to force myself away from these nightmares, Franky comes in the house after being gone all night.

"Where have you been?" I ask her.

"Out, I do have a life outside of this house you know." She smiles mockingly. She steps away from me dropping something from her bag. I pick it up as she turns to try and take it from me. "That's not yours, Kayla."

"No but it is my husbands. What are you doing with Nick's wallet?"

She sighs looking away from me, "He left it in my car." I stiffen and face her straight up. "We both told you that we are old friends and he trusts me. He has been very conflicted about what has been happening."

"Happening? What's happening?" I snap.

"You know he is ... well he finally feels like he is at home now. He is too afraid to tell you. I told him that you and Eli are becoming quite close and although he is not happy about it he does feel that maybe it is for the best." She pauses with a deep sigh. "Nick and I were each other's first loves, and that is just something that can't be broken easily, Kayla." She inhales deeply stiffening her back in front of me. "I hate to tell you this but Nick is meeting with lawyers to divorce you so he can marry me. I am sorry to tell you this way but maybe it is much better than hearing it from some attorney. He still cares for you deeply but you have to know that you two are just not right for each other. You are not right for him."

"I don't believe you." I say shaking my head.

"You don't have to, Nick is arranging for me to move in with him and Dennis is making arrangements to announce our engagement at the Masquerade. I would encourage you to embrace your relationship with Elijah, I know Nick does not fault either of you for what you have done."

"We haven't done anything!" I yell at her.

"Calm down, your children are nearby. I will start packing my things but if there is something you would like to share with Nick, let me know and I will be happy to pass it on to him."

"You will pass it on to him? I want to see him, you tell him I want to see him."

"I don't …"

"You tell him I want to see him or else." I demand.

"Okay, I will tell him." She shrugs with a mocking expression.

I leave her and run to my room, our room and release the frustration I could not let her see.

It is only a few days later that I get divorce papers from Nick, along with a letter telling me how sorry he is. How much he appreciates the time we have spent together but wishes me the best in my new journey without him. I destroy the papers and refuse to believe it. They come again with a more forceful letter and again I destroy them. I finally get a call from Savage asking to meet with me and though Ryan has forbid me to go anywhere near him, I have to go.

Savage awaits me at fancy café in the city, his bright smile shining in the afternoon sun. I was hoping Nick would be with him, but I am still hopeful for some kind of explanation of what is happening. I walk up with a scowl and have a hard time sitting down next to him. He breathes deeply looking over me with accomplishment. *I hate him.*

"Kayla, you are being too stubborn for no good reason. Nicholas has moved on, and he would very much like for you to do the same." Savage says as if I should have no problem doing this.

"I am not moving on until I talk to Nick." I say to him.

"He doesn't want to talk to you, you have disgraced him by having another man in your bed. You are lucky that he is forgiving enough to allow you to stay in his house, that he isn't forcing you to give up your children."

"I am not sleeping with Eli, he has been nothing but a friend to me."

"So you say, however, it really doesn't matter. I have made arrangements for him to be happy with another woman. She is more suitable for him, you understand."

"No!" I demand slamming my fists onto the table.

He leans in towards me growling his anger, his swirling eyes sit me back on the edge of my seat in fear. "I don't care what you want, or what you believe, I am giving you one chance and one chance only." He concentrates hard telling me of all the horror he wants to inflict on me *"Leave."* He says with a fiery breath. "Leave and never come back. Never come near my grandson. If you do not listen and follow this warning then I will not only torture you to death, but I will kill your son Brayden, take young Nicky for my own use and make Ryan my prisoner until he is transformed into a loyal follower." I try to speak but he hushes me quickly, "Choose your words carefully, my dear. You have a lot to lose, and I have no problem taking it from you. Nicholas is now mine, and he has no desire for you any longer. Be happy with the man you have before I take him, too." He finishes his drink and waves his hand to a man who nods in his direction. His car pulls up across the street. "You have a choice. You can go home now and rescue the man you have or you can chase after the one you had. I assure you, Mr. Stevens only has minutes before he succumbs to his untimely death." Confused, I stand, watching him go towards his car. The door opens, and Nick steps out and allows Savage to step in before getting in himself. My mind begins to spin out of control. Nick glances my way but seems to look right past me before he gets into the car and leaves.

"Nick," I say, not even having the energy to scream for him. "Eli?" I rush out of the restaurant and home.

When I arrive home, Elijah's car is there. I run into the house, searching and calling out his name.

"Kayla?" Ryan yells at me. "What's wrong?"

"Where is Eli?" I ask him.

"Upstairs taking a shower I think. Why?"

I run upstairs and bang on his door, screaming for him, but there is no answer. Ryan takes it upon himself to beat down the door, and we both rush into his bathroom where he lies in the shower, bleeding profusely.

"I'll get the doctor," Ryan says.

"Oh Eli, I'm so sorry." I drag him to me and hold his head out of the water. "What happened?" I ask him, but he is too dazed to respond to anything. We get him to a hospital and wait as they repair the deep stab wounds he endured. He never saw it coming. He never had a chance to defend himself. To make matters worse, I find Brayden with a bloody blade lying on his chest and a note predicting that he would be next. He was sound asleep, and I would have thought dead if I hadn't scared him awake with my cries. I hold him and Nicky close, afraid to let them wander more than a few inches away from me.

I don't know what to do. I don't know where to go. I am lost, lost and alone. The ragged breaths escaping my lungs give me no reassurance or strength. Once Elijah is strong enough to come home, I make a decision that we have to run. I have to protect my sons, and I can't allow anyone else to be harmed by that man. I can no longer be stubborn for my own good when it effects so many others.

Chapter 39

Savage

Nicholas is coming along quite well. He remembers nothing of his past except what we tell him. "Good Nicholas!" I yell as he fights off another attacker with ease. "He's getting stronger by the day, Rabbie." Rabbie nods, enjoying the show along with me. When Galena comes in with a sour face, I instantly groan. "What is it now?"

"The bunker has been attacked." I turn towards her, forcing her to step back in fear.

"When?" I yell at her.

"A couple of weeks ago," she says, cowering in front of me.

"Weeks ago? Weeks ago! Why am I just now being told?" I scream at her.

"I was hoping to have answers for you. I was hoping to have the culprit in hand before I told you. I knew you would be upset, so I decided …"

"You decided," I growl at her. "Since when is it your responsibility to think and decide anything?"

Nicholas runs up on us, out of breath and taking a stance in front of Galena. "What is going on?"

His protective ways have not diminished any I see. "Galena was just telling me that we have been attacked at our safe house, which must be a mistake since no one but she and I know where it is."

"Also, Gideon is missing," she says, cowering further behind Nicholas.

"What!" I yell, raising my hand at her, but Nicholas stops me before I can strike her. I push him aside and strike her several times before he stops me. "Nicholas, do not stop me again."

"I will stop you every time. There is no need for that. It doesn't accomplish anything."

"Nicholas, you don't understand. This is our family's safe haven. It holds our secrets, our interests, and … And she let someone find it. You must have been followed, Galena!"

"I wasn't followed. There is no way. And if someone did follow me, you know they could still have never found it or even knew what it was," Galena yells back.

I pace away from her, trying to understand how this could happen. "Gideon, he must have gotten free. He would have called Luvis. It must be him, but why hasn't he rubbed it in our faces already. Why is Gideon remaining hidden? There is something else about this, there is someone else that we don't know about." Then, it hits me. My biggest fear, Rein. If he is behind this, then we need to step up our efforts. If it is Rein, he will use everything he has gained to go to the High Council and have me banished. It will ruin us, it will ruin everything I have worked for. The only chance we have is … I look back at Nicholas as he looks over Galena and helps clean her face. I need to hand over the realm before Rein can bury us. If I make Nicholas the controller then Rein has nothing to gain by going to the High

Council. I just need to make sure if I step down as head of the family that I have complete control of Nicholas. The way he sticks up for Galena, I am not sure I can yet. His protective nature is still managing to come through. He should be craving blood by now. I need to get him more kills. No, no, I need to get him some *powerful* kills. Some kills that will feed his hunger on a higher, more addictive level. "Galena, you find out who is behind this, and do it quickly."

"Grandfather, if you trust me, why don't you let me handle it? It might be good for someone with fresh eyes to take a look at the situation, and it might give me a good opportunity to learn more about the family?" Nicholas asks.

"Very well, Nicholas. Handle it from here. Galena you back him up. I want to know who did this, and I want them taken care of as soon as possible."

I send them on their way and send out word that I would like to see Ryan. I would have liked to have saved him for a better purpose, but now, I think he can best serve me as a casualty for Nicholas and a great test of his loyalty to me. I send out word that Nicholas wants to see Ryan at a secure place. I give Ryan every reason to believe his brother is in grave danger and needs his help to survive. That should be enough to lure him into the lion's den. *Now, to deal with Kayla.*

Ria comes in, cowering to me already. She is such a disappointment. "Tell me what I want to hear."

"She is scared and packing. I believe she is going to leave. It worked. Now, can I go back to being me and getting to know Nicholas?"

"No. The only value you have supplied so far is stabbing that friend of Nicholas's and putting the fear into Kayla by putting a target on her child."

"I also organized the attack on Ryan's house!"

"Oh, you did that, did you?" She nods, avoiding my glare. "No, you didn't. You had your lover do that for you. You would never do anything that might cause you to break a nail."

"Still, Marius would have never done it if I hadn't of asked him," Ria says with a calmer tone. "What do you want me to do? Kayla is leaving. There isn't much else for me to do now."

"I don't want her to leave anymore. I want her dead. If she is busy running, she will never see you coming." I hand her a blade to strike her with. "You only need a second to strike her. All you need is a scratch, and she is done. You can get out of there before they realize what is happening. If you do this for me, I promise you will want for nothing for the entirety of your life. I will even grant your father a permanent position as Lord. He will not have to worry about attacks from any other Lord as long as I back him." She stares at the blade in her hand with a shaky grasp. To ease her mind, I pull out a large diamond ring and place it on her finger. "Ria, do this, and I guarantee you that Nicholas will be yours and you can have the satisfaction of eliminating the one competition you have, and with this beautiful ring on your finger." Her eyes rise to mine with a sparkling smile.

"All I have to do is kill Kayla?" she asks.

"All you have to do is scratch her, and she is dead," I say with a smile as she beams with excitement.

With the anticipation of Nicholas killing his brother and Kayla being removed from this world, I move forward in meeting with The High Council. I walk in front of them with respect. They each nod towards me with suspicion but do not seem to be ready to pass judgment, so it would seem I have beaten Rein to the punch which pleases me. "My dearest

Council members, I am here today to ask that my grandson, Nicholas, be allowed to take over my realm." They each sit back in shock. "I understand this seems sudden, but as you all know, I am not getting any younger. It is time for me to step down and enjoy my retirement while I can. I assure you, Nicholas is everything you could hope for in a Lord. He will be a symbol of leadership. He will be what the realms have needed for centuries. Nicholas is all that of the Lord's passion and strength put together. He, my grandson, is the answer to the battling and wars between the realms; he is the answer to all that you have been searching for," I say, stepping back to wait for their anticipated questions. It doesn't take long. They ask me about Nicholas's ability to serve properly which I assure them he will have no problem, especially with me to show him.

"Isn't he young to be taking over such a powerful realm?" one member asks.

"Nicholas is young, yes, but no younger than Luvis, and you allowed him to take over for his father," I say in return.

"Luvis's father died suddenly and was brought up from a boy knowing the responsibilities. As I understand, Nicholas has only learned of his recently." They seemed to be more troubled by my request than I anticipated. "I don't understand why you feel assured of his abilities so soon? Are you ill, Lord?"

"No, I assure you I am in great health. I simply don't want to be like the others and serve beyond my time. I prefer to be available to teach him properly, be at his side as he grows into the position." They all sit back and discuss amongst themselves, nodding and seemingly feeling positive about the idea.

"I think we need to meet with Nicholas to discuss his abilities and what is expected of him," the leader of the Council says. Nicholas will have to pass their grueling questions before they allow him to fully take over. I agree to the meeting but put off the date as late as I can. That will give me until after the Masquerade to find out who is behind Gideon's disappearance. Handing over my realm to Nicholas will give him power over me, and I am not anxious to give up that power just yet either. If I am able to proceed with my plans and take over the other realms sooner, there will be no need to hand anything over. I can go on having power over everything and everyone.

Chapter 40

Galena

I have watched over Nick for days. Although he still shows some concern for me and Father, he shows little emotion and rarely looks at me directly. He is killing without any trouble; he no longer forces Delin to handle agitators. Nick is stronger than ever. His eyes are focused, and as Father speaks, he nods and acknowledges the need for every attack. When Father feels Nick is ready, we plan our first attack against Amery. He will never see or understand the magnitude of what is coming for him until it is too late.

Father has me lead the attack, while he and Nick cover my wings. Despite all that has gone on and my reluctance as of late to follow my father's orders, I can't wait to get a hold of Amery and avenge my mother's death.

"Wait," Nick says suddenly. "Wait, and let them come to you." I look Father's way, and he nods. So, I wait – impatiently. "See. Here they come."

I look up, and sure enough, Amery's army walks right in. Steadily, I await the moment and signal, "Go".

I taste blood, over and over again, while searching for Amery, and once I see him, I become so excited I can think of nothing else but getting to him. I run at him with everything I have while Amery smiles wide. The sudden impact of Timber slamming into my side sends me flying into the water.

"Thought you had us Galena, didn't you? You're mine." Timber's strength overpowers me quickly.

As hard as I try to get away, I can't. He forces me into an awkward position and holds me out in front of him, leaving me vulnerable to Amery's will. All I can do is search for help. "Father!" I yell, reaching out for him, but he shakes his head, staying in his protective area. However, when Nick hears my cries for help, he instantly searches for me. He catches sight of me and rages like I have never seen. Timber is lifted off the ground by him as my father screams for Nick to return to him. Amery is on his way, and the two together could surely kill Nick, by doing nothing more than forcing him into the water with them. The two of them can stay under water forever, suffocating Nick to death.

"Galena! Protect him!" Father yells as I fall to the ground, gasping and trying to regain my strength.

Powerless against my nephew face to face on the ground, Timber has no choice but to run. A fish demon, Timber runs straight into the water where he can surely be safe from Nick.

I look back at Amery as he eyes Nick with hunger, so I take a protective stance in front of him. Nick, however, runs after Timber. "Nick no!" I yell, watching Amery smile and dive in after them.

"Nicholas!" Father yells, rushing from his protective guards to try and catch Nick, but he is too late. He is underwater with Timber and surely going to die. "This is your fault!" he yells at me. "Why are you still standing here?! Go get him!"

"But I can't swim," I yell back.

"I don't care! Distract him so Nicholas can survive." I walk to the edge of the sand, trembling. "Go Galena!" I step into the water and push forward until Nick suddenly rises out of the water with a large, dramatic inhale. His breath his heavy but he seems unharmed. I look down at his hand as he rises further and see Timber's lifeless body being dragged along behind him. Father smiles wide and steps forward.

"Well done, Nicholas. Well done," he sings.

I look up as the water runs down Nick's face. His eyes lift towards us, the swirling red storm within them pushes me backwards and off balance onto the ground. "Thank you, Grandfather. It was nothing." I look over at Amery rushing out of the water as his wide eyes watch Nick. He briefly glances my way before being pulled away by the rest of his army, retreating to save themselves. I look over at my nephew as Father looks fondly over his kill.

"Thank you," I say to him as I help myself up off the ground.

"Next time, pay attention to what you are doing, Galena. I can't always be there to save you, but I must say, it was enjoyable to feel this one's heart stop beating," Nick says with a moan. "Now... when can I kill another?"

"I can taste supremacy," Father whispers joyously while I fear for the worst.

Chapter 41

Kayla

No one seems to understand my silence lately, I am afraid to say too much because I don't want anyone to argue with me. I have begun making arrangements to leave and run to the beach hideaway Nick created for us a long time ago. I only hope that it will be far enough and safe enough. Ryan is suspicious and begins to question my focus. He tries to start many arguments with me but I don't take the bait. I have lost interest in discussing battle plans when I know the best thing to do is run. I have nothing left; I have no reason to fight anymore. I have lost Nick, I have lost the war to Savage and now all I want to do is hold on to what I have left. Savage has sent messages to see Ryan but I am scared to give them to him, I don't want to lose him too. My fear is causing me to question everything I do. I want to box my sons, Ryan and Elijah all up and hide them from Savage forever. I am afraid to be here one more day, to sleep in this house one more night.

I enter Elijah's room to check on him before leaving to finalize my plans to get us all out of here. He is sound asleep when I adjust his blanket on him but he quickly wakes up and grab's my hand. "What are you up to,

Kayla?" I shake my head. "Don't do that, you have made a decision about something and it is not one that Ryan or I would approve of or you would talk to us more. You have been silent for days and while usually I would welcome the change, right now I find it to be unsettling. Tell me what is going on?" Elijah holds my wrist with no sign of letting go despite him still being weak from the attack on him.

"I met with Savage?" His eyes widen as he tries to set up. "Lie back down Eli, I am still alive aren't I? He threatened the boys, he is the one that ordered the attack on you. He will kill Brayden and take Nicky and Ryan if I don't leave, if we don't leave. He will kill you Eli. He will take everything if I don't run and stay away from Nick forever."

"Nick would never allow that and you know it." Elijah says.

I shake my head, "No, I saw Nick and he looked right through me. He doesn't want anything to do with me. Chills went down my spine when he looked my way Eli."

"You're giving up?" He says not seeming to understand at all.

"It is not giving up, it's cutting your losses and saving what I have left." I say while he shakes his head at me. "Don't shake your head at me."

"Fuck Kayla What have we been fighting for? We have been doing all this for what? So we can run? That is not you. I don't know what has gotten into you. You have one set back and you run?"

"It isn't one set back. He loves her now. He has always loved her. I was just a fill in," I say as he looks at me confused.

"Who, Franky?" he asks. I nod and explain the story that she told me. "Oh no… he does not. I don't care what she says. Nicky has no interest in her. Something is wrong, Kayla. Something is seriously wrong for all this to be happening. How can you not see that?"

"All I can see is that someone nearly killed you and my son, and even if I was here, there would have been nothing I could do to stop it. I can't stand back and watch you all die. I can't allow my son to be taken away and used as a tool for Savage's desires. I won't do it, Eli." He stares at me with disappointment, and I feel ashamed. Instead of arguing with him, all I can do is walk away.

"Kayla!" Elijah yells after me. He calls out to me again, but I ignore him and continue on with my plans to leave, to run away, to leave my husband forever.

The arrangements are made for us to all leave tomorrow night. Now, all I have to do is go home and tell everyone what time to be on the plane. I decide to stop by my sister's grave one last time to say goodbye. I will miss being able to visit her and take care of her grave, but it is for the best. There isn't much I can say, and I don't bother trying to argue with her tombstone. I simply lay her favorite flowers down and place a kiss from my lips to her name. Before I go home, I take time to lay flowers at Nick's mom's grave too. I assume he will never bother to do so himself now that he is loyal to Savage.

"Saying goodbye are you?" a woman says to me from out of nowhere.

I step back, readying myself and my gun. "No need to worry, Kayla. I am not here to harm you. On the contrary, I am here to help you."

"Who are you?"

"My name is Kamini. I am what they call a Punisher. I work in similar circles to Mr. Savage, but we are not of the same kind or of the same mind." I look over the woman with suspicion. She is beyond intimidating with her long dark hair, bright sparkling eyes, and rich dark skin. I cannot bring myself to look directly at the beautiful woman. "I can understand your trepidation, but I assure you, I have much to offer you if you will give me a chance to explain." I step back with little interest in what she has to say. I have already made up my mind, and I don't want anyone to try and talk me out of it. "I can help you battle Savage and regain your husband," she says, stopping me in my tracks.

"How can you do that?" I ask, looking her over once again.

"I'm going to teach you how to use your own power, your own skills." She paces around me. "I am going to show you how to find the strength within yourself to battle him, toe to toe."

I shake my head, "It's not possible; he is too strong for me. And why does it matter ..."

"Do you really believe your husband has left you for another?" I don't bother answering her. "You foolish girl, you have let your insecurities creep back into your head. Don't let your mother's voice detour you from what you know is right. You're better than that, and you know it."

"I don't see how having a brave face can get me very far with Savage."

She laughs, and continues, "A brave face? Is that all you think you have? After all that you have been through, it's a brave face that you think has pulled you through?"

"No, Nick has always been there too, or he was always there."

"He is still there; he is trapped right now. I will admit, he will be lost forever if you don't act swiftly and precisely. You need to do just as I tell you if you want to save him," she says, standing with an assured look about her.

"I don't understand what I can possibly do. Nick doesn't want anything to do with me anymore. He looks right through me," I say, shaking my head at her nonsense.

"Nick is under the spell of Savage's poison. He has no control over what he wants right now." I look over my shoulder at her as she smiles wide. "You heard me right. He's been poisoned. His heart is hardening, and if we don't get to him before it finishes, he will be forever Savage's loyal warrior." I sigh, wondering what I could possibly do and how can I do it while still protecting my sons, Ryan, Elijah ... "Kayla!" she yells suddenly, forcing me to look up at her. "He has gotten into your mind and made you believe that he is stronger than you, and it is not true. He is scared of you! Why don't you see that?"

"Because I am nothing! I am nothing more than a tired woman who has a family to care for, to look after. I cannot risk losing my sons. They are all I have. I can't let him take all that I have left," I yell back at her, returning my focus back to my feet.

"He already has, Kayla. He has you running, and he can take whatever he wants from you, whenever he wants, when you are too scared to fight back. He will take from you and then take from you again until there is nothing left and there is nothing left of you. He doesn't need a weapon to kill you when he can get you to destroy yourself." I raise my eyes up to hers once again. "Fight, Kayla, fight. Don't run or you will surely lose everything." My head begins to spin, and I am not sure how I can find the energy to even continue this conversation.

"I need to go home and rest. I need some time to think," I say as she stands silent. "You're not going to stop me?"

"Leave if you want to leave. I won't stop you. I don't have the power to do that. All I can do is show you how to fight, but if you don't want to, there is nothing I can do," she says, standing in the wind and judging my every step away from her. I turn completely away and walk towards my car. "Will you start drinking like your mother now?" she asks, remaining in her place. "Search for love within the arms of any and every man that shows you any attention? Will you hate your children because they remind you of what you have lost?" I immediately spin around, eyeing her down.

"I will *never* hate my children! I am not my mother. She was a horrible person. She hated everything and everyone. She blamed everyone for her problems when all she had to do was ..."

"Was fight? Not give up every time things became difficult?" Kamini asks with a smile.

"This is not the same situation."

"Isn't it?" I have to close my eyes and tell myself to breathe. "You know you have it within you. You know he still loves you. Just think about it. None of it makes sense. I can help you, Kayla. All you have to do is fight and stop running."

"I don't know how. I ..."

"No, there is no more 'don't or can't.' There is only, 'I will. I will fight.' I will meet you here tomorrow at this same time, and if you show up and say, 'I want to fight,' then I will help you. I will help you protect your family and your friends and get your husband back. But if you don't show, if you decide you don't want my help, then I will walk away and let you run." She steps towards me. "I want you to think about this when you go to sleep tonight, Kayla. Ask yourself how strong your love is for him. Will you fight for him like he has for you? Is Nick worth fighting for?"

Her words echo in my head, all the way home and on into my bed. Nick is worth more than I can even put into words. Can I fight? Can I fight and win? Will I fight? Kamini's words haunt me throughout the night, sneaking into my dreams over and over until I wake up in a cold sweat. I dreamt of running, and I dreamt of fighting, and in the end, my fears crept in again, and I dreamt of dying. The question is: Will I die running or will I die fighting?

For Nick ... I would die fighting the devil himself.

www.ingramcontent.com/pod-product-compliance
Lightning Source LLC
Chambersburg PA
CBHW070859180626
46817CB00003B/840